GIRL
FALLING

Also by Hayley Scrivenor

Dirt Creek

GIRL
FALLING

A Novel

HAYLEY
SCRIVENOR

FLATIRON
BOOKS
NEW YORK

GIRL FALLING. Copyright © 2024 by Hayley Scrivenor. All rights reserved. Printed in the United States of America. For information, address Flatiron Books, 120 Broadway, New York, NY 10271.

www.flatironbooks.com

Grateful acknowledgment is made for permission to reproduce from the following:

The quotations on pages vii and 51 are from *If Not, Winter*, by Sappho, translated by Anne Carson, Vintage, 2002.

Designed by Jen Edwards

Library of Congress Cataloging-in-Publication Data

Names: Scrivenor, Hayley, author.
Title: Girl falling : a novel / Hayley Scrivenor.
Description: First U.S. edition. | New York : Flatiron Books, 2025.
Identifiers: LCCN 2024030919 | ISBN 9781250362179
    (hardcover) | ISBN 9781250362186 (ebook)
Subjects: LCGFT: Thrillers (Fiction) | Queer fiction. | Novels.
Classification: LCC PR9619.4.S396 G57 2025 | DDC 823/.92—
    dc23/eng/20240708
LC record available at https://lccn.loc.gov/2024030919

Our books may be purchased in bulk for promotional, educational, or business use. Please contact your local bookseller or the Macmillan Corporate and Premium Sales Department at 1-800-221-7945, extension 5442, or by email at MacmillanSpecialMarkets@macmillan.com.

First published in 2024 by Pan Macmillan Australia Pty Ltd

First U.S. Edition: 2025

10 9 8 7 6 5 4 3 2 1

For my mother, Danina.

To the friendships that mess us up.
And the ones that save us.

Eros shook my

mind like a mountain wind falling on oak trees

SAPPHO, FRAGMENT 47, *IF NOT, WINTER*

TRANS. ANNE CARSON

GIRL
FALLING

1

WEDNESDAY, SEPTEMBER 6, 2017

Why would my best friend want to destroy my life?

———

The cliff the three of us were standing on curved down to the valley the way your ear joins your neck, the rock shining yellow and blood orange in the sun. The smell of damp earth growing warm. I was doing everything I could not to think about the question that had been running through my head since the night before. I was pretty good at that: pushing stuff down. I reminded myself that I was in love, that everything was better since a woman named Magdu had arrived, slipping into my life, filling it, changing its mood and temperature. It made what Daphne had done harder to accept, I realized. Now I knew that things could be better, different than they had been.

I took five deep breaths.

On a day like this, you looked across the valley and everything was too sharply in focus, all that detail demanding to be noticed at the same time. Bright blue sky that made you forget about mist and cold, a gentle breeze blowing.

"Let me check your gear," I said.

Magdu turned to me, eyes wide, and raised her arms up and away from her harness. *My beautiful girlfriend.* I'd said it so often that now it just made Magdu roll her eyes. I tugged on the front loop, resisting the urge to stand closer, to make it an intimate moment. Daphne was nearby, though out of earshot.

Read the room, Finn, I thought.

"Now, check mine," I said.

"I don't know what I'm looking for," Magdu said.

It wasn't like her to be this nervous.

"Yes, you do, Mags," I said gently.

She looked down at her feet.

"This is your belay device," I said. "Your rope will feed through as I belay you down. We want to check that this"—I pulled on the carabiner looped through the front of her harness—"is properly attached. It needs to connect these two loops together and be closed tight." I let my hand move from the harness to her hip, hooked a finger in her pocket. "All Daphne's gear is self-closing, so I've put you on that. If you ever need to be rescued, the climber who rescues you will transfer you onto their gear by attaching to you here."

"Rescued?" Her eyes were wide again.

"Don't worry, Mags. I've got you. Remember what we talked about."

It was an easy climb, perfect for a newbie. I would set up two ropes and go down first, abseiling down from the anchor. Then Daphne would come down at the same time as Magdu while I was on a fireman's belay below. It meant Magdu would always have someone with her, and I'd be right there, ready to take over and stop her descent if something went wrong. The cliff had a gentle angle, with good handholds. It'd been Daphne's idea: something fun for the three of us to do together. Now we were here, I wanted to make the best of it.

"There it is," Daphne said from behind me, and I jumped.

She laughed and leaned down to rifle through her bag, then looked up at Magdu. "You better hope Finn knows what she's doing," she said with a wink.

Magdu stiffened.

"I'm just kidding! Finn's been doing this since she was little." Daphne unfolded to her full height but still had to reach up to muss my hair. "I mean, she may only be twenty-six, but she's got years of experience. Right, Finnbo?"

Daphne turned away and I let her go. I couldn't meet Magdu's eye. Magdu leaned close and squeezed my hand, and I was reminded why I loved her.

Men's laughter rang out. The sound of clinking gear. A group of them were setting up, prepping for a harder climb than we were doing. A whole cliff face for them to choose from, and they'd chosen the climb right next to us. One of them kept looking at Daphne. He was tall with dark hair and a deep tan I knew wouldn't finish at the line of his sleeve, because he looked ready to take his T-shirt off any second. It was important to carry a knife in case you had to cut a rope, but he didn't need one as big as the folded blade dangling from his belt. He had white teeth that flashed when he smiled. One of those men so handsome they don't look real. I wanted to push against his shiny teeth with dirty fingers. I wanted to shove him into a shrub and watch him struggle to get out. The worst part was the suspicion that if he turned his charm on me, I could be won over.

I blocked out the men. Blocked the dull ache in my belly that told me my period was coming. My tooth hurt too, a throbbing that

I ignored. Daphne's blue helmet, blond braid snaking out from under it, bobbed in the corner of my vision. She was checking her gear, holding out her slings for inspection. She was the more talented climber, and she knew it. But I was more experienced, and we'd discussed the plan, had agreed how we were going to tackle the climb. We were here to get out of our heads and into our bodies.

I stepped into my harness and pulled the straps tight, and my belly and back felt better with the pressure. Locked in. Safe. Daphne sent me a meaningful look and I smiled at her, trying to refuse it, make it a simple thing. Daphne would always drag me into a secluded corner anywhere we went. She wanted to go deep, her hand wrapped around mine, her gaze steady on my face, her blond hair in her eyes. I thought of what had happened the night before. Pushed it down. I didn't want to be drawn in by Daphne at Magdu's expense. Not again.

I strapped on my helmet and walked toward the cliff edge to check the ledge below for climbers. A sheer drop, rock surging down into the valley. A gut punch of fear, a pulse felt in your back molars. Who could stand here without imagining what would happen if you went a little bit crazy, for even a second?

Magdu kept well back, running her hand along the straps of her harness, not looking at me. She pulled her inhaler from a jacket pocket and sucked on it, back arching and hands cupped like someone trying to light a cigarette in strong wind. She turned back to face the gaping hole of the valley. The tension from the car, from the previous weeks, had followed us here. But it was going to be okay. It had to be.

I turned. Daphne had wandered closer to where the group of young men were setting up. The handsome man towered over her, a full two heads taller. He reached for something below her waist. I tensed. Then I saw that he was holding the knife that I'd bought Daphne in high school, the handle engraved with a pattern of leaves.

It was on a cord, one end tied through a belt loop. I wanted to slap it out of his stupid hand.

I had to attach our ropes to the anchor that would hold our weight as we abseiled down.

"Daphne," I called.

It took her a second to turn toward me.

"Can I grab the rope bag?"

The bag was Daphne's responsibility. She'd done a ropes course. It was one that I was qualified to teach, but she'd chosen not to learn from me. "Teachers need authority, you know?" she'd said with a shrug. I understood. She meant she needed someone who wouldn't go easy on her like I would.

"Daphne," I called again.

"It's by the boulder," she yelled, without shifting her attention from the guy.

———————

There were permanent slings around two trees either side of a large rock. I checked the webbing on both for damage, but all the gear along this series of climbs was well used and well maintained. Our anchor would be equalized between the three points—the two trees and the boulder. Three points of contact to keep the three of us safe. I walked my red rope and Daphne's blue rope, now both securely attached, to the edge. I called down, "Rope!" and waited a moment before throwing them over one at a time.

Magdu was bouncing on the balls of her feet now. As if shaking off the heaviness I'd noticed in the car: a quiet sadness that scared me.

"It's beautiful," she said. "Just beautiful." Her arms spread wide, indicating the landscape. Magdu ran toward good feelings. I loved that about her.

———

Down at the first ledge, the sun was warm against my back, a stronger breeze now, caressing my sweaty neck. I turned to look over my shoulder, the incredible view stretching away from me, the rumpled edges of the valley crowded with bush. I breathed deeply, relishing the smell of eucalyptus and the feeling of calm I got on the rock. Here, I could focus only on what was in front of me.

When I turned to face the cliff again, some grit fell into my eye. I'd left my sunnies on the dash of the car. Rookie error. I blinked and looked down, my hands ready. I heard Daphne's voice above me say, "Coming down," and I instinctively widened my stance, preparing for her and Magdu's weight to come on to the two ropes. I held one in each hand. "On belay," I called back, hearing my words bounce up the rock.

A gentle tug on the blue rope told me at least one person's full body weight had gone over the edge. I closed my eyes, trying to squeeze out the grit.

There was a snapping sound. A scream, a body moving toward me at speed. Instinctively, I pulled hard on both the ropes in my hands, but the body—no longer attached—was in freefall. Arms and legs flailing. Shiny black hair. Magdu's orange jacket moving past me on the ledge. I grabbed for the detached rope without considering the consequences, wanting only to stop the body from falling. The heavy line whipped and thrashed on its way down. I was tied in at the bolt, or I would have tipped back and off the ledge. I twisted to look down, to follow the orange blur. I could no longer hear her.

It had all happened in the time it takes a door to slam closed.

———

From where I stand now, I picture the three of us still together at the top of the cliff. *Run*, I want to say. *Leave, while you still can.* I want to ask Daphne why she did all the things she did. I want to understand what happened. To smooth it out until it resolves, like a map on which you finally recognize the landmarks around you. I can't go back to that moment, can't change what happened. The best I can hope for is that I will find what I have always needed; what I realize I am looking for even now: a story I can live with.

2

BEFORE

The first time I spoke to Daphne Bennett, we were in year ten at Indra High and she was crying in the girls' toilets because her little sister had died. The two of them had only transferred to the school a month earlier. It was rumored that the young girl had killed herself. Everyone said it quietly. There was something unnatural about a girl dying, something that made you want to be still and small, so the universe didn't notice you and start getting ideas.

It was September. A wet day in the mountains. So misty you could *see* the edge of the wind as it surged through the trees at the fence line. Our mountain town was two-thirds of the way along a chain of mountain towns that snaked ever higher and ever deeper into the national park. Old towns, with old buildings. Most of the grand old estates in Indra had been bought by commuters from Sydney or people who'd retired here, but some still belonged to the same old families. There was also a Kmart. Tourists liked the Kmart because they could buy cheap beanies and gloves if they'd forgotten or lost their own, but it was families like mine, who lived year-round in the mountains, who kept it in business. We bought cheap fleecy blankets and shitty heaters that were expensive to run and fell over, singeing old rugs that smelled of dog hair. Kmart was all about having something kind of good now because there was no point waiting for something better. I'd overheard an American family at the Kmart once. I thought it was strange, to travel all the way from America and then go to a store you could go to at home. The mother told the father that she hadn't thought Australia could be like this, warm clothes piled high in her arms. She must have meant cold.

The afternoon I met Daphne, I'd asked to be excused from English class, supposedly to pee. In reality, I needed a break from the words that swam and flashed before my eyes like koi in some old lady's garden pond. An old lady in a stained cardigan who forgets to feed her fish and then sometimes feeds them twice a day. That was the sort of detail I thought of, specific like that. The teacher always told me off because my sentences were too long, my handwriting too difficult to read, with what she called *feral spelling*.

When I opened the door to the toilets, I heard the sound of crying. A girl was sitting on the floor near the sinks. She was tiny in that way some girls are. The tiles were cold when I sat down next to her. I did it without thinking. She didn't flinch or move away. She was a mermaid in a tank: an otherworldly creature that mortals like me would never usually get to see. Even crying, she was beautiful. I wouldn't be able to tell anyone about it after, at least not in a way that they would believe.

When Daphne told people the story of how we became friends, she would say that no one else had any idea what to do with her— they fled, or looked away. "But Finn did exactly the right thing," she'd say. "She came and sat on the floor next to me and put a hand on my shoulder and didn't say anything."

I do remember brushing her long blond hair back from her face, the rightness of the action. A tap dripped and the small, echoey room smelled like cheap disinfectant and vanilla Impulse. Up close, Daphne had a particular smell that I would learn the name for later. It was neroli oil. From a little blue bottle she said was very expensive. Her mother's mother had also worn it. I tried it on once, but it didn't react with my skin in the same way it did Daphne's—instead of smelling sexy and citrusy it smelled sour, like something left too long in a jar. Daphne said we have our own, private chemicals and that changes how things smell on us.

"It's Daphne, right?" I said, breaking the silence in the bathroom.

The blond girl snorted. "Mum was going through a sacred womanhood thing," she said, her voice still wet and thick. I nodded, not wanting to let on that I didn't know what she was talking about. "She wanted to name me after a figure from Greek mythology," she continued. "Of course, Daphne had her daddy turn her into a tree to avoid being raped by Apollo." She rolled her eyes. "Ultimate power move."

I had absolutely no idea how to respond, so I smiled.

When I was a kid, I thought that remembering something was like pulling it from a filing cabinet, or maybe finding it in a crowded bucket. But by fifteen, I'd figured out that there was nothing neutral about what we remember and how we remember it. Most often, we lose the memories we need and keep the ones we'd most like to discard. What I would never tell Daphne is that the first thing I thought of when I'd heard her name was *Scooby-Doo*, the pretty girl with red hair who wore purple a lot. That's the kind of person I was. A *Scooby-Doo* person. Not a Greek mythology person.

"I don't know why my little sister Brianna got a normal name."

She'd stopped crying. The idea of her dead sister hung in the air between us. I pulled my hands into my lap, losing my nerve. It'd been natural somehow, at the beginning, but I was catching up with myself. This wasn't the sort of thing that I did.

I don't know how long Daphne and I spent on the floor of the toilets. I do remember that she stood first and offered me a hand up. We went off to our separate classrooms. As I watched her walk away from me, I envied Daphne, and her mother who liked Greek myths. Even if Daphne's sister had died. When I got home that afternoon, the house would stink of white wine. Mum reckoned that you weren't a problem drinker if you weren't on the spirits, so she bought boxes of wine and hid the brandy bottles at the bottom of the recycling. She did this so carefully she might have been hiding them from herself.

Daphne's orange-blossom smell lingered in the school corridor, but already the interaction felt like a dream: one that would start to fade before you could pull yourself out of bed.

3

WEDNESDAY, SEPTEMBER 6, 2017

After they brought us back from the cliff, Daphne and I lived through three silent lifetimes in the police station waiting room. There was an empty seat between us where Magdu should have been sitting. I couldn't look at Daphne, couldn't say anything. We'd been told not to talk to one another anyway. A cop kept an eye on us from the front desk. I sat, rocked, cried into my own chest. My tooth ached and I felt swollen and pink and raw. I felt a century older than my twenty-six years, my bones growing into the chair. When they finally came for us, we were taken into two separate rooms.

I followed a uniformed policeman down a long hallway.

"Righto," said an older man, who was already in the interview room. Even though he was sitting down, I could tell he was tall. The skin on his face was red, and weirdly loose. Like someone who'd lost a lot of weight quickly. "Let's get on with it."

The other cop, a younger officer with dark skin, sat down in the seat opposite me. He had a tiny Aboriginal flag on his name tag.

"My name is Senior Constable Dale Gosling," he said. "Can you please state your name and address for the tape?"

"I'm Finn Young. Finnlay Young. I live at one forty-one Indra Street." Something coated my throat, made it hard to swallow.

The older man leaned toward the device at the center of the table. "Also present, Sergeant Gary Oakland."

When the older man had settled back in his seat, the young officer looked at me. "Tell me about today."

My head moved side to side in a *no* motion as he spoke. I had to concentrate to get it to stop.

"What happened?"

I sifted through the images of the moments after Magdu had fallen, riffling them like you might a deck of unfamiliar cards you are trying to memorize. It had taken a long time to steady myself to climb back up the red rope. Then hours of waiting until the helicopter had finally negotiated the long drop into the canopy, wind from the rotor whipping at my face as I craned my neck looking for movement in the stretcher as they lifted Magdu up. I caught the shake of the head between the man in the harness next to the stretcher and the cop who stood alongside me, a little way back from the cliff edge. That cop had kept himself between me and the void. I wanted to be with Magdu, to catch her in midair, to jolt her alive again with the thwack of my body hitting hers. I didn't want to believe what that shake of the head signified. Told myself it could've meant a lot of things. I let myself think of Magdu in the hospital. Of how we would complain about the disinfectant smell and the constant beeping; of how she would slowly recover.

"We were doing Kamikaze Koala," I said. Then, seeing the confusion on his face, I explained, "All the climbs have dumb names like that. Whoever does a climb first gets naming rights."

I described how I'd attached two ropes to the anchor and gone down first on my red rope, so I could belay from below. When Magdu had fallen, I'd been at the midway ledge on the cliff.

"I heard Daphne call out that they were coming down, so I looked up. I got dirt in my eyes. There was weight on the rope in my right hand, so I called back, *On belay.*" I shook my head, blinked. "I figured it was Daphne coming down, because the weight was in the blue rope. Then I heard a rope snap."

"So, at first you thought it was Daphne who'd fallen?"

"I didn't really have time to think about it," I said. "But before I went over the edge, she was tied into the blue rope and all the weight had just gone out of that one. She'd been standing on the right, and that was the right-hand rope, so I guess I assumed it was her. But then I saw Magdu fall past me, on my right."

Senior Constable Gosling leaned in. "What happened after Magdalene fell?"

"She never uses that name. Her name is Magdu." I whispered the words urgently, like they mattered, like they could change something. "I was tied into a bolt on the ledge. I stood there watching, listening, for ages. Eventually I realized I should climb back up, but—"

"Could you speak up?" He nodded with his head to indicate the device between us. "For the recording."

"Sorry," I said. "Um . . . I could hear Daphne screaming, but I couldn't hear any sound from Magdu." I'd stood on the ledge for a long time, calling to her. "I decided to climb back up. I assumed Daphne had called Police Rescue, but I couldn't be sure. She was yelling down to me and I couldn't understand everything she was saying. It was an easy grade, but it took me forever to get to the top. I couldn't make my hands work properly." I took a breath as fresh tears slid down my face.

The young cop, Gosling, gave me a few seconds to compose myself before asking, "Did you think she was dead?"

"I wasn't sure."

It was the truth. I'd stood at the belay point, calling to Magdu for what felt like hours.

"How old was the rope? Was it her own gear she was wearing?"

"The blue one is Daphne's rope. It's pretty new. Same with the gear Magdu was wearing," I said. "I checked that myself."

"Who set the anchor?" Dale asked.

I managed to stutter, "I—I did. There were permanent slings around two trees at the top of the climb. But I did all my checks." I'd seen my anchor point, still where I'd attached it to the undamaged slings, when we'd been herded away from the cliff edge by the police. I knew there was no problem with the anchor. "It wasn't supposed to be like this. I promised Magdu I'd keep her safe." Tears were flowing freely down my face now.

The cop wanted to know about the other people on the cliff. I told him about the four men I'd seen. They'd been on a climb called A Blowjob for Blinky, but I didn't tell him that. The natural result of climbs mostly being named by young men was that it set my teeth on edge to say some of the names aloud.

I described the man I could remember: the one with the white smile and the big knife. The one who'd been talking to Daphne—flirting with her. I didn't tell Gosling this either. Everything felt important, yet I also had a sense that I should keep moving. That I was walking along a narrow track very high up, and I shouldn't look down.

The older, flabby-faced cop—Sergeant Oakland—spoke. "Let me ask you this, Miss Young." There was a sneer on his face. He seemed bored, in an aggressive way; a kid getting ready to throw a tantrum in a supermarket. "Was Magdalene an experienced climber?" Of course this man wouldn't bother to use the right name.

"No," I said, swallowing hard.

Sergeant Oakland shifted in his seat. I could smell tomato sauce. "Great," he said, addressing his remark to his colleague. "Another group of weekend heroes who think they know what they're doing, and then we get to come in and clean it up." He leaned back, crossing his arms.

It was Wednesday, I wanted to say.

Magdu was dead. Magdu was dead. Magdu was dead.

I couldn't look Oakland in the face. "I'm certified. We both are. Daphne and me, I mean. We're local. This shouldn't have happened."

"Do you know when the blue rope was last safety-checked?" Dale asked. His voice was kind.

I shook my head.

"We'll be having forensics look at both ropes." The older man narrowed his eyes. "You and your friend could be looking at negligence charges. This is no joke."

Fear, shame. I'd done something wrong. Then anger. Of course it wasn't a fucking joke!

I remembered Mum crying in a room like this one, sitting next to me as I answered questions. Mum crying as two men picked at her. A female officer speaking to me slowly, like I was five years old. Bright light shining off dirty metal surfaces and shit tea in polystyrene cups. My gut clenched, stapling my insides together.

"We're trying to figure out how the blue rope failed," Gosling said. "It may have been a manufacturing issue." He added softly, "We're just doing our jobs. We need to establish what happened."

His words hung between us.

The older detective looked at his watch as Senior Constable Gosling asked a few more questions. I held a hand to my throat as I spoke.

It took a long time for a person to fall. Magdu had been moving all the way down, arms flailing, banging against the cliff wall, trying to grab hold of something as she plummeted toward the trees, the ground.

Dale Gosling had a kind face. Magdu would have liked him.

Fuck you, I thought. *Don't pretend to be nice to me.*

After we'd circled back over what had happened so many times that I'd almost confused myself, Gosling looked down at the recording device on the table. "Okay, it's six oh three p.m. and I am terminating this interview."

Oakland said, "Don't leave town, Miss Young," before hauling himself out of the chair. He wasn't looking at me when he said it.

The door swung closed behind him.

I heard the thud of Magdu hitting the valley floor. Then silence. That was the worst part. The trees making a huge church of themselves, the light holy and terrible. Calling Magdu's name and hearing nothing but Daphne's screaming.

The younger cop was still gathering his papers. "Uh, yes. As stated, I am terminating the interview. It is now"—he looked at the clock on the wall behind me—"six oh four p.m." He leaned over and clicked off the machine.

I looked at him. He noticed and cocked his head to one side: a question.

"Do you need someone to—to see her?" I asked, hating myself for the need in my voice.

The words *identify the body* did not belong to Magdu and I would not say them.

He gave me a pitying look and stood up. "Her uncle has already agreed to come in," he said.

"Magdu's uncle doesn't know about me and Magdu," I said.

"Okay," Dale said, voice neutral. "I'll keep that in mind."

"I'm not saying you should hide it or anything, it's just . . ." I wanted her uncle to know. I wanted everyone to know.

The cop nodded, not in agreement but thinking it over. He put a hand on my shoulder. "I can see she was special to you," he said quickly, before dropping his hand.

Fuck off, I thought as he continued to look at me. I resisted the urge to push past him and run. I felt numb and small. I might wash away, a bottle cap being swept down a gutter in a stream of water. Just as worthless.

"After you," Dale said, holding the door open.

———

Back in the reception area, I waited for Daphne. *Negligence charges.*

A few minutes later, she returned from her own interview and sat beside me. I was desperate to know what the police had asked her, what she'd told them, but the numbness was still there. I couldn't make my lips move, couldn't shape the words. She let her body rest against mine, her head on my shoulder. I could smell her shampoo. I put an arm around her. Holding her like this meant we didn't have to look each other in the face.

Daphne turned her head, so her mouth was near my ear. "I never would have told her," Daphne whispered. "I might have pretended like I was going to, but I was just being a bitch. You know that, right?" The words were flat, no anger or plea or apology in them.

I said nothing, just sat there motionless, Daphne's head on my shoulder.

We were still sitting like that when Daphne's mother arrived. Daphne leaned away from me, settled her head against the wall, closed her eyes, so I stood and stepped into Carol-Ann's out-stretched arms. We'd been close, once. I let myself fall into her, let her soothe me. We must have been like that for a while, because when we pulled apart I saw that Daphne and her dad were outside, standing by their car.

"We can give you a lift?" Carol-Ann said, her mouth tight with worry.

In that moment, I longed to have her lead me to their car and usher me into the back seat, do up my seat belt, run a hand through my hair.

I shook my head. "My mum'll be here soon."

I walked with Carol-Ann through the doors of the police station. It was getting darker outside, and a wall of gray cloud had started to roll in. I shivered in my jacket. My head was still throbbing with what Daphne had said.

"I'm so sorry, Finn. Daphne's told me how crazy you are about Magdu."

I didn't know what to say. Carol-Ann and I had never spoken about Magdu. The two of them had never met. Now they never would.

"We can wait with you until your mum gets here? Or I can call, see how far away she is?"

"I think it would be a good idea to get Daphne home," I said, nodding my head in the direction of the car, like she might need me to clarify who I was talking about. "I'm all right."

Daphne had her face turned into her father's chest. He looked at me over the top of her head. His arms moved up and down in time with her sobs.

Carol-Ann squeezed my shoulder. "We'll talk soon, okay? You should try to get some sleep. God knows you girls could use it."

I smiled grimly, and watched as Carol-Ann walked over to the car and slid into the driver's seat. The three of them drove off into the fading light.

———

I'd lied when I told Carol-Ann my mother was coming to get me. I hadn't given the police her number. "Can you please take me back to my car?" I'd asked. That was where I wanted to be: alone in my car where nobody could see me.

After Daphne left, I waited inside the station until someone was free. Eventually a young, mercifully silent cop drove me to the Goat Track car park. When he brought the car to a stop, I stepped out, patting my zippered hip pocket. I could feel my key chain. A stupid, dinky plastic thing in the shape of the Tasmanian Devil from *Looney Tunes*. I pulled it out and examined it, with its wide grin and eyes that pointed in different directions. It felt wrong in my hand, like when you're in a dream and look down and realize that you're holding a weapon and are suddenly afraid.

The cop performed a three-point turn in the tight space and I lowered myself into the driver's seat of my car. The cop watched me in his rearview mirror. I started my engine and he drove off in front of me, picking up speed on the rutted dirt road before turning toward town.

The rain started, pattering against my roof, coating the windshield. I took the same turn, not sure where I would go, relieved to be in the moving car, to be leaving the cliff edge behind.

4

BEFORE

Magdu had come into my world like the invitation to a party you didn't know was happening. The day I met her, we were short-staffed, Ryan yet again too hungover to show up to his shift at the visitor center. He'd been the one who got me the job—at a time when some people might've thought it was strange I wanted to work in the national park, given what had happened to my family—so I couldn't be too mad at him.

It was a big group for that day's walk. They stood talking and laughing, bunched along the visitor center's wraparound veranda. You'd think you'd want the guide at the front, but with a bigger group like this, it was better to follow at the rear. I was familiar enough with the path to know when to call up the line and tell people to wait at the fork.

A pretty, round-faced girl in her midtwenties had fallen right to the back. I'd noticed her walking with an older woman, and assumed the two were related. They both looked South Asian, with a similar curve to their cheeks. It was a warm day, and the young woman held her bright orange puffer jacket in her hand. The close-together ridges of the ribbed stuffing reminded me of the hose that runs out from the back of the washing machine. The light caught her shiny black hair. I tugged at my shirt, which was a bad shade of green—on me, at least—and had the floral logo of the visitor center embroidered over my heart. I zipped up my vest.

"How are you going?" I asked, nodding at the path stretching ahead of us.

I was close enough now to see the sheen of sweat on her face. She was a head shorter than me.

"Fine. All under control."

I recognized the wheezy strangle of someone trying not to breathe too hard.

Her hips and chest curved to match the roundness in her face. Her skin looked like it would be firm to the touch. I could smell her sweat under another smell I couldn't identify. Together, they made me want to stand closer to her.

"Oh, well, that doesn't sound good," I joked.

I slowed my pace a little.

"I mean, we're all in nature to let loose a little, right?" I was like this with women I found attractive: I flipped into a mode of speech as unsexy as it was annoying. A car salesman with a lot full of cracked engines and rust.

She looked skeptical. "So, you're telling me there are people who find this genuinely relaxing?" There was an American twang in her voice I hadn't noticed at first.

It was only gentle sarcasm, I thought, designed to pull me in rather than make me feel stupid. Or that's what I hoped. When I didn't reply she said, "That would explain why my aunt wanted to do this." She said "aunt" with a flat "a" that made the word rhyme with "pant."

"People come from all over to walk around here. We're incredibly lucky to have this on our doorstep." I gestured to the open valley that had come into view between the trees. I glanced down at the track, trying to keep my voice casual. "Do you live nearby?" I was holding my stomach in.

"I'm local," she said.

"Oh, great!" I said, cringing at the enthusiasm in my voice. *Play it cool, Finn.*

She raised one eyebrow. My gaze fell on her full lips, puckered in a funny little smile.

"Is this your full-time job?" she asked, raising her chin slightly to take in the small gaggle of people in hiking boots fanned out ahead of us.

"Sort of," I said. I also worked at a café in town, but for some reason I didn't want to tell her about that.

"I thought I'd seen you at Jimmy's, making coffee," she said. That American accent again. She said "coffee" the way they said it in the movies.

I would have noticed her. Then again, when we were busy I called out orders without looking up to see who was taking them.

"My name's Magdu, by the way," she said, stopping and sticking out a hand. "Magdu Fernandes."

I took her hand in mine. A cold sensation poured through my body.

"Hi, Magdu. I'm Finn."

Her eyes crinkled like she could tell what I was thinking and it amused her.

"Finnlay Young."

She held my hand for a beat longer than a normal handshake. We started walking again.

"What gets me is that you think it's going to be mountains,

because it's called the Blue Mountains, but it's really just a big hole," Magdu said, raising her shoulders in mock confusion.

It was nice to be able to walk alongside each other, not looking at Magdu but aware she was there. We fell into a good silence, the kind you have with someone you know.

———

Later, back at the visitor center, Magdu found me again. Almost everyone else had wandered off after the orange slices and water we offered at the end of walks, even in winter, which I thought was a bit weird, though everyone always seemed to enjoy it. People like free food, I guess. Even oranges.

"So, maybe people ask this all the time . . ." Magdu said. She had her hands in the pockets of her orange jacket. "But will you come for a drink with me?"

For a moment my mind was stuck in a different scenario, one in which she had asked, "Can I use the staff toilets?"

Magdu smiled, showing teeth that were white and straight.

"I'd like that," I said.

I gave a silent prayer of thanks to my haircut. In the six months since I'd got it, I'd noticed more women had approached me, or at least smiled at me in a certain way from across the room. My short hair settling a question.

"Where's your aunt?" I asked.

"She had to get back to the store. I told her I'd walk back into town."

I shifted my weight. "Ah yes, because you love walking so much."

She screwed up her face.

We looked at each other for a moment.

"Do you mean now?" I asked.

"Got anything better to do?" She smiled again and took her hands out of her pockets.

———

I took Magdu to the Wild Colonial. It was an old-style bar, with bronze and polished wood that shone in the light from the green-glass lampshades. They did cheap pints before six p.m. on a Friday. I held the door for Magdu when we arrived and someone else slipped in front of her, taking advantage of the opening. I grinned sheepishly. What was I trying to do? Why did I try to play the gentleman with women?

The bartender was a guy who'd been in year twelve at Indra High when I was in year seven. I was sure he wouldn't recognize me because the older kids never remembered younger kids. I was distracted by him and raised my hand to the small of Magdu's back as we walked toward the bar. The way you scratch an itch, without thinking. She looked at me sideways. Smiled.

———

"My family are from Goa, but I grew up in the United Arab Emirates," Magdu told me over our beers. "I came here for university when I was eighteen. I got my permanent residency a few years back, which was an insane bureaucratic process. The next step is to become an Australian citizen. The UAE is home, but I can never get citizenship there."

I nodded, hoping it looked like I knew what she was talking about. "So, what brought you to the mountains?" I asked.

"I was living in Indra with my aunt and uncle at first, before I found a share house in Sydney for undergrad. Then I moved back here when I started my Master of Psychology. It's a low-residency course, so I only have to go to campus every few weeks." Magdu sat tall on her bar stool. "It's cheaper here, and I like the mountains. Sometimes I worry I won't be able to do another winter, but it's a great excuse to stay inside and watch a movie with the heater on, you know?" A look flickered over Magdu's face as if she'd said too much.

I jumped in, wanting her to feel comfortable. Wanting her to as-sociate me with comfort. "Do you like studying psychology?" I asked. I wanted to ask, *Do you like me as much as I like you?*

"I do." She looked down at my hands, which were ripping my coaster into shreds. "Don't worry, I'm not analyzing you." She laughed.

"How long have you been in Indra?" I was hoping she couldn't see the heat creeping up my face.

"I moved here when I was twenty-eight. So, two years."

"Oh, I didn't realize you were older than me," I said.

Magdu laughed. "Yeah, it's the good skin." She looked at me, leaned in close. "That bother you?" she asked, her voice soft. "It *is* catching, you know. Aging. We catch it from everyone around us. Like, if people weren't there to watch us get older, would it happen? We treat aging as if it's a disease, which is kind of weird." She placed her beer back on the table. "I enjoy getting older."

The gap between twenty-five and thirty seemed too wide. Magdu might lose interest if she thought I was too young. I still thought of myself as a *girl*. Except when some old dickhead at the pub called me one. I smiled, thinking of how mad that made me.

"What are you smiling at?" Magdu asked, leaning closer.

"I was thinking that I don't necessarily enjoy getting older, but I don't like it when other people treat me like I'm young either." I lifted my chin, looked her directly in the eye. "I'm probably scared that my body will change as I get older, and I'll no longer be able to do certain things."

"I've never had a physical peak to look back on fondly," she said, laughing. "Maybe that's why it doesn't bother me."

I wasn't sure what to say. I'd never seen anyone as beautiful as her, sitting on that low-backed bar stool. In those early days I didn't give out compliments as freely as I should have.

"What about you?" she asked. "Where are you from?"

"I grew up here." I took in the sweep of the pub with a wave of my hand, though I meant Indra more generally. "I'm endemic to the area," I said, borrowing some of Daphne's botany-speak.

She raised a single eyebrow again. It was very sexy when she did that. "You know you're white, right?"

I feigned horror, looked down at my hands, fingers spread wide, looked back up at her. Luckily, she seemed to think that was funny.

"I know I'm only a couple of generations deep, but I was born here, and most days I think I'll die here."

Magdu leaned in, placed a hand above my eyebrows. Her eyes widened. "And how long do you have left?" I liked the feel of her hand on my forehead.

"I know, I know. I'm being dramatic. I'm a mountains girl, you know? It gets to you, all the mist."

Magdu's hand moved down to the sensitive skin above my top lip. "You've got something."

She wiped away some beer with her thumb, then brought the thumb to her mouth and licked the foam. I resisted the urge to look around the pub to see if anyone else had noticed. She laughed again. It was joyous, like when the sun hits a point high enough that it floods into a room where you've been sleeping.

"I dated a guy once who used to suck the mustache part of his beard after he'd drunk something," I said. "For quite a while, I'd find myself sucking my top lip the same way."

"It's funny how we end up copying people's little mannerisms like that." She wiped at her own lip with a thumb. "How long were you dating this guy?"

"He's not even an ex, just a guy I was sleeping with for a while."

"So you're bi?" There was no judgment in her voice, only curiosity.

"I am," I said, struck as I always was by both the rightness of the word and my own embarrassment in admitting it out loud. Faking a bravado I did not feel, I lifted my chin again and said, "Is that a problem?"

Magdu raised her hands. "Hey, not to me."

"It's been an issue before," I said. "With the last girl I dated."

Thank god for Beth. It had been a gift, that short-lived relationship. I could say casually, "Yeah, I dated a girl who was obsessed with that movie," or, "I used to date someone who was into that; *she* . . ." I enjoyed seeing the flicker of realization in people's eyes. The thought that I shouldn't need that, that it should be enough for me to know what I was, niggled at me. But it was important for other people to acknowledge it, to mirror back to me what I knew about myself. The word *bisexual* felt right, the correct note played on a piano.

When I was dating Beth, I could get annoyed by the GP who asked if I might be pregnant and, when I said no, asked how could I be sure, because hadn't I said I was sexually active and not using condoms? Is it bad to say that I enjoyed that shitty medical center interaction? Like a real queer person against real ignorance? But then I happened to get the same doctor another time and had to say yes, I was using condoms when having sex with boys. (I knew if they were having sex with me, I should think of them as men. But I didn't: they were boys. The same way I thought of myself as a girl because someone with their shit as poorly together as me didn't think of themselves as a woman).

The truth was I'd never been in any kind of long-term relationship. I'd dated that one girl and several boys in ways that were so casual it was hard to tell when the dating started and stopped.

"Finn?" Magdu placed a hand on my shoulder.

Something about the way she said my name, the way it shimmered in the air a little after she'd spoken, made me sit up straighter.

"Sorry." I wanted to reach up and take her hand, but I didn't. "Guess I spaced out for a second."

"Ah. I'm boring you," she said with an American-inflected solemness that made me smile.

I mustered the courage to put my hand on top of hers.

Magdu turned her hand so that her fingers slid into mine.

I took a sip of my beer and placed it back on the table before replying. "I can honestly say I have never been less bored in my entire life."

Magdu swiveled on her bar stool, inviting everyone to see what a good time we were having. Her fingers tugged on mine as she reached the far point of her swing. She leaned into me a bit as she swung back around.

"So, do you think you'll stay in Indra?" A lot hung on Magdu's reply.

"Well, my mother would hate it here . . ." She winked. "So that's a plus."

I took another sip from the beer, making sure I didn't suck my lip after. "She's never visited?"

"She's worried about leaving the UAE. She thinks if she leaves, they won't let her back in. She's having a house built in Goa, because they'll have to leave Dubai when my dad stops working, but it's hard when you're not there in person to supervise. There's always something going wrong, something that needs more money. I told her maybe she should move to Goa now and rent, but she wants to be near my brother."

"Did you like living in the UAE?" I asked.

"In the Emirates, we lived our whole lives inside," Magdu said. "I am not an outdoorsy person, but I love the potential here. Even when you go to the shops you're outside in a way that is different. And with the crappy insulation, you get the weather indoors. I was so cold my first winter. I moved here and I was like, *What have I done?*"

"But now you know it gets better in summer," I said.

"Yeah, yeah," she said. "Although the moist air isn't great for my asthma, no matter what time of year it is."

We fell silent for a moment. I said, "When was—" at the exact moment she said, "Do you—" and we laughed.

"You go first," I said.

"Do you have any siblings?"

I shook my head. All I wanted to think about was a plausible reason to get my hand back into hers.

———

I walked Magdu home after the pub.

The weatherboard houses were in colors that looked optimistic in the foggy night. The yellows and greens and pinks were ruins from a lollipop land swallowed by rain and gray clouds. It had been a warm day, but the temperature had dropped and now the mist was steam coming off the top of the small buildings and trees. A whole town on the boil. Low-lying garden beds in bloom. Daffodils. The thin stalks with the yellow heads made me think of people listening to music, bobbing their necks to a rhythm only they could hear.

I loved walking past houses, assessing how much I wanted to live in each one. A single feature could knock a house out of consideration. I let myself search for perfection because I knew I'd never own a house, certainly couldn't afford one in the town where I'd been born and spent my whole life. Not even a shitty house like the one I lived in.

Magdu was also looking at the houses, considering them. I'd only had the one drink, and so had she. Still, everything was warm and delicate. My heart was an egg yolk held by fingertips while the white part slips wetly away.

As we walked, I had my hands in my pockets. Magdu moved along beside me. My hands tingled. A police car coasted through the intersection ahead of us and I had the strange desire to be stopped. I wanted to be asked to account for my actions, to list what I'd done that day. I wanted to be seen from the outside. *I just had a drink with a girl named Magdu who's from Goa originally, though she grew up in the UAE. She has an American accent because she went to an international school. Her real name is Magdalene, but she only* ever *goes by Magdu.* I thought about what we would look like together, her dark skin and thick hair, her soft body, and me, taller and leaner but bottom heavy, obviously a woman, no matter how much unisex hiking gear I wore, my short hair tucked under a cap. I liked this version of myself, the one that walked next to Magdu. I wanted someone to see it. But wasn't that fucked up? Was I congratulating myself on her being brown, on what that said about me? Or was it because she was a girl, because we were both girls together, and that was something, wasn't it? If I tried to tell her any of it, I knew it would come out wrong. It was the feeling you get when you pull your car over so that an ambulance can pass you. Good, righteous.

The more we walked, the calmer I felt. I pulled my hands out of my pockets.

I knew that when I walked her to her front door, she wouldn't invite me in, that we wouldn't have sex that night. I sensed that the fact she wanted to wait was a good sign.

We said goodbye at the little gate leading to the line of flats. She looked down the path toward the row of doors before she leaned in to kiss me. Her lips were soft and she tasted of beer.

Heading home, I walked fast, like my chest was going to lift up and away from my body if I undid my vest, a balloon let loose at a birthday party.

I knew the day I met Magdu that I wanted to marry her. There wasn't a doubt in my mind. If I could be a different person, someone worthy of her, then I'd convince her to marry me, and I would spend the rest of my life making her happy. Maybe wanting to be a better person is what true love does to you.

5

WEDNESDAY, SEPTEMBER 6, 2017

I drove straight home from the cliff. Our house was an old fiberboard place, small on its big block, the driveway at a steep angle. It crouched beyond the light of the nearest streetlamp, but I didn't need light to see the lines of mold and discolored paint, the crappy aluminum windows in their sagging frames. I opened the back door with the key attached to my stupid Tasmanian Devil key chain, kicking my shoes off onto brown tiles. It smelled of damp, but also dinner. Spaghetti Bolognese.

I could hear *A Current Affair* through the walls as I approached the lounge room.

Mum kept her eyes on the screen as she spoke. "That's a relief! You weren't answering your phone."

I burst into tears.

Mum stood, eyebrows pulled high on her forehead. "Oh, Finn. What's happened?"

The TV showed an intro to a story on dangerous neighbors. Mum extended her arms and I sank into her. A man on the screen was shoving a cameraman who was trying to film him. His outstretched hand covered the lens, the warm, pink color of white skin held up to the light.

Huge sobs made my body shake.

"Magdu is dead. She died, Mum. She fell."

Mum's eyes were wide.

"I was on the ledge and I had to climb back up and I was afraid the whole time that she was dead and she was."

Mum fumbled for the remote and turned the television off.

I howled and buried my mouth in her shoulder. She placed her hand on my head, drawing me into her. She smelled of Bolognese sauce and cigarette smoke. I squeezed her tight, comforted by the small rolls of fat at her waist.

"What happened?" Something small and tight in her voice. "Did she trip?"

Yes, was what she wanted me to say. *She tripped.*

"She was tied in, coming down after me, and the rope just *went*," I said. There was so much mucus behind my words that when I breathed out shakily a bubble of saliva popped. I wiped my mouth.

Mum straightened her arms, shifting back to get a better look at my face. "How could that have happened?"

"I don't know, Mum. I don't know." I burst into fresh sobs. "She was fine, everything was fine, and then Magdu was *gone*." I buried my face in Mum's dressing gown.

She seems like a lovely girl, Mum had said when she first met Magdu. I'd never brought Magdu home, but the three of us had met for coffee at a place Mum liked, and they'd got on well. Who wouldn't love Magdu?

Mum smoothed my hair with her hand. "And what was Daphne doing?" she asked quietly.

I jerked away from her. "What do you mean?"

"It's just a question, love."

I sat down heavily on the lounge. "She was clipped in too, on a different rope. They were coming down together."

Mum had never liked Daphne.

"Where is Magdu now?" Mum asked, as if I might have left her at the bottom of the valley.

"I'm . . . I'm not sure. The police came. They had to get Magdu out with a helicopter. They took me and Daphne to the station."

Behind Mum, on the side table next to her TV-watching chair, tea seeped up the string, moving up and over the lip of the cup. It marched toward the square paper label. Soon, it would drip onto the table and then there would be a stain to match the dozens of others. The thought made me tired. I wanted to find a cave, crawl inside, and sleep. I would come out when the world was clean and new, instead of dirty and tired and old.

"Why didn't you call me?" Mum asked.

I looked at her.

"Jesus, I need a cigarette," she said.

Mum didn't smoke in the common spaces: the kitchen, the lounge room. But I knew she smoked in her room when it was cold and she couldn't be bothered going outside. It was always freezing in our house at night.

The old fear—that she would have a glass of brandy with her smoke—moved through me.

She seemed to decide against the cigarette. "Do you want some tea?"

I sank deeper into the couch.

"Let's go into the kitchen." Mum pulled me up by the hand. "You need lemon balm."

Lemon balm, which Mum grew in pots on the kitchen window-sill, was her answer for everything. She claimed lemon balm tea had helped her to stop drinking. I never said anything when she said that.

She made the tea and I held the cup between my hands, the ceramic hot against my palms.

"Could you eat anything, do you think?"

My stomach flipped at the thought of food. Mum must have seen the look on my face because she didn't push it.

Spencer waddled in from the hallway, inserting himself under the table, placing his wet nose in the open palm I held in front of my knee. His face had gone gray, in that way it does when golden retrievers get old. We sat together until I'd drained the cup.

———

Mum helped me down the hall, like I was a sick old lady. She pushed open the door of my room.

"I've got it from here, Mum," I said. I didn't look at her.

She rubbed my back and said, "Okay, love."

It was all I could do not to lie down directly on the floor and close my eyes.

"Mum?" I said.

She was standing in the doorway. "Yes?"

"Are you okay?"

She smiled. "I'll be fine, love. Don't worry about me."

She walked back toward the kitchen.

I stepped forward to shut my bedroom door and came face-to-face with the picture of me and my little sister that hung in the hallway, arms around each other's shoulders, wide smiles with teeth missing.

My bed was covered in clothes. I'd tried out a few different climbing outfits before deciding what to take to Magdu's. I'd wanted to look capable for her. It took all my strength to push the clothes off the bed with a sweep of my arm. I kicked out of my pants, left them where they landed.

I threw myself down on top of the covers.

I could hear Mum somewhere in the house.

Another sound, a different one. It took me a second to place it. My mobile vibrating. I dug through the pile of clothes I'd swept off the bed and found the phone. The screen showed Daphne's name. The smell of her neroli oil filled my nose.

"Finn. It's me." She took a big, gulping breath. "I'm coming over. We need to be together."

I was glad Daphne couldn't see me, because I couldn't shift my face to match what I was trying to say. "I'm sorry, Daph. I can't." I couldn't give her what she needed. Before she could say anything else, I said, "I've got to go, okay? I'll call you. I can't talk tonight."

I couldn't ask the questions that burned in me, and I couldn't see her and not ask them.

I wanted to know what had happened. What had gone wrong up there on the clifftop after I'd belayed down? Why had Daphne put Magdu on the blue rope? I'd seen with my own eyes before I went over that Daphne herself had been tied in on that one.

I hung up, my heart racing, acid in the back of my throat. It was hard not to give Daphne what she wanted, but she'd understand, would forgive me. I took five deep breaths, counted them.

I stared at the phone, afraid it would ring again. Then I opened the bottom drawer of my bedside table and put the mobile inside.

Magdu wouldn't be here for her birthday. She would've turned thirty-one on the thirty-first of October. The thought was hot water on a fresh burn. I thought of the smooth swell of her cheeks. When you saw her from the side, and if she turned away from you slightly, her cheeks hid her nose. Her wavy hair that she'd kept shorter than her mother knew—she wore it up on Skype, she told me—but not so short that people assumed she was anything but straight. *That's why I have to be so forthright*, she'd said with a laugh. *I can't hope women will approach me like I approached you.* Magdu had never even kissed a boy. *I always had male friends in Dubai, and every so often one would fall in love with me, but I never cared. I thought it was so boring. I was pretty cruel to some of them.* I knew she'd never been cruel. She'd have been firm, clear, if she didn't like someone that way. She was still friends with all of them. They played *Dungeons & Dragons* online, read the same fat fantasy and sci-fi books. I pictured her with her headphones on in her teenage bedroom, lost in unreal lands. *A nerd and a loser from the start*, she sometimes said. "Yeah, well, you're *my* loser," is what I always said back.

My body pounded with adrenaline. I couldn't stay here, in my bedroom, in the house. I had to know what had happened. I needed to see where she had fallen. I needed to try to understand what had gone wrong.

———

It was dark in the car park for the cliff. I'd driven away from the house with my lights off until I got close to the cross street. I hoped Mum hadn't noticed me go, as I hadn't brought my phone. Another bit of pain and worry she didn't deserve.

I got out and leaned against the car. The trees seemed to press in around me, extending into the sky as if they were reaching for something. The moon was full, stars loosely strewn between winding branches. My head was tight, tears leaking from my eyes. I kept having flashes of Magdu falling. She dropped through an endless canopy, suspended in the thrash-horror of the fall, reaching out for something, anything, trying desperately to stop herself. For a moment, I'd almost jumped after her, had actually tugged against my harness. We had that kind of love. The kind where, when she fell, my first urge was to follow.

A hand on my shoulder made me gasp. I wheeled around.

It was Daphne, her hair pulled up into a ponytail, rain jacket on over jeans and a jumper. Her voice rang out in the clearing. "What the fuck are you doing here?"

It felt like all the air had been squeezed out of me. I didn't want to be in my own body, needed to be somewhere else.

"I don't know." It was the truth. "I suppose I had to see it again for myself."

I looked past Daphne, scanning the darkened car park. There were no other cars. "How did you get here?"

What I couldn't ask was: *What are you doing here?*

Daphne put her hands in her jacket pockets. "I walked."

I pictured Daphne back at her place, angry that I hadn't let her come over. It would've taken her at least an hour to walk here. She must have left home straight after she called me.

Daphne was a notorious insomniac. She'd told me that on the nights she couldn't sleep, she walked. She went out on the tourist trails, following a path to the visitor center where I worked, enjoying the silence and the silvery silhouettes of the trees. I worried about her, walking alone in the dark, but she said it was the only thing that helped. Hours of walking. Sometimes, when I slept over, she would poke me awake to tell me how smug and happy I looked sleeping. I didn't mind. I'd roll over and go to sleep again.

"Did the police tell you we could be in real trouble?" Daphne asked. "I haven't been able to stop thinking about it."

I wanted to say, *What did you do?* I could almost picture myself saying it out loud. *And what did you tell the police?*

Instead I looked down at the ground. "Yes, they said that to me too."

My heart was beating so hard it pushed against my sore tooth. *We had agreed Magdu would go on my red rope.*

Daphne pulled her hands out of her pockets and smoothed her ponytail. "Finn, did you say anything to the cops about the guy I was talking to?"

"No," I said. I was cold, wished I was wearing another layer.

"That's good. I don't want the fact that I was flirting with some random guy to make the cops think I was negligent."

Why was she talking about this? I wanted her to tell me why she'd put Magdu on her rope.

Daphne wiped at my face with her sleeve. "I can't believe it." Her eyes filled with tears, and I put my arms around her. She pressed her face into my shoulder. "Everything happened so fast." A cold wind blew through the car park, stirring her hair. "It could so easily have been me."

This was my chance to ask. Something in me hardened for just long enough to get the words out. "What happened up there? Why did you put Magdu on the blue rope? I saw you before I went over; you were tied in on that one."

The air went out of the space between us. Daphne took a step back from me. "So, what are you saying?" Her voice was high and strangled. "It would have been better if *I* died?"

I started sobbing. Couldn't stop it, couldn't make it quieter.

Daphne lowered her voice, almost apologetic. "I'd left my Prusik in my bag, so I untied myself. When I came back, Magdu was having trouble. She was nervous, wanted me to check her rope and belay device again. I thought it would make her less anxious if I untied her and then talked her through it again. I moved her onto my rope; it's newer and I thought she'd find that reassuring. I explained what I was doing step by step as I attached her, and it seemed to help. Then I said I'd wait on the top while she went over."

I swallowed hard. Everything Daphne was saying made perfect sense. Once you were tied in, it was a pain but not that big a deal to untie and retie. And I would have done the same thing, talked Magdu over the edge before joining her. It was always the scariest part of abseiling, when you committed your weight fully to the rope.

"Did you see anything wrong with either rope?" Daphne asked.

"They were both fine when I went down," I said.

Daphne grabbed my hand. My skin prickled. How beautiful she looked, no makeup on. Her skin shone white in the moonlight. According to Daphne, the ancient Greeks were always going on about white skin in their poems.

I ran my free hand through my hair. I thought of being alone in her bedroom the day before the climb. The things I had seen there. The fall had wiped them from my mind. The way you forget something when you move from one room to another. You can only remember that you're supposed to be remembering something. Daphne told me once that's an evolutionary thing. She said it was something about moving from an area of dense vegetation to an open plain that made your brain reset, ready for predators, and that's why I can never remember what I went into the kitchen for.

I stopped crying and took some deep breaths. When I squeezed Daphne's hand, it remained limp.

"Why didn't you want me to come over, Finn? What's wrong? Why aren't you talking to me?" She wasn't accusing me, but asking me. Her eyes met mine. "Are you worried that they know what happened before?"

Something in my belly dropped. She was right. That was what scared me the most.

Daphne held me by the arms. "They don't, Finn. I would never tell them that."

My shoulders slumped. I was sick with relief. Of course she hadn't said anything. Daphne was the one who kept me safe, who kept my secret.

I pulled Daphne into a hug. Neroli oil. The smell of it was in her hair, on her skin. She was smaller than I was, and I liked the way that felt for a moment.

Daphne took a step back and pulled something from her pocket. "When were you going to tell me about this?" she said.

A small, maroon velvet box. Inside it, I knew, was my grandmother's wedding ring, a simple gold band with three small opals embedded in it. I'd hidden the box inside an old climbing shoe, shoving it in the pocket behind the driver's seat. It was silly of me to leave it there, but who would steal a single climbing shoe? I hadn't been planning to use it the day of the climb, but when the moment was right, I wanted it close to hand.

Daphne was crying. "What is going on? You've been acting like you can't talk to me about stuff for months. And then I find this."

My body was ice, heavy and slow. "Why did you take that?"

"Fuck, Finnbo. You act like you've never lost control. Like you've never wanted to look inside a box you knew you weren't supposed to."

I thought about what I'd found in a drawer at Daphne's house only the night before. A million years ago.

"Don't you ever just *do* something?" Daphne said. "Because you can?"

"Is this supposed to be you apologizing?" The venom in my voice surprised me.

Daphne crossed her arms. "You're right. We both know you understand all about losing control."

She shook her head, unfolding her arms as if she hadn't meant what she'd said, that it wasn't what it sounded like: a threat.

A pleading note in her voice. "I almost died today, Finn. I could use some compassion."

"Why did you take the ring, Daphne?"

Daphne threw up her hands. "It was a dumb joke, all right?

Besides—a wedding ring? I'm your best friend, and I love you, but you can be a little intense." Daphne reached up and pushed a lock of hair back behind my ear. "I needed to make sure she could hack it. That she wasn't going to break your heart."

Daphne handed the box back to me, a peace offering. She held my hand as I took it, fingers closing around the maroon velvet. I didn't want to fight with Daphne. I wanted her to tell me how to be. The belief that Daphne knew better than I did almost never went away.

Her voice was low, gentle. "After everything I've done for you, how could you possibly think that I don't have your best interests at heart?"

Daphne wrapped her hands around mine, the velvet box hidden now under two layers of skin.

6

BEFORE

In high school, Daphne and I had nothing in common. Until we did.

The first day I came back to school after my sister died, Daphne grabbed me by the arm and wheeled me around, marched me straight back out the school gate. I'd spent a week sitting around with Mum at home, only going out for the funeral. Even with English for first period, I'd been keen to come to school, to do something normal. At the same time, I felt freakish. Ugly and small and pink from crying.

"You get to do what you want," Daphne had said. "Everyone's going to give you a free pass. Let's go smoke this."

The smell of the joint she was holding in her hand wafted over. It was an old Looney Tunes bit, when one of the characters smells a pie cooling on a shelf, the smell indicated by two little lines that dance, and follows it, nose first. Suze and I had a set of those cartoons on VHS. We'd watched them until the videos went hazy in some places.

Daphne and I skirted the school grounds, found a place near the bus shelters where we couldn't be seen from the road or the class-rooms. We huddled together between some pathetic bushes. There were old chip packets and bottle caps on the ground, little offerings to a garbage god. It was still September, the air crisp even though it was sunny. I'd walked with Daphne every lunchtime since the day we'd met. We'd roamed the school, getting to know each other.

"This is the problem with Australian public schools," Daphne said, gesturing to the rubbish on the ground. "They lack a certain *ambiance*." She pronounced the last word with a strange emphasis. Daphne often sounded as if she were from an earlier generation. Something full and round and juicy about the things she said.

We laughed. It felt bad to be laughing, but it was also good to be fifteen and laughing. Daphne tossed her long blond hair. I found it hard to look away from her. The collar of her bright white school shirt folded crisply over her school jumper. She wore the school tie, which she loosened. We threw our bags down on the ground and she lay on the patchy grass.

When people talked about Daphne's sister's suicide, they said that the girl had been unhappy at her new school. I'd thought, *She's punishing her parents for making her move*, and it had made me sad because it was such a permanent punishment, one that had wiped the girl out forever.

I lay on the ground beside Daphne.

"Is it true what they've been saying?" she asked. "Did your sister kill herself?"

I froze. I didn't read newspapers, but I knew that Daphne's sister's death had been in them. Recently enough for people to say my sister must have seen the stories, had to have been stewing on it.

I was grateful to be lying beside Daphne, so I didn't have to look her in the face as I spoke. "Yes," I said.

"She jumped from a cliff?" Daphne's voice was clear and loud. I resisted the urge to look around us to see if anyone had heard.

I wanted to tell her about going camping, about waking in the early hours to find that Suze was no longer beside me on her bedroll in our tent. Mum's face when the cops came. Her keening when they said they'd found the body on a rock shelf. Mum and I going in the ambulance with Suze, her face and body covered with a gray blanket. How I'd had the thought that someone would wash that blanket without ever knowing it had been tucked around my thirteen-year-old sister. I wanted to tell her all the things that roiled inside of me. I couldn't, so I just nodded.

"I was so angry at my sister," Daphne said. "For what she did. That's the part no one lets you talk about."

Daphne lit the joint, took a long, expert drag before handing it to me. We lay on the ground passing the joint between us—not every three puffs, like you did at parties, but after each puff. Time slid away. My body went floating off from itself.

"Is this what it feels like?" I managed to ask, looking over at Daphne, who had her eyes closed and her hands on her chest. I was too stoned and sad to be self-conscious. "Grief, I mean?"

"Yes," she said.

I was having difficulty keeping my eyes open. I levered one eyelid apart with my fingers. Daphne must have been watching me because she broke into hysterical giggles.

I thought of Dad, long skinny legs and his smell of earth and sweat, of loamy forest floor. After he'd left, Suze and I stayed with him for a weekend every month. He'd got together with a new woman not long after leaving Mum, and after a while she would be there too. Her name was Gwendoline and she told us to call her Gwen. ("Might as well be Guinevere or bloody Saffron, I mean *honestly*," Mum had said more than once after she found out.) I suspected they'd met before Dad left, but I never asked Gwen about it because she would have told me the truth.

After a while, I found I could open my eyes again. Daphne stretched her legs in the sun, hitching up her skirt so the gold light spilled across her thighs. I held my breath, heard the sound of cars driving by in the distance.

"Tell me about your sister," Daphne said. She reached over and took my hand in hers. "How old was she again?"

"Thirteen." The sentence *She was thirteen when she died* played in my head. Shame bubbled through me. What a shitty fucking sentence. "She was almost exactly two years younger than me. Her birthday's only two days after mine. I loved being the big sister."

I remembered Suze sitting at the low coffee table in the lounge room a couple of weeks earlier, her mouth turned down in a frown of concentration as she worked on her homework. The creased lines in her forehead made her look more adult. You could already see the kind of woman she would grow up to be. She was lean, like Dad's side of the family. I would look at her cast-off clothes and think that one of my thighs would only just fit in the space her jean shorts made for her hips and bum and both legs.

Dappled sunlight on my face. The smell of weed and of Daphne and of something in the earth and the plants.

"What are you thinking about now?"

Daphne's words were expensive-sounding. Different from the flat nasal sounds of me and my family. *Suzanne.* My sister Suze could swear with the best of them.

I was suddenly ravenously hungry.

"God, I could go for a packet of chips right now," Daphne said. In the moment it was evidence of a connection, proof that I could tell her anything.

Tears trickled down my face. I scooped them into my mouth, keeping the side of my palm tight to my cheek, which seemed both the most natural thing to do and very important in the moment, so that my tears didn't touch the ground.

"I don't know," I said. "I don't make sense to myself anymore. I can't come back. There's no home to come back to anymore."

Daphne began to recite something, the rhythm of it flowing over me like warm water.

He seems to me equal to the gods that man
whoever he is who opposite you
sits and listens close
to your sweet speaking

and lovely laughing—oh it
puts the heart in my chest on wings
for when I look at you, even a moment,
no speaking is left in me

no: tongue breaks and thin
fire is racing under skin
and in eyes no sight and drumming
fills ears

and cold sweat holds me and shaking
grips me all, greener than grass
I am and dead—or almost
I seem to me.

———————

"What was that?" I asked, blush spreading from my face up into my scalp, a line of bushfire heat moving through low scrub.

"It's a fragment from Sappho. There's about a million different translations, but I like the part that goes, *It puts the heart in my chest on wings.*"

I was speaking to a creature from another planet. I'd never known anyone who recited poetry. I tried to think of something intelligent to say. "I like it too," I said. "It makes me think of that Red Bull commercial. You know: *Red Bull gives you wings.*"

Daphne smiled and took me by the hand on that scrappy bit of ground near the school, my palm wet from my tears. She didn't pull away. I wanted to ask about Daphne's sister Brianna, about how she'd died. Daphne had told me she was angry at her sister for what she'd done, and this information—*she'd told me a secret*—glowed inside me. I couldn't form words, and not because I was stoned. Daphne was inside an elegant force field, a ring of ancient magic that fizzed and buzzed. And it was okay. It was okay to be outside the force field, so long as I could sit alongside it, my hand in Daphne's. I was afraid of what being close to her meant, what it said about me that I could sit with her, take comfort from her hand in mine. But even if I'd wanted to, I knew I didn't have the strength to stand up and walk away.

7

THURSDAY, SEPTEMBER 7, 2017

In the moment before I opened my eyes the next morning, my body was light. And then, in a sick rush, something vital slithered out of my guts and through my fingers as I tried to cover the hole. I'd driven Daphne home from the car park. I'd come home to bed, returning the ring to my bottom drawer. I'd dreamed of darkness, of Magdu falling. And then my sister was in the dream. She was down in the valley with Magdu's body. I heard her laughing, the sound of it rising through the trees.

I swung myself out of bed and stood. I swayed, unsure if I could keep myself upright. Anger swelled. How could I have forgotten, even for a second? I looked at the clock. It was after eight. How could I have slept in after what had happened? There was something wrong with me. Magdu deserved better.

I pulled on a pair of track pants and walked to the bathroom. I'd automatically stepped into the slippers by my bedroom door. I kicked them off next to the sink, let my bare feet rest on the freezing lino. I needed to feel the exact spot where my body ended. Something in my chest was rotten and putrid and stinking. It was going to burst the same way Mum had seen the carcass of a goat burst on her parents' farm when she was a kid.

My belly throbbed, heavy and full. I pulled down my pants and underwear and sat down on the toilet. My period had arrived. Yesterday's thick ache was from another lifetime, and it took a moment to understand the dark, mucus-y blobs on faded material. That dull pain, someone punching my stomach from the inside. The metallic twang of blood in the small, cold room. It was satisfying, when I bled. The feeling that I'd made something, done something. I threw the ruined underwear in the small flip-top bin next to the toilet, burying it under some scrunched-up tissues. I wouldn't usually throw away underwear, but it seemed ridiculous to try to save it when Magdu was gone.

I spent a long time brushing my teeth. Flossing. I hated flossing. Hated smelling what was left on the waxy string afterward, but couldn't stop myself. My tooth throbbed.

There was a high horizontal window in the bathroom up near the ceiling, and I could see the morning sky through it. The weather of the morning before seemed like a distant memory, like there had only ever been rain and anybody who thought differently was fooling themselves.

I staggered to my bedroom and threw back my quilt to check if I'd got any period blood on the sheets. I hadn't, but the tug in my belly grew stronger. My tits ached. I squeezed one reflexively, the short, sharp pain a relief from the duller ache. I found an ancient pad in my top drawer, the bright pink packaging a remnant of high school. I ripped it open, tearing the tabs and pushing it into a clean pair of underwear. I couldn't be bothered with my menstrual cup. Grim satisfaction at creating more waste, something to fuck the world up a little bit more. I lay down in my undies and T-shirt, pulling the quilt over me.

———

I woke again to a knock at the front door. The sound was sharp. Authoritative. Not the limp-wristed tap or cheery rat-a-tat-tat of one of Mum's friends. They would know to use the back door, anyway. My tongue felt for my sore tooth, a stab of pain when I pressed it, and I raised myself up on my elbows. For a moment, I thought about getting up and answering it, but I heard Mum's footsteps in the hall.

"Mrs. Young?" A man speaking.

"Yes?" Mum had her Jehovah's Witness voice on.

Once, when she'd heard from Candace up the street that they were doing the rounds that day, Mum had answered the door in only her dressing gown, tied in such a way that when she leaned forward to accept the pamphlet the whole thing had come undone. Maybe it was only a coincidence, but there hadn't been any more Jehovah's Witnesses since then.

"Hello. I'm Senior Constable Dale Gosling. I was hoping to speak to Finnlay Young? I've tried calling but her phone seems to be off."

It was the lean cop from the day before. I sat up in bed, then lowered myself back down again.

My room was the closest one to the street, right by the front door, and his voice carried through the thin walls like he was standing next to me. "We need her to come in and answer some more questions."

Cold metal ran through my veins, threatening to break the skin.

"It's not a good time." I pictured Mum standing on the front step, her hands on her hips. "She's sleeping."

"It'll be quick," he said.

"Given everything she's been through, surely it can wait?"

"It won't take long," he insisted. There was a "dealing with the public" tone in his voice, a weary politeness.

"That doesn't make her any less asleep, though, does it?" Mum's voice was firm. "Give me your card and I'll have her call you when she wakes up."

The man paused before responding, as if weighing how hard to push the small woman in front of him. "She should have my number, Mrs. Young, but I'll give you this in case."

I rose and pulled on clean track pants. Spencer barked in the hallway. I opened the door and he slipped into the room like someone arriving just in time for an appointment, heading straight for the bed.

I stepped into the hallway behind Mum.

"I'll come," I said. "I'm coming."

Mum turned to face me. "Do you want me to go with you?"

It was drizzling and we didn't have an awning over our front door. The cop was getting damp standing there.

"No, it's all right." I looked at Dale Gosling. "I'll follow you in my car?"

"I'll meet you at the station." Looking down at my tracksuit pants, he said, "It'll give you a minute to get changed."

When the cop turned away, Mum grabbed my hand and squeezed it.

I turned to her. "It's all right, Mum," I said. Acid swirled in my gut. "It's going to be all right."

————

I slid into the car a few minutes later, dressed in jeans and a hoodie. I saw Magdu's bag sitting in the footwell of the passenger's side.

She'd taken a small daypack out to the cliff the day of the climb, but she'd left her faded black canvas tote in the car. *Keep talking, I'm diagnosing you* was printed on one side; it had been a gift from someone in her master's program. I was suddenly relieved that the car had not been stolen, that no one had taken it with Magdu's bag inside.

My hands were on the wheel, and yet at the same time I was peering down on myself and the car as if from a great height.

When I arrived at the station, I had to lock the car manually by depressing a button in the driver's-side door then holding the handle up as I slammed the door closed. My clicker was broken, had been for years. Other people didn't have to do this. Their clicker broke and they fixed it.

I walked into the waiting room, unsure if I should say I was there to see Senior Constable Gosling. Felt a stab of fear, wondering if Daphne would be there too.

Why didn't I want to see her? The ends of my fingers tingled when I thought about it.

A voice came from the direction of the reception desk. "Finn?"

Dale wore a short-sleeved shirt, smooth forearms visible. There was no fat on him and the uniform suited him. He looked strong but quick, someone you wanted on your side in a fight.

"Thanks for coming in again," he said, leading me down a corridor to a small room.

It was a different room from the one I'd been taken to the day before. There were some children's toys in the corner and a battered couch. We sat at a scratched wooden table, on chairs that belonged in a kitchen.

"I'm sorry you had trouble getting hold of me," I said. "I wasn't thinking. About my phone, I mean." I could hear the pleading tone in my voice.

The older man from the day before, Sergeant Oakland, came in, shutting the door behind him. He looked too big for the room. I sat up straighter in my chair.

This man is looking for someone to blame.

Oakland sniffed, rubbed his nose. "What was Magdalene's state of mind on the morning of the climb?"

I took a breath, looked down at the table. "We woke up at her place around six thirty," I said. "Which was early for her."

Magdu hadn't slept well the night before, I could tell. We'd agreed that we would make an early start on the day of the climb. I was used to getting up early—for work, for climbing, out of habit—but Magdu struggled. She liked to sleep in, to burrow deeper into the blankets while I went out into the cold world. It was nice, having someone to leave in bed.

Dale clasped his hands in front of him. "How did she seem?" he prompted.

———

Magdu and I had sat at the kitchen counter, listening to the kettle boil. I'd checked the weather forecast and seen that the conditions were favorable. It was quiet, the way it is when you're awake before the rest of the world.

I poured coffee from the French press, adding two sugars and milk to Magdu's cup and placing it in front of her.

She spoke softly but deliberately. "Sometimes I get so angry at myself for thinking I can do this."

"Do what?"

"Life."

"Jeez, you are really not a morning person, huh?"

I smiled because I wanted her to smile, because this was not normal for us. She was the one who did the reassuring. She was the one who said that everything was going to be okay.

———

"What did you two talk about?" Dale asked.

"She was tired." It wasn't an answer to his question. Oakland shifted in his chair and sniffed again.

———

I'd stopped on my way past her, rubbed her back with an open palm. There'd been something I didn't like in the room. Someone was about to say we needed to talk. Maybe it would even be me.

"Do you ever feel like things keep stacking up, going further and further into the future, and you're never going to catch up? That you'll never be finished?" Magdu was hunched over, speaking into the countertop.

"You mean like when you wash all the dishes and then someone brings a big pot you didn't see?" I teased. It was something Magdu did to me all the time.

Her tone was cold. "No, not like that."

"You're working too hard," I told her, trying to wrench us somewhere other than wherever this was.

She raised a hand, as if to stop me from coming any closer. "Everyone else in my course seems to be managing."

"What's wrong, Mags?"

"I don't know if I have what it takes to do my job out in the real world. Who am I to think I can help people?"

I'd felt a rush of love so total I had to take Magdu in my arms and hold her. I would never let anything come between me and the woman I loved. I wanted her sadness, I wanted to hold everything for both of us.

"You are going to be amazing, Mags."

———

"She was worried about her placement," I said aloud, aware I'd been quiet for a while. "She had one coming up as part of her master's course."

Dale made a note on the pad in front of him. "What in particular was she worried about?"

"That she wouldn't be able to keep up. It was ridiculous. She's one of the smartest people I know," I said.

———

"Ready to go?" I'd asked, after Magdu had managed to eat some toast. The best thing would be to get going. Get it over and done with.

"Why are we even doing this, Finn? How is it we've ended up following Daphne's plan?"

"That's just kind of what happens." I smiled, wishing I'd said something else, something encouraging.

"I'm so tired, Finn." Magdu burst into tears.

"Baby." I didn't know what else to say. This was not like Magdu. She was brave. We had practiced. The day before, she had been ready and excited for the climb. This wasn't fear. This was something else.

I put my arms around her, let her cry into my shirtfront.

She pulled away after a little bit, her hands still linked behind my back.

"We don't have to go," I said, though I couldn't imagine making that phone call to Daphne. I shouldn't make promises I couldn't keep.

"It's nothing, honestly." She reclaimed her hands to push hair out of her face. "You're right, I'm not a morning person. It takes me back to being a teenager, having to get up at the crack of dawn, my time not being my own."

————

"She said that morning reminded her of being a teenager."

"She said that?" Dale interrupted. "That she felt like she had when she was a teenager?"

"Yeah," I said, unsure why this was important. "I assumed she meant, like, getting up early for school or whatever. But she was nervous. That's all it was." I should have seen how nervous she was. I should've put a stop to it all. "Why are we talking about this?"

Oakland broke in. "We've had an opportunity to speak with her family, who told us that Magdalene attempted suicide once before, in her teens. That kind of thing is relevant to our investigation." He looked at his colleague, like he was sick of Dale pussyfooting around. "It would have been useful if you'd told us."

"Suicide?" A sick rush. Someone pulling out your chair as you go to sit down. "But it's not true. Magdu wouldn't do that."

I looked at Dale, who was looking down at his notepad. A numbness spread through me. I couldn't even be angry at what the older man had said. It was happening far away.

"Did Magdu have a knife?" Dale asked gently.

"No." I looked between the two cops. "I didn't give her one because I didn't think she'd need it. And in an emergency she might even have got herself into more trouble. If something went wrong, I was right there."

A wave of shame moved through me.

"Why are you asking me this?"

Oakland spoke again, before Dale could answer. "The way I see it, either you fucked up, or Miss Fernandes had decided it was her time," Oakland said. The raw hostility of it was strange and slightly absurd. "We'll be undertaking a forensic assessment of your gear, to rule out the first option."

"How's Magdu supposed to have . . . tried?" My words were almost a whisper. "Before?"

Oakland leaned back. "I can't disclose that information."

Something inside me twisted, turned cold. I knew that life had been hard for Magdu sometimes in Dubai. But that didn't make her suicidal. She would have told me.

I crossed my arms. "I don't believe it," I said. "I can't."

Oakland turned to Dale. "This is a waste of time."

I looked to Dale, then at Oakland. "Wait, what about the guys who were on the cliff?" I could hear the desperation in my voice. "Are you looking into them?" Acid rose up in my throat, and my heart pounded. "If you're asking me about a knife, then you should know that one of them had a big knife, and he came close to where we were climbing."

Daphne had asked me not to mention that she'd been talking to him, but surely that didn't mean I couldn't mention him at all?

"I was going to ask you about that." Dale plucked a photo from a folder on the table. "Is this the man you saw on the cliff?"

Same bright white smile, dark hair. "Yes."

"His name is Brendan McNamara. He was the one who called the police. Apparently, Daphne Bennett wasn't able to get reception on the cliff top and refused to leave you. The group of young men walked back to the car park, and then drove to meet police at the top of the track."

"Are you talking to them as well?" I looked toward the door.

The older man sniffed again.

Dale's voice was low. "They provided statements to one of our officers at the scene and were then asked to leave to make room in the car park for emergency vehicles."

"Okay," I said. "But will you talk to them again?"

"Is there something you need to tell us?" Dale asked. "Why do you think we should speak to them?"

I stared into the corner of the room, trying to remember. "Before I was getting ready to belay down, Brendan was checking out my anchor. I think he wanted to say something snarky about it." Not that he'd had anything to say when he'd seen my knots. I knew what I was doing.

"Did he touch the anchor?"

I shook my head.

"But Magdu would never hurt herself," I said. "You have to believe that."

Sergeant Oakland snorted and stood up. He slapped his hands on the table and I jumped in my seat. "Please keep your phone on in the future, Miss Young." He towered over us for a few moments before turning and leaving the room.

I looked at Dale Gosling, letting my eyes fall on his name tag again. A gosling was a baby goose. Once, Mum had taken me and Suze to her cousin's farm for Christmas. Suze was three years old, so I would have been five. I'd got Barbie roller skates. The farm's concrete driveway was weedy and cracked but I wanted to try out my new skates. Only, a flock of geese had come around the corner of the house and seen me. Scared, I tried to go faster, but I fell and the geese went for me, pecking at my face and hands. My father was supposed to be watching me, but it was Mum who heard the screaming and came out. She lifted me up and away from the birds.

"You've spoken with her parents?" I asked when I saw Dale was getting ready to stand too. My heart thudded in my chest. "Are they here?"

"Not yet," Dale replied. "Magdu's mother is in the air now." He looked across to the closed door. "She's traveling alone."

"What about her aunt?" Magdu's aunt Priya was the only family member I'd met.

"She and Magdu's uncle have been informed."

The acid was back. "Can I see Magdu?"

Dale rubbed the back of his head, wincing. "Like I told you yesterday, Magdu's uncle has formally identified the body. Her family members have expressly said they don't want anyone else to see her."

He looked at me the way people had looked at me and Mum after Suze's death. I'd wanted to punch the pity off their faces. "Can they stop me?" I asked.

I hadn't showered since before the climb. I could smell my own rancid sweat, wondered if Dale could smell period blood in the small room.

"I'm sorry." Dale cleared his throat. "The family has a right to decide who can have access."

"She was *my* family," I said softly. I didn't sound persuasive to my own ears. It was melodrama. A bad episode of *Home and Away*. I'd been preparing for the rejection but that didn't make it any easier. Why would the cops help someone like me?

After Dale had walked me to the waiting room and left me there, I thought about what they'd said. I thought about Oakland, the way he'd spoken to me. Usually, everyone got very quiet around suicides, like the family might break if you talked too loudly. Something sharp sank from my lungs down into the pit of my stomach.

I learned later you weren't supposed to say "commit suicide," because it was like "committing adultery" or "committing murder." It implied that it was wicked, a sinful act. Still, it was the language the cops used for Suze when I'd come to this station with Mum.

The thing is, my sister didn't commit suicide.

8

BEFORE

I told Daphne the truth about my sister a week after that afternoon on the grass. It was October. We'd skipped school and were hiking along a track that started in the bush reserve behind Daphne's house. Daphne was telling me about the psychologist her parents had been forcing her to see since her sister died. She'd been making me laugh by doing an impersonation of the woman, who insisted that Daphne call her Jo. The psychologist was always asking, *And what does that bring up for you?*

Daphne's long hair was tied back in a plait that was almost as thick as her wrist, if not mine. As it swayed in front of me, I had to resist the urge to take hold of it, to wrap it around my arm like a guide rope, tucking it up into a neat loop the way my father had taught me.

I took a breath, and then I said it: "My sister didn't commit suicide."

"What do you mean?" Daphne stopped and turned to me.

She was in a white T-shirt and shorts, her blond bangs plastered to her face with sweat. Out of school uniform, she looked older than sixteen. Her tanned legs ended in scuffed hiking boots.

We'd been welded together in the week since I'd come back to school after my sister's death. I spent more time at her place than my own. As if sensing it might make me feel more comfortable about talking, Daphne started walking again.

She turned to look at me over her shoulder. "Finn?"

It was a hot day, and when I opened my mouth the dry wind sucked the moisture out of me. Shame scorched through me. "We were talking, right before she died," I said. "It was nighttime, and Mum was already asleep in the other tent. Suze and I were fighting about something stupid to do with my dad." I slowed and took out my water bottle. Fiddled with it. I came to a stop next to Daphne. "I wanted her to listen to me."

———

There'd been no warning on the night Suze died. Nothing to indicate what was coming. Well, there had been a sign. At the edge of the ridge track was a faded national park sign that read BRINKLEY'S LEAP, but I'd ignored it.

When Mum left our camping spot to buy booze, she was gone a long time. I made spaghetti on the camp stove, stirring half a jar of pasta sauce through it after attempting to drain the saucepan with a tin plate held to the edge. The pasta slopped around, nearly sliding off our plates and into the campfire. Suze had been quiet, her sandy blond hair pulled away from her face in the intricate braids she'd figured out how to do when she started high school the year before.

It was September, but that night had still been cold enough that you could see your breath. Long after Mum had returned, drunk her booze, and fallen asleep, Suze got up. I heard the rustling of her sleeping bag, the *pzzzt* of the tent being unzipped. When Suze didn't come back, I went outside to find her.

We were camped in scrub at the edge of a rock platform. You weren't technically supposed to camp here, but rangers never seemed to come into this part of the park. It meant waking to beautiful views over the valley. Suze was sitting on a camp chair that she'd pulled onto a section of the cliff that jutted out from the main rock like one of those mushrooms that spread out in a semicircle from the trunk of a tree. She had on a bulky jacket of Dad's. She must have hidden it when he left, or he just forgot it. Despite the cold, she only had her nightie on underneath. Her long legs stretched out in front of her. She was looking down at them, examining them as if she'd never seen them before.

"You're too close to the edge, kiddo," I said. "Shift it back a bit."

Her head whipped around to look at me. She gripped the arms of the camping chair, pulled her legs up into the coat. "I am so *sick* of you telling me what to do."

"Jeez, what's up *your* bum?"

I had a memory of Suze's first day of school. Putting her hair in pigtails. Suze standing on tiptoe to kiss me on the cheek at the door to her kindergarten room. Now, as she stood up and out of her chair, she was as tall as me, and would only get taller.

"Can't sleep?" I asked.

She looked at me for a moment, then turned away, toward the valley, as if I hadn't spoken. My skin itched beneath my jumper. I rested a hand, my fingertips like ice, between my neck and the scratchy wool.

"C'mon, you must be freezing without trackies on. Come back into the tent and get warm." I moved closer to her and put my free hand on her shoulder.

Suze was still not looking at me, but even in profile I could see her eyes narrow. "Quit telling me what to do. You're not my mother." She spoke out to the empty space over the valley. It was like she'd ripped off my clothing and I was standing there in my underwear.

I took a breath. "Suze, I know it's all a bit shit . . ." I gestured to the tents. "I don't want to be here either."

Sometimes, I wondered why Mum didn't leave us girls at home. I was fifteen, Suze thirteen. We were old enough to stay by ourselves. But I knew she wanted us close to her. And she didn't want us to tell Dad that we'd been left alone. We never spoke about Mum's drinking with Dad.

"But we can make the most of it, can't we? Go for a walk in the morning while Mum sleeps it off?"

Suze was still gazing out into the inky blackness. Only the tops of the trees shone with reflected light from the moon. Everything else was dark. The valley was beautiful in that way things you can only see part of often are.

"You have no idea how much I fucking hate you," Suze said, keeping her eyes on the void. She said it calmly, as if she were saying we needed more firewood. When I didn't respond, she continued, "And you think I owe you everything. I can't fucking *stand* you, Finn."

I'd heard of people climbing with a ring on their finger. The band of metal getting caught somehow, shearing the finger off, something that had so recently been a part of them falling to the ground, never to be seen again. That's what it felt like, as if part of me had fallen away.

I loved my sister, had always looked out for her. She'd always been the one thing I was doing right, the one person I wasn't letting down. I couldn't feel anger, just a deep sadness.

Suze turned and leaned toward me. "You *embarrass* me."

Tears sprang into my eyes. "Why are you saying this?"

Her face was screwed up now, the skin tight and white with fury in a way I'd never seen. "If it weren't for you"—she pointed an accusing finger—"I could go and live with Dad. He said I could. But then he talked to fucking Gwen and *she* said it wouldn't be fair, that they couldn't take both of us so they shouldn't take only one of us."

I knew my dad wouldn't have thought about it like that. He made exceptions for Suze. Suze was Mum's favorite, too. And that wasn't how it was supposed to go in families. We should have each been one parent's favorite, even if they would never admit it. And it didn't matter that I was the one who brought Mum tea with four sugars when she was hungover, the one who got her up for her supermarket shift.

"Aren't you going to say something?" Suze crossed her arms, disgust on her face. "You're so fucking *slow*."

I stepped back, tears rising, wanting her to stop saying these awful things.

"You can't even *read*," Suze said. "Why would anyone want you around?"

Suze stalked away from me, away from the tents and toward the blackness. The moon was bright enough that I wasn't worried she would walk off the rock ledge, but my body tensed, the way it does when you see someone up high.

I walked toward her.

"Fuck off," Suze said, oblivious to her distance from the edge.

I bridged the space between us quickly. "You're too close." I grabbed a fistful of our dad's jacket, trying to tug her near to me, away from the drop-off.

She twisted away, pulling her arms out of the jacket, corkscrewing out of my grasp the way she'd perfected at five years old. But she must've stepped on a rock or something in the dark. She lost her balance. She screamed but it was so quick. The scream silenced by a cracking thud.

I was left holding my father's jacket. Dark navy with canvas pockets and a faint smell of woodsmoke.

I got as close to the edge as I dared and looked down. In the moonlight, I could see Suze on a rock ledge around twelve meters below. Her neck was . . . wrong. I called her name and strained my ears for any response. The valley was still ringing with the sound of impact, filling me up like breath. There was no way a body could be shaped like that and still be alive. Blood was pooling around her, eating up the light reflected by stone.

I turned, ran for the tent. Suze wasn't in there. I'd thought that she might be, like returning to a save point in *Zelda* on our cousin's Nintendo 64 after I died. Finding everything as it had been. I zipped the door closed behind me.

I was holding the jacket. I pulled off my jeans and crawled into my sleeping bag, kicking the jacket down between my feet, the material so cold it felt wet. I could hear Mum still snoring in the next tent.

A wave of tiredness hit me like a punch to the face. I fell asleep the way you slip into fever; had strange and terrible dreams that someone was chasing us, me and Suze and my mother. Then we reached an open field and we'd got away. The three of us walked, holding hands, across the grass.

———

I looked at Daphne, unsure what would happen after I told her all this. I smelled the air.

"It was the sort of thing she did all the time as a kid, twisting out of her clothes like that. You could never catch her. She was like an eel." I wanted to freeze in this moment, before Daphne's reaction. "It was my fault. It was all my fault."

Daphne's gaze held my own. "What happened when you woke up?"

———

It was lighter inside the tent when I woke, and it hadn't happened. Sleep had severed the connection between me and the event. It was a dream I'd had.

I unzipped the tent, the sound so loud you could hear it from miles away.

"Mum? Where's Suze?" Panic in my voice. The panic was real. Suze was not where she was supposed to be. Something was very wrong.

I opened Mum's tent and the smell of booze hit me. Mum raised a groggy head from her sleeping bag, wincing at the early morning light.

"She's gone for a quick pee, love."

"Mum, it's been too long." There was a whine in my voice. "Please, get up."

Mum shuffled out of the bag, her thighs white in the glowing green light of the tent.

She pulled on her pants, stepping into them, missing one leg and nearly falling sideways so that I had to reach out and steady her. I was irrationally angry at her for being slow. If we hurried, we might find Suze.

We headed out in different directions from the tent, calling Suze's name, shards of morning light cutting through the thin scraggle of trees pushed up against the rock shelf.

The expression on Mum's face when we both arrived back at the tent was grim.

"Okay, I'm going to call the police." She dug around in her handbag for her red Nokia phone. "Should I call emergency or the local station?"

"I don't know," I said.

Mum called triple zero. The connection was bad. She told them the road she had followed, that she didn't know quite how far down we were but that we were camped close to the edge of the valley.

"They're on their way," she said when she'd ended the call.

We sat in silence for a few moments, then she stood.

"You stay here, love. I'm going to do another loop."

When the police arrived, I was sitting alone out the front of the tents. I'd restarted the fire to have something to do with my hands.

"You're not meant to light fires in the national park," an older cop said. I could hear the other cops calling to each other as they walked through the scrub.

I looked at the fire, then back at him. "Sorry. We didn't make one before now," I lied. "Just while we were waiting."

As if clocking my age and remembering there was a missing girl—my sister—the man's expression softened. He smelled of after-shave. It reminded me of Dad. He would have to be told. Who would tell him? What would they say?

I was crouched by the fire. Mum reappeared and stood next to me. The three camping chairs, damp with morning dew, were arranged in a semicircle at our backs. I'd only noticed after Mum had wandered off to search again how odd it looked to have one chair sitting closer to the edge, so I'd dragged it back nearer to the tents. My heart pounded. I shouldn't have done it.

"What was she wearing?" the police officer asked, stepping between us and the fire. We were both staring into it, heads frozen in the same position.

Mum ran her hands through her hair, looked at me.

"Her nightie," I said.

The soft white nightie with the scalloped satin edge that kicked up a little bit. Too short for her, but she'd refused to throw it out. And Dad's jacket, which was now bunched in the bottom of my sleeping bag.

As I moved to sit down in one of the camp chairs, I could smell the alcohol coming from Mum's tent. I knew the police officer would smell it too from where he was standing, would smell it on her breath.

He guided Mum away from me, close to the edge of the clearing. She waited there as he searched the tent and found Suze's diary. Whatever he read there made him tell Mum to stay where she was. He walked past me, looked out over the edge of the cliff. I saw the moment he saw Suze, watched as he made a call on his radio. He walked back to my mother, warning her not to move. I caught snatches of what they were saying, but couldn't make out whole sentences. I first heard the word "suicide" in the deep voice of the cop, the word standing out in the drone of the rest of the conversation.

Later that day, a woman from social services led me into a room at the police station and asked if I felt safe with my mother. I was so angry, so filled with rage, that I could only mutter, *Of course*. No one thought to ask if I might be the problem.

The tears came then. I crouched on the track, covered my face with my hands. I didn't want to lie to my mum anymore. I had to tell her, tell everyone what I had done. For two whole weeks I'd said that I'd been asleep, that I'd woken up to find Suze gone. What was wrong with me? I'd stayed silent as everyone else assumed that Suze had jumped. I had no idea what she wrote in her diary, and Mum wouldn't tell me.

I waited for Daphne to turn and run, to leave me here and go straight to the police. Instead, she lowered herself onto the path beside me, let her body weight shift into my side.

We sat together in silence, in the shade of the gums that towered over the path, my heart thudding in my chest.

Daphne looked up at the sky. "It was an accident, right?"

"Yes." I needed her to understand that. I hadn't meant to hurt anyone. "I told Suze to stay away from the edge." The words sounded worthless. If I hadn't been talking to her, she would never have got so close. "I was trying to warn her. And then . . ." The hissing shame inside screamed at me to run, to run and run until no one would ever find me.

A hot wind whipped through the trees that surrounded us, the sound of their dry leaves like crackling applause.

"When Mum woke up, she said we should look for Suze, and I didn't know what to say." I risked a look at Daphne, her face solemn but calm. "So I didn't say anything."

We were still sitting in the dirt.

She was quiet for a long, long time. I brushed away ants that crawled on my leg, waiting for her to speak.

Daphne picked up a gum leaf, twirling it in her fingers. She took a deep breath. "Something happened at my old school. I haven't told you about it. I did something . . . bad. My parents and I don't talk about it. We moved here for a fresh start." Daphne kept her eyes on the leaf as she spoke. She was trailing it over her kneecap and down her leg now. "Brianna was *so* mad at me. She never knew why exactly we had to move, but she figured out it was my fault."

I wanted to ask what had happened, to see if her badness was anything like mine, but I didn't feel I had the right. I couldn't believe she was still here, still talking to me.

She watched the leaf in her hand as if it were something she had no control over, like she wanted to see where it would go next. "I don't even know why I did it. I never meant to. But I couldn't stay at my old school."

Daphne tore up the leaf. The smell of our sweat mingled with the sweet, sharp scent of eucalyptus.

"And I decided, when I came to this new school, that I was going to be a different person. I threw away all the CDs I listened to, all the stupid magazines. I was going to dedicate my life to something stronger, something older. I bought every book I could find on Greek mythology. And then I bought some botany books. I figured if I was making a new person, I might as well make her well-rounded. I held them and I looked in the mirror, and I thought, *This. This is who I want to be.*"

Daphne scattered the shredded pieces of leaf. Some of them were taken up by the wind; others fell to the ground.

"Now is the most dangerous time to be telling you all this, because it's still so new. But we're both at the beginning of who we could be."

Daphne's voice sounded so even. Where was her anger? Her disgust with me?

"Have you heard of the ship of Theseus?" Daphne asked.

I shook my head.

"It's a philosophical question. It asks what happens if you take a ship and you replace every single bit of it—every plank, every rope. Is it the same ship?"

I didn't understand why Daphne was talking about this. Waves of guilt moved through me in the sickening way they'd been doing since that night. I was ready to go to jail for what I had done.

"But I'm a bad person," I said. "I did the wrong thing. The worst thing you can do."

"I think what happened was a terrible accident. I know you. I know you would never hurt your sister."

I wrapped my arms around my knees. "Why did I lie to my mum? Why did I do that?"

Daphne looked at me steadily. "Because you wanted to protect her. And now you have lied, it would be so much worse for her to learn the truth. She would lose two daughters." She raised a hand to her neck, spoke like what she was saying caused her physical pain. "They put people who've done what you've done in bad places. Places where there are no walks like this." She gestured to the track around us.

I curled into myself, rocked in the dirt.

"Finn," Daphne said. "You can't tell anyone else about this, okay?" She placed a hand under my chin. "This could ruin your life. I know, because something like this nearly ruined mine." Her face was set, determined. "I'm not going to let that happen to you."

It was the same as when I'd met her in the girls' toilets. We were somewhere different, where the rules of the regular world didn't apply.

I ducked my head. "But my mum . . ."

"It would kill her, Finn."

Daphne didn't know my mother, had only met her once, but she was right. The police had already been so hard on Mum. If they knew that I was responsible for Suze's death, they would definitely take me away from her. The certainty lodged in my gut. Worse, she would have to visit me in prison. Or maybe she wouldn't be able to bring herself to do that.

After a long while, Daphne spoke again. "I knew as soon as I met you that you don't see the world like other people do." Her hand fell from my chin to my knee. "You're a good person, Finn. You just need to change the way you think about this, like swapping one plank out for another in Theseus's ship. Visualize it: actually replace it. You've already got a story, which is what everyone else imagined happened. Now you need to make that the *only* story."

I felt the heat from her hand on my skin.

"Like I said, when I came to Indra High," Daphne said, "I decided I was going to be an entirely new person. And I have. Do you remember the poem I recited to you, the day you came back to school, after your sister?"

"Yeah." *It puts the heart in my chest on wings.*

"You never would've guessed that I'd only memorized that poem the night before. Right?"

I widened my eyes to show my agreement.

"People see what they want to see. The most important part is that you believe it. It's possible, Finn."

Once, in winter, I'd been standing at one of the park's lookouts and seen a bird emerge from the mist that filled the valley below. The bird, small and bright and quick, was as unexpected as a fish jumping clear of a stream. Something unanticipated and free.

"You're not going to tell anyone?" I asked.

She stretched out her legs, let her hands come to rest in her lap. "Your secret is safe with me. And now you have my secret in return."

I looked at her. She was so beautiful. Strong and young and good.

Daphne stood up, pulled me to my feet. She looked down the track, in the direction we'd come.

"Nothing you can do will bring her back. You need to think of it as suicide. Even when you're alone, you have to talk about it that way in your own head, all right? Think it until it's true, Finn."

We walked on along the hot track into the next part of our lives. I was lighter, lightheaded, and Daphne moved alongside me, setting the pace.

———

I worked hard to do as Daphne said. To push and shape my pain into a different configuration. I grieved my sister. I slept so much in the weeks and months afterward, hoping to wake up and find it was all a dream. People told me over and over again that I had to be strong for my mum, that I was all she had left now.

I discovered a selfishness inside of me I hadn't been aware of before. That's what saved me. Or ruined me. But I don't think I could have found it without Daphne, without her ship.

It takes a long time to understand that you're never going to see someone again. I kept seeing Suze out of the corner of my eye. I would get annoyed with her when I couldn't find something of mine and then I had to remind myself that she was dead. That she had killed herself.

9

FRIDAY, SEPTEMBER 8, 2017

Early on Friday morning, Mum knocked on my bedroom door and walked in without waiting for an answer.

"Sweetie." Mum's hands raked through her hair, like she was trying to make herself presentable. "Magdu's mother is here."

"*What?*"

"She's waiting in the lounge room."

———

When I walked into the room, a woman dressed all in black was sitting on our couch. Mum was in her armchair. Neither of them was speaking.

"Finnlay?" the woman said, a shaky note in her voice.

"Everybody calls me Finn," was all I could think to reply.

The woman crossed her hands over one another and placed them in her lap. She looked down as she spoke. "I am Sunita Fernandes—Magdu's mother."

Sunita was a sharper version of her soft-edged daughter. She wore a long skirt, an expensive puffer jacket, and gold jewelry at her wrists and ears. A gold crucifix around her neck. She looked like a woman-doll whose stuffing had been removed.

"Oh." I couldn't find any other words for her, and the single sound hung between us.

"We need to speak," she said.

Mum stood up from her chair. "I'll put the kettle on," she said, looking at me.

I nodded and she left the room.

"I'm so sorry we had to meet this way, Mrs. Fernandes," I said.

Magdu had been coaching me on her mother, and I knew I should be formal, polite. "I cared about your daughter, and I can't believe she's gone."

A hand fluttered to her throat. "I wanted to meet you."

I gave her a watery smile.

She continued, "I wanted to meet the person who thought it would be a good idea to take my girl out into the Australian wilderness and put her in such danger."

I ducked my head.

"I would never have taken her if I thought something bad would happen to her." I sought Sunita's gaze. "You have to believe me."

Sunita closed her eyes, shutting me out. Where was the moment when Sunita took me into her arms and acknowledged what we'd both lost?

I was crying. I tried to breathe, tried to pull oxygen into my lungs. Sunita had opened her eyes, letting them rest on the wall the way you do when you're on the train and don't want to get involved in whatever drama is playing out near you in the carriage.

Then, as if reaching a decision, she pulled herself up to her full height and looked at me. The set of her shoulders reminded me forcefully of Magdu. "I know about you and my daughter." She didn't say it like an invitation, more like a shield that she was holding up between us.

I thought of the impression of her mother that Magdu would sometimes do. She would let her mouth get fuller, like she was talking with a grape tucked between her tongue and the roof of her mouth, her hands making uncertain gestures in ways that clashed with what she was saying. She would say, "Of course," but her hands would be flapping as if to wave me away.

There was a beat of silence, broken when Mum came in with the tea things on a tray. "Milk and sugar?"

"No, thank you, Mrs. Young," Sunita said.

Mum looked between the two of us, as if sensing the electricity in the room.

"Call me Rita," she said, helping herself to two sugars.

I turned to Mum. "You'd better get ready, or you're going to be late."

I didn't want her to see this, to hear it.

I could see Mum considering this, wondering if she should call in sick to work. I realized that was what she must have done yesterday. Mum never took time off work, and two days in a row was unthinkable.

Mum looked at Sunita, who sat motionless on the couch, then said, "All right." Slapping her thigh gently with one hand, she stood.

Like me, her face was pinched from sleep. She was also wearing track pants and a dark jumper, our shared home uniform. At least I had showered the night before, but we still didn't look like a family you would want to belong to. I was aware of everything wrong with our small, dark lounge room.

I imagined Magdu's parents' flat in Dubai. I pictured Sunita's bedroom, a place Magdu wasn't allowed to enter. I might've looked around when the family was out. Walked barefoot on thick carpet, opened drawers. It would be weird in the way rooms belonging to other people's parents are.

I remembered a day when Magdu and I had walked along the main street of Indra. Magdu had laced her fingers through mine and we swung our hands between us, the way you sometimes see parents do with little kids. It was rare that Magdu would hold my hand in public, and it was good. Pure and shining and good.

Magdu stopped and turned to look at something behind us. Two cops with bulky vests on and guns at their hips were standing on the street talking to someone I couldn't see properly. A grubby blanket thrown over a pair of legs.

"Why do they have to stand over him like that?" Magdu said, eyes fixed on the three men. "I'll bet you someone in the shops has complained. What does that achieve? Where's he supposed to go?"

I squeezed her hand. I'd seen the police and the man when we walked past them, but I'd tried not to look, my face blank, my brain eager to get us onto an empty stretch of pavement.

The police were walking away from the man now. Magdu's body relaxed.

"You're a saint," I said.

Magdu shrugged, her hand still in mine. "I'm paying attention." There was something cold in the way she held herself now. "We should get rid of the police altogether," she said, turning and setting off again, tugging me forward.

"What do you mean, get rid of the police?" I hadn't told her about Suze yet, so I couldn't explain that I hated the police for what they'd done to Mum.

"We should take the money spent on police and give it to social workers. Instead of punishing people with drug problems, we treat and support them. The money that gets pumped into the prison system could change so many lives for the better. So many black and brown people end up in prison while white defendants receive noncustodial sentences for the same crime. There are women, mothers, locked up for unpaid fines. Basically, they're put in jail for being poor. The whole concept of fines is messed up. There's one kind of justice for people with no money and another for people who can afford to buy their way out of it."

"Okay, sure. But what happens to people who do bad things?"

"In Norway, prisoners can go to work, live lives. Everything is geared toward rehabilitation, helping you to reenter society, instead of how you can be punished."

"But what about murderers?"

"That would be only a very small percentage of the current prison population."

"But wouldn't they need to be kept away from other people?"

She was looking at me. "You think I'm nuts, don't you?"

I looked to the cops, then back at her. "Of course not!"

Magdu yanked her hand away.

"What's wrong?"

"I think that's my uncle over there." She grabbed my arm and pulled me into the narrow alley that ran alongside the bakery.

"Where?" I asked.

Magdu shrank closer to the wall as a tall Indian man drew level with the laneway on the opposite side of the street. He had a strong jaw and a long, straight nose and walked quickly, a newspaper tucked under one arm.

"He'd be on the phone to my mother before the two of us could make it back to my place," Magdu said, shoulders up around her ears.

I'd met Magdu's aunt on the day I'd met Magdu, as Priya had been on the walk I led, and we'd gone for tea together since then, at a place in town that did scones with jam and cream. Magdu introduced me as her friend, but she let slip something about me staying at her place. Smiling, Priya had taken Magdu by the wrist. "I wouldn't speak with your mother about such things." She said it in a nice way, like it was our little secret.

I walked to the entrance of the alley and poked out my head. Magdu's uncle had passed us now.

"It's safe to come out," I said.

———

Sunita spoke, breaking me out of the memory. Her words were so quiet I had to strain to hear them. "Sometimes your job as a parent is not to give your child what they want." Sunita's self-possession was total. Her face completely still.

"Will you please let me see her—her body? The police say I'm not allowed. I would really like to say goodbye."

Magdu's mother looked as if she'd been slapped. "Absolutely not."

Rage flared in my belly. Magdu had wanted me. This woman knew it. I knew it. It was tangible, something I could hold in my fingers.

Sunita continued, her voice louder now. "When Magdu was a small child and we went back to Goa, she was always bringing home stray dogs. She wanted to help them. But she let them go when I told her to." She folded her hands. She'd said what she came to say. When she raised a hand to her throat again, I saw that it was trembling.

A sound made me turn toward the hall. Mum was standing in

the doorway. "I understand that you're upset, Mrs. Fernandes. I've lost a daughter too."

She pressed her lips closed, unable to go on. Mum never put the words "Suze" and "died" in the same sentence, even all these years later. She could handle the abstract concept of Suze, and the abstract concept of death, but not together.

As if my mother hadn't spoken, Sunita turned to me. "I wish Magdu had never met you." She said it without malice: a simple statement of fact.

A moment of suspension, of total quiet, then Mum said, "I think it's time you left, Mrs. Fernandes."

———

After Sunita had gone, I stood with Mum in the lounge room, filled with an anger that pushed down the wave of sadness that threatened to knock me over. Sunita hadn't even really looked at me. Like I wasn't worth her while.

"I'm sorry, kiddo," Mum said, drawing me into a hug. "You don't deserve this, not any of it." The sentence was muffled, spoken into my neck.

"You're going to be late," I said. I didn't know how to thank her. I never could.

Mum sighed and let me go.

At the back door, she stopped and looked back at me.

"Shit." She was flustered suddenly. "You have that dentist's appointment booked for today. I can call and reschedule for you?"

"It's all right, Mum," I said. "I'll sort it."

I put a hand on the doorframe, nudging her out toward the driveway. She looked at me like what Sunita thought didn't matter and hugged me, tight. It wasn't right, that I was all Mum had. She turned, and I shut the door behind her. I let out a breath and sank to the floor. I'd spent a lot of time imagining meeting Magdu's mother, but even the most nightmarish scenario had never looked like what had unfolded in our lounge room. Outside, an engine started up. I listened as Mum's old car groaned out onto the street, straining to hear it long after it had driven out of range.

10

BEFORE

I'd been so nervous on the night Daphne and Magdu first met. Two versions of me were going to have to exist in the same place at the same time.

Magdu squeezed my hand as we pulled into a spot out in front of Daphne's neat house.

"Have you heard the one about the two cowboys trying to get to a town over a narrow mountain pass?"

"No," I said, wondering where this was going.

"They stop in the village at the base of the mountain to ask for directions. The villager points them toward the pass, but warns them to be wary of one particular section. 'It comes up on you real fast, around a blind turn. Two men can't ride abreast there, it's too narrow,' the villager says."

Magdu had given the cowboy in her joke a Texan accent. "'Well, dang,' says one of the cowboys, taking off his hat and wiping the sweat from his brow. 'Where would you even find a harness for that sort of thing?'" She cracked a smile. "You get it? Because he thinks the villager is talking about riding a breast, like a booby bucking bronco."

I groaned.

Magdu sighed. "Like throwing pearls before swine, I'm telling you."

I made a high-pitched squealing noise like a pig and she laughed.

I wanted this good mood to last, to cover the evening like sprinkles.

"Is it weird I've met your mother but not your best friend?" Magdu asked.

I shrugged. "I don't know. She lives in another city, so maybe it's not that strange."

"But she's coming back, right?"

"She's back in the mountains full-time now to do her fieldwork."

Daphne had started her winter break early. She'd done the coursework she needed to do for her PhD, so she'd be sticking around for the rest of the year, maybe longer.

I was checking the time on my phone when Daphne appeared at her parents' front door.

"There you are!" she called.

She strode toward us, her blond hair shining in the streetlight, and threw herself into the back of the car. When I turned to look at her, she leaned between the gap in the front seats, took my face in her hands, and kissed me full on the lips.

Then she turned to Magdu. "So nice to finally meet you!"

There was a silence before Magdu spoke.

"You too," she said. "I've heard so much about you."

———

The Silver Fish was a high-ceilinged music venue near the train station that had been there since before I was born. It had sticky carpets and a wall of music posters on either side of the bar.

We were there to see an artist called TimeKeeper. One of his songs had been on almost constant rotation on the indie radio stations and the station they played at the supermarket. The song was so upbeat, you got caught up in it before you knew what was happening. I didn't know any of their other songs, but I'd thought it would be good to go somewhere noisy, so Magdu and Daphne wouldn't have to talk too much. Magdu and I had been dating for almost three months. With Daphne away at uni, it'd been easy to keep them apart. If I was honest, I didn't want the two of them talking about me. The familiar, greasy feeling of guilt and shame. Like I'd betrayed them both.

We arrived just as the first act was starting, and I was relieved to find that, just as I'd hoped, we could stand there, holding our drinks, nodding our heads without speaking.

Although I only drank one light beer, it went straight through me.

"I'm going to the loo," I yelled in Magdu's ear.

She gave me a thumbs-up. The music was a wave of sound roaring in every crevice.

Daphne was watching us. I pointed in the direction of the toilets, and she nodded.

After peeing, I looked at my face in the fluorescent light of the bathroom. My skin was rubber. I had a pimple coming in and dry skin around my nose. I'd borrowed a shirt of Magdu's and wore it over a white singlet. I tugged at the shirt, straightening the collar. I washed my hands, rubbed them on my jeans, and rejoined the others.

Almost immediately, Daphne took Magdu by the hand.

"I'm taking Magdu to the bathroom," she yelled over the music.

I wanted to follow them, but it would look strange.

It was fear I was feeling, I realized. I tried to breathe deeply. I thought about everything Daphne had given me, everything she had made possible. In year eleven I'd studied ancient history at Daphne's urging. Above the door of the classroom was a poster of a Greek ship, with a striped sail and a carving on the bow. In my dreams I held it in my hands, pushing it out into the sea, peace washing over me. I imagined every tiny perfect detail of the boat, and every detail of the night my sister had killed herself—the smell of woodsmoke, the sound of Suze's scream, the moonlight eaten by blackness, cold stone—and they made each other stronger. There were moments when I *could* forget the accident, could swap it out for something that hurt less.

The support act had finished, and after a short pause the main act took to the stage. I was glad the first song wasn't the one everybody knew—I didn't want Magdu to miss it. I rubbed the back of my neck with my hand and closed my eyes. The music thumped in my chest. I had an urge to be outside. If I kept my eyes closed long enough I might float upward, be caught by the winds until I was high above the valley, the smell of wet earth, small creatures moving in the dark below me.

I asked Daphne once, when we were in high school, *Do you ever get the feeling that you're about to be voted out of the human race?* Someone else would have laughed, but Daphne looked me dead in the eye and said, "I know exactly what you mean, and it's fucking terrifying."

Magdu was walking toward me through the crowd. I shot her a big smile, swept up in the song as it crested, filling the bodies around us. But she didn't meet my eye. I could see Daphne following, several feet behind her.

"Mags!" I called, thinking that maybe she hadn't seen me. I stepped into her path. "What's wrong?" I had to yell to make myself heard above the music.

Magdu shook her head. "I'm going home."

I frowned. The people around us all had blissful expressions. Some of them had their eyes closed, hands raised.

"What is it?" I said.

"I need to go home, Finn. Let's talk tomorrow. I don't want to talk about it now."

"What happened?"

Magdu shook her head, pushed past me toward the exit. Daphne reached me as I was about to follow Magdu, put a hand on my shoulder to restrain me.

I turned to her. "What the hell happened in the bathroom?"

Daphne shouted over the music: "How could you not have told her about your sister?"

I pictured my small Greek ship, Daphne raising it high above her head then smashing it to the ground. The sound of wood splintering, pieces of it spraying across the dance floor.

After our first date, when Magdu had asked if I had any siblings and I hadn't mentioned my dead sister, I'd never found the right time to tell her about Suze. And after a while, I realized that one of the nice things about spending time with Magdu was that she didn't know. And of course, I'd never even dreamed of telling her the truth that only Daphne knew. I'd got so good at doing what Daphne had told me to do. Maybe that was why I was so reluctant to raise the subject of Suze with Magdu. I hadn't wanted to tell her the story I told everyone else. She deserved better.

I felt dizzy, blood pounding in the space behind my eyes. "What did you tell her?" I yelled back.

Someone had turned to look at us. Or maybe they were only looking for someone they knew, but I grabbed Daphne's arm and led her a few steps away from the stage.

Daphne gave a strange little smile, recognition dawning on her face. "Oh, Finn. I didn't tell her *that*. That's just for you and me."

"Why in the hell did it come up, then?" But I was shaking with relief. For a moment I'd thought that Daphne would be careless, would say something that I wouldn't be able to explain away.

"How could I have possibly known you hadn't told her about your sister's suicide?" Daphne spoke directly into my ear, her breath tickling the hairs on my neck. "If you didn't want me to mention it, you should have said." She tossed her long hair over one shoulder. "Don't crack up on me now, Finn."

"Should I follow her?"

"She'll be okay." Daphne had me by the arm, pulled me closer. I twisted around to see if I could spot Magdu near the door. Daphne's familiar smell: flowers and warm metal. "Stay with me."

The opening bars of the song, the one that everybody knew, started up. I was sad that Magdu was missing it, but also kind of angry. She shouldn't have run out. Why would she leave before this song?

Daphne looked at me, eyebrows raised. She hadn't done anything wrong. I couldn't leave her here. Hadn't I just been thinking about everything she'd given me? Magdu had said we could talk tomorrow, and we would. It would be fine.

"Okay. I'll stay."

Daphne had made an innocent mistake. Of course she would presume that I'd told Magdu about my sister who'd killed herself. Why would I keep it to myself?

A woman came out onstage to join TimeKeeper. She was dressed in black and wearing a gold headband with black spikes on it. I must have noticed that there was a woman's voice on the track at some point, but it was only now that I realized she was singing her side of the story. What she was describing sounded unfair. In a high voice that sometimes got lost in the crash of cymbals and the whooping of the crowd, she sang about a man who wouldn't look her in the eye, who wouldn't fight for her, who gave her no choice but to leave.

A couple more songs, including an encore, and then the crowd was filing out. Some deep, animal part of me wanted to say to Daphne, *You knew I hadn't told Magdu yet.* The sentence hissed in my head. But I realized that I wouldn't be able to hold my own against Daphne if she told me I was wrong, that I was imagining things.

Daphne nudged me with an elbow, like she could read my thoughts. "Look, babes, if you want me to lie for you, you have to warn me in advance. I don't think that's too much to ask, is it?"

I stood silently. The smell of stale beer and the sound of voices emptying out into the night.

Daphne flicked her hair away from her sweaty neck. Her earrings were tiny, dangling pomegranates, bought on a family holiday to Greece. She'd given me a similar pair, forgetting that my ears weren't pierced. "Your sister dying brought us together. It was a horrible thing to happen but it's part of your life. Our life. If Magdu can't handle that, then she needs to move along."

She said it like she was joking. Daphne had sensed a weakness and, smiling, she went for the jugular—that was what she did.

My throat constricted. I wasn't going to get what I wanted from Daphne. The solution was to change what I wanted, what I felt. It was so much easier that way.

Daphne draped an arm around my shoulders. "Now, listen." She leaned and pointed toward a guy who was propping up the bar. He had a bottle-brown corduroy shirt on with the sleeves rolled up. Everything on his face was exactly where it should be, and he knew it. "I'm going home with that specimen of a mountain man. And I don't want you to worry."

Daphne had been staying with her parents since she got back, so I supposed they were going to his house. She pulled me into a hug, snaking an arm around my waist, kissing my cheek. She pressed her lips against me for a second too long. My heart raced until she released me. I listened to the sound of my own breathing as Daphne walked toward the bar. I felt a cool breeze brush my skin. Like walking farther and farther into a canyon, getting more and more lost. You keep telling yourself that you're in control, that there's no need to turn around and retrace your steps, but it's only when you cut and run, when you accept that you've failed, that you're able to find your way again.

I watched as Daphne turned back at the exit, her arm around the guy's waist, and waved goodbye.

As soon as I got back to my car, I realized I should have gone straight to Magdu's. I'd wasted too much time with Daphne.

But Magdu was a night owl. She'd be awake, right? The idea feathered through the meat of my heart, followed immediately by another question: What if she didn't want to see me?

———

Magdu's building had green trim around the doors and windows. The walls were a fleshy beige, the color of a 1970s prosthetic limb. I knocked on Magdu's front door, the first in a single-story row that stretched back from the street. I rapped the metal door knocker against the wood a few times before she opened up. I grinned at her stupidly. Her face didn't move.

Magdu's studio apartment was warm—not just in temperature, but in atmosphere. She had rugs and green plants in ceramic pots. Her dresser was crowded with body butters and perfume bottles, and she had an ornate brass bedhead—an adult's bed. I slept in the same bed I'd had since I was a child.

I delivered the lines I'd been reciting in my head all the way here. "Magdu, I'm sorry. I should have told you. I know I should have." I hadn't thought any further than that.

"Come in," she said, standing aside. Her face gave nothing away.

I stepped inside. "I'm so sorry," I said again. "I didn't feel comfortable telling you at first, and then by the time I did, it felt like it was too late."

Magdu bit her lip. "I left because I felt like an idiot, Finn. I don't even know if I'm mad at you. I'm guessing you had your reasons for keeping it to yourself."

It was good that she was meeting me halfway, that she wasn't going to try to play it cool, wasn't going to pretend. My body relaxed.

"I know it sounds dumb, but I think I liked who I was without that part of my history. But I want you to know all of me. I do. I'm sorry."

"I'm sorry too. I shouldn't have left. Daphne got under my skin."

I ducked my head. "Yeah. She'll do that."

Disloyalty. Daphne tucked away somewhere, listening to what I was saying. An urge to check my phone, to make sure it hadn't called her, that she couldn't hear us right now.

"I mean, there was that whole kissing-you-on-the-mouth thing. And then she made me feel that I didn't know you at all and, well, I thought, *Maybe I don't. Maybe I'm not as important to Finn as I thought.* I think that's why I reacted the way I did. Why I left."

Sadness bloomed in my chest. "Magdu, you are the most important thing to me. I'm sorry if I've ever made you doubt that."

I took a step closer to her, hugged her, pulled her down onto the couch. "Suze was two years younger than me," I said.

Magdu put up a hand. "We don't have to talk about this now."

"I won't go into too much detail tonight," I said, putting a hand on her leg. I tried to picture the ship in my mind, but it was flimsy, insubstantial. I couldn't tell the lie to Magdu. "But I want to tell you something about her."

Magdu sat back, letting gravity slide her into me a bit, not leaning on me, but not pulling away either.

"Suze was so impulsive, so funny. She wasn't afraid of what other people thought." I stopped. Suddenly, I missed my sister so badly I couldn't hold it inside my body, like it might explode out in a million directions.

"She sounds like an interesting person," Magdu said gently.

"She was," I said. "I'm sorry you had to find out about her from Daphne."

Magdu turned to face me. She wasn't Daphne, I reminded myself. I would have to be a different person with her, a better person. I needed to be the version of Finn that Daphne had made possible when she'd told me to forget my secret.

Magdu let her whole body come to rest against mine. We sat that way for a few silent minutes. I listened to her breathe and felt a calmness come over me.

I spoke again. "I know Daphne can be a little tricky." I raised my shoulders, knowing "tricky" wasn't quite the right word but aware that I couldn't think of a better one.

Magdu leaned away and tugged at her hair tie, her hair falling loose to her shoulders. She ran a hand through it. "I've been thinking since I got home. I'm a problem for Daphne. She's upset because now she knows she can't have all of you whenever she wants. She can tell that I love you."

It was the first time either of us had said "love." My hands clenched and released.

"Say that again." My voice was low.

Magdu raised a hand to the back of my neck. "Finnlay Louise Young, I love you."

She stood, pulling me up with her, bringing me close.

"I love you too," I said. "I've been wanting to say it."

There were so many shiny things that reflected the light from the lamps. We were inside a box of chocolates, everything warm and rich and golden.

Magdu placed her hand on my belt. Her fingers curled over, nes-tled between the pants and the skin over my hip bone. A charge traveled the length of my body.

I wanted champagne. I wanted to be the kind of woman who'd brought a bottle of champagne with me. I could become that kind of person. I could see it, bottle dripping with condensation in my hand.

Magdu kissed me. I was taller than her. I put my hands in her hair, gently pulling her head back so I could kiss her more deeply. She liked when I did that. Her hands were under my shirt. I took a step back so that she could lift it off me. She helped me to squirm out of my sports crop. Laughter.

I reached for her belt buckle, undid it. She dropped her jeans and stepped out of them. I reached behind her, ran my fingers along the line where her underwear cut across her bum.

"Hey," she said, guiding my hand to the front of her low-rise underwear.

Magdu breathed into my ear. Her arms were around my neck. I could smell her, the sharp, marine scent of her deodorant.

It was only a few steps to the soft smoothness of her bed. Magdu lay down, her knees bending over the edge of the bedspread. I slipped out of my jeans, kicking them under the bed with my socked feet. Magdu didn't keep anything under there, just smooth, polished floor-boards that weren't even dusty.

"I love you," I said again, as much for the floorboards as for the miracle of her body on the bed.

Magdu had pulled her own underwear off. I tugged at her shirt. She sat up, letting me lift it over her head. Her stomach mounded with the contraction of muscle, her belly expanding over her pubic hair. I unclasped her bra.

Magdu's breasts fell gently away from each other, moving in the direction of the mattress. I took one nipple into my mouth, let her feel my teeth a little, before coming for the other one.

Magdu pulled my underwear down. We were kissing. I cupped her breasts, then moved a palm down her body. She ran her fingers through my hair.

I held the curve of her, waiting. My palm already slick. I raised my second hand to her hip.

Magdu bucked and I was rewarded with a sound like she was in pain as I applied gentle pressure, felt myself slide into the place the wetness was coming from. Her hand found my thigh. She moved it across, her fingers teasing my pubic hair, inside me in the moment it took to breathe out.

She kissed me again and it sent another wave of wanting through my body. I was rocking against her hand now, lower half of my body twisted.

Fucking, fucking, fucking. Everything tasting of our sweat. The edges of me dissolving into the edges of her. Taken up. Thrown down. Passing through the middle of the circle and starting where we'd begun, feeling the curve of the universe, which was my body and her body.

———

When we'd got our breath back, Magdu spoke as if there had been no pause in conversation.

"Can I tell you something, Finn?"

I nodded, honey in my joints.

"I was involved with an English girl named Hannah for a few years, back in Dubai. She was an expat, living with her family. I'll be honest: I didn't think I would ever fall in love with a white girl again after Hannah. There were things I didn't want to have to explain, or feel again, or describe."

Magdu smiled. My whole body was calm. I'd stopped vibrating.

"Then I met you," she said. "And it feels simple. Maybe that's why Daphne upset me so much—because for a moment it wasn't simple."

The room had cooled. I tugged at the quilt until Magdu shifted her weight and I could pull it out from under her. I dragged it over us, her skin warm against mine.

It had been simple with Daphne, once. My body was gripped with the certainty that Magdu would not be able to live with the truth. Magdu could never love me if she knew what I'd done. How could I tell her that the only reason I was still here was because of Daphne?

I said nothing, folding my body around Magdu's and falling into sweet, sticky sleep.

11

FRIDAY, SEPTEMBER 8, 2017

After Mum had gone to work, I sat in the empty lounge room. The sound of rain on the roof. Once I'd tuned in to it, I realized it must have been coming down since before I woke.

Spencer came in, like he'd been waiting for everyone to leave.

I took his muzzle in my hands. "You're a smart boy, aren't you?"

The rain was relentless now. If we'd settled on today instead of Wednesday it would have been too wet to climb, and I would have been driving home from Magdu's house after a day in bed, because Magdu never wanted to go outside when it was raining. I felt an intense longing for that version of myself, going about her life.

I thought about my dentist appointment. My girlfriend was dead. I should cancel. My tooth throbbed and my whole body was raw. The thought of making the phone call was harder than sitting up and finding my car keys.

———

"Hi, Finn." The young receptionist smiled at me. Her eyebrows were perfect, her makeup expertly applied, like it was a salon instead of a dentist's office. I've never understood how people can be so well groomed. She was beautiful in the way an intricate garden is, everything inside strictly controlled lines. There would be weed killer involved. "Take a seat. He won't be long."

I was called in a few minutes later. As I lay back in the vinyl dentist's chair, the dental assistant clipped a bib on me, letting a hand linger on my shoulder. She smiled. She had a pixie cut and high-arched eyebrows. I couldn't remember her name, but she was nice to me. I burst into tears.

"I'm sorry. This isn't . . ." I was surprised by the sound of a choked laugh.

It was me. I'd laughed.

Why had I thought it was a good idea to come? I could have rescheduled the appointment. What the fuck was I doing?

"It's okay. Let's take some deep breaths." She took a deep breath herself, counting the out breath for me in a way that made me want to start crying again, but I managed to hold it together.

"Better?" she asked, smiling. "Think you're ready to start?"

"Yes."

"Then I promise we'll get it over with quickly."

I couldn't tell her that my girlfriend had died. I'd never even mentioned having a girlfriend.

I lay back and waited for my dentist. He was a short, slim man with frameless glasses. The first thing I'd noticed about him was his small hands. In their gloves they looked positively dainty, like he was born to be a dentist. I wondered if small hands was something all dentists wished they had, or if it was something that only a patient—a nervous one—would notice.

The assistant sat on a little stool near a computer screen. "Has Dr. Priat explained what's involved with a crown?"

"No," I said. He usually talked me through stuff before he started. Told me clearly how much things were going to cost. Gave me a month to pay. These were the things I liked about him.

She winced. "It's a bit of an involved process. You'll need two appointments. After this first appointment we'll send away for the crown, a cover for your tooth that we'll put in place to prevent further decay."

I nodded, twisting my hands in my lap.

"Today we'll be working on the damaged part of the tooth," she said. "It's not super fun, I'm afraid. You'll get a temporary cap to cover it until the next appointment."

I nodded again. My knuckles tingled.

"I'll see where Dr. Priat has got to," she said, and left the room.

I heard voices at the end of the hall, could hear a kid squealing in the waiting room. I stared at the ceiling. Rectangular white blocks of what might've been chipboard, or some other light material. Plastic grooves and gravity held them in place. Maybe I could make my escape that way.

All I wanted was for Magdu to be waiting for me to come home from the dentist. I wanted this to be something I could talk through with her afterward.

The nurse came back into the room. She sat down on her stool and rolled it toward me. "So, do you want the good news or the bad news?"

I gripped the arms of the chair. "What?"

"Unfortunately, Dr. Priat hasn't made it in today," she said, relentlessly perky in a way that was starting to piss me off. "Some kind of emergency."

The content of her words hit me a second after her tone.

"He's not here?"

"No. But the good news is that our most senior dentist happens to be free now, so we won't have to cancel your appointment."

I thought of the young man with small hands who was my dentist. I'd imagined him at the end of the hallway on my way in, slipping his gloves on, chatting to someone in the tearoom, laughing. "I'd like to reschedule," I croaked.

"If we don't do the first stage today, we'll have to cancel that *and* the second appointment. And then Dr. Priat is going to be away for almost two months for a family holiday." She placed a hand on my shoulder. "It's nothing to worry about. We'll look after you." She glanced back at the screen behind her right shoulder, where she'd brought up my X-rays ready for the dentist. "Besides, I don't think it would be a good idea to delay treatment any longer."

"Really?" Tilted back in the dental chair with a little blue bib covering my chest, I was not speaking from a position of power.

"Try to relax. Dr. Couto should be here any second." She smiled again.

At that moment, a tall man in a crisp white lab coat stepped into the room.

"My name is Sandeep Couto, Finnlay. I will be doing the first part of your crown today."

I just stared at him without speaking.

"I'll bring up Dr. Priat's notes," said the nurse.

The dentist—strong jaw, long, refined nose—nodded.

It was the man I'd seen on the street that day with Magdu. Her uncle.

It was strange to think of this man bending over Magdu, nodding at an officer. I could imagine him saying, "That's her," like she was a victim in an episode of *The Bill*, which Mum had watched religiously when Suze and I were small.

Magdu's uncle said, "I'm going to use the needle now, to numb the area." I pushed my head back into the seat. I didn't want this to be happening but was unable to stop it.

He placed his blue-gloved fingers in my mouth, exposed the gum. The sharp prick of the needle and then a sensation that was a mixture of pressure and heat.

He stood, checked something on the screen, spoke to the nurse in a low voice. All the things they did when they were waiting for the anesthetic to kick in.

Dr. Couto pulled a stool toward my chair from a far corner and sat down. Said loudly, "Let me know if you experience any pain, okay?"

Strange, spiky warmth spread through my jaw.

I closed my eyes and saw Magdu's face as I'd abseiled down away from her, leaving her on the clifftop with Daphne.

The dentist stood, picked up a drill.

I pressed my palms into the arms of the chair. My face was wet with tears.

It's often described as a whine, the sound of a dentist's drill, but it was more of a possessed beeping: a garbled, high-frequency emergency message. The nurse was bending over me, sucking at my saliva with a small vacuum. I read her name tag: *Ashley*. I wanted to ask Ashley to make it stop, but my mouth was too full of implements.

I focused on opening my mouth wider and listened to the absurd, high-pitched robot language of the drill. The robot sounded pissed.

I had a clear memory of Mum bringing out my eleventh birthday cake, a cigarette in one hand as she triumphantly set down the mound of icing and candles. The cigarette must have pressed against the table, because when she pulled away there was a burn spreading on the plastic tablecloth. It burned quickly but without a flame, a portal opening. Mum had slopped Fanta on it, laughing.

My chest was a spreading burn. I didn't know how much longer I could stand it.

"Ainsley?" came a voice from the reception.

The nurse looked up. I must have misread her name tag.

Magdu's uncle paused the drilling. "Jacinta must be having problems with the booking software again."

The nurse sighed. "Will you be all right on your own for a few minutes, Doctor?"

He inclined his head. "I need to take the cast. That's a one-man job."

She strode out of the room. I could hear her footsteps moving down the hall.

He had me sit up and spit. I ran my tongue around the inside of my mouth. There was a huge hole. It felt too large, like too much had been removed.

"Sit back for me, please," he said, and I did. He ran a gloved hand over the crater in my mouth.

"Do you know who I am?" he asked in a quiet voice.

His fingers were in my mouth, so I could only nod.

He was opening my mouth wider, like he wanted to see the damage he'd caused.

What the fuck? My heart slapped against the cavity of my chest.

He kept his voice low. "Magdu Fernandes is—was—my niece. I know you think you cared about her." I made a low groan in the back of my throat. "But we are her family." His fingers were still in my mouth. There was a quality in his voice, something cold that might have been sadness. My heart was about to leap out of my chest. "Her parents value their privacy. I only hope you will make it easy for my sister-in-law. That you won't post on Facebook or say anything that could hurt her."

My mind was racing now, trying to understand the meaning

behind his words. Did he mean they didn't want me to say Magdu had been my girlfriend? Or was it that they didn't want me saying that the police thought it could be suicide? Of course I wouldn't tell anyone that. I knew it wasn't true.

He removed his fingers. I could feel sweat in the small of my back. I struggled to sit up, my hands gripping the arms of the chair so tight that my knuckles were white.

"Please, lie back. I need to work quickly, before the anesthetic wears off."

Was that a veiled threat?

I stared at the air vent in the ceiling.

Dr. Priat would always tell me to raise my hand if something hurt. Would Magdu's uncle stop if I raised my hand? I flexed my fingers and toes.

"Please stop fidgeting," Dr. Couto said.

I forced my hands to be still.

He swiveled away. When he came back he was holding a piece of plastic with a creamy paste inside of it.

"Keep your mouth wide open; I'm going to insert this. It's very important you don't move or speak."

The head torch he'd attached to his glasses shone into my eyes. He hadn't given me sunglasses to wear, like my usual dentist did.

Long minutes passed. I tried not to drown in my own saliva, swallowing in awkward gulps. Where was Ainsley?

"Okay, I'm taking the tray out now," he said.

I leaned forward and spat into the little sink. Sitting back again, I took a deep, shuddering breath.

"Open wide, please," Dr. Couto said.

He pushed something into my mouth and I heard the sound of a tooth snapping.

The dental assistant walked back into the room.

"All good in here?" she asked chirpily.

I pushed my tongue into the space where my rotten tooth had been. It was a piece of smooth plastic.

"All done," he said, turning and spreading his blue-gloved fingers wide. Jazz hands.

My heart pounding, the side of my face numb. I couldn't look Magdu's uncle in the eye. What had he done without Ainsley there to see him?

I waited for something else to happen, for him to tell the assistant to leave the room again, for him to yell at me, but he just stood and left the room.

"All right, Finn?" Ainsley asked. "The cap will feel weird at first, but you'll get used to it. And we'll get something more permanent in there soon."

I staggered to the front counter. Usually, whoever was on reception asked how it had gone. But the receptionist must have seen something in my face because she gave me my invoice without saying anything. I had no idea how I was going to pay for it without my shifts at the visitor center, but I couldn't make myself care at that moment.

I walked out of the dentist, woozy and tender, that strange numbness I hated. I was breathing heavily—from the shock of seeing Magdu's uncle as well as the treatment. It had been awful, but going to the dentist was always awful. It was the fact that I'd had no control. But he hadn't done anything to me that my normal dentist wouldn't, had he? The thought that he'd taken more of my tooth than was necessary, or that he'd left something bad and rotten under the cap slinked through my brain. As if in response to the thought, an ache shot through my jaw.

I didn't trust myself to drive in this state, so instead I walked to the center of Indra, passing tourists and laughing families and old people. I resisted the urge to bite down hard on the inside of my swollen cheek.

I walked until I saw the library, the shop that sold plus-size women's clothes and, tucked behind that, the hippie store.

A bell chimed as I entered. I was hit by a wave of incense.

Magdu's aunt was sitting at the counter, looking at her phone. Priya was even shorter than Magdu. She wore a black turtleneck under an Indian tunic and pants.

"It must have been you," I said.

She looked up. "Finn?" Standing, she opened her arms.

I was surprised, leaned awkwardly across the counter. Despite the slab of wood between us, it was good to feel the pressure of her arms against mine.

I pulled back.

"Why did you tell your husband about me and Magdu?"

"No, Finn—I would never do that." Her eyes were wide and earnest. "It was Sunita. Sandeep had no idea."

A wave of nausea. Heat creeping down my jaw, into my neck and chest. "So how did Sunita find out?" Before Priya could answer I added, "That's why she said Magdu couldn't bring a friend home with her to Dubai for Christmas, isn't it?"

"Honestly, I don't know. I don't know about that. But please, don't let us fight." She hugged me again.

It was a physical relief to see Priya: someone Magdu had trusted, who had known Magdu since she was a baby.

We stood like that for a full minute. Tears were running down Priya's face.

She pulled away, pressed her sleeve to her cheek. "Even at her worst, I never thought that this could happen."

"She never told me that she tried to kill herself when she was a teenager," I said, wanting Priya to contradict me.

Priya looked around the empty shop before speaking. "I had the impression that she wanted to be found." She paused. "She needed us to see how much she was suffering. That was the only reason her mother agreed to let her come and live with us."

I'd known that Magdu lived with Priya when she first came to Australia, that she'd commuted to Sydney when she started her undergraduate degree. Something squeezed in my stomach.

I thought of how quiet and fearful Magdu had been on the day of the climb.

Priya spoke again. "She'd been doing so much better in Australia. It was a gamble, of course, coming all this way. When she first arrived, she was like a zombie. But I tried to get her out, more and more. She was interested in her studies. I think it made her feel less alone. She got her own place, which was good for her. And then she met you. I noticed such a change in her. Maybe she didn't tell you any of this because she wanted to put it behind her."

Priya had stopped crying. She wiped her face again, turning practical. "I'm flying out in a couple of days," she said. "I tried to get a seat on the same flight as my sister, but it wasn't possible. She'll be flying on Wednesday with . . . Magdu." The small dimples in her cheeks, a feature she shared with Magdu, looked out of place on her distraught face. I wanted to touch them.

I would never see Magdu again.

Why hadn't Magdu told me that she had wanted to die? That she'd attempted suicide before leaving Dubai? Had I made her feel she couldn't tell me things? Had she sensed that I was holding something back? I thought of Suze and bit the inside of my cheek.

"Are you sure your husband didn't know about us?" I said.

Priya shook her head. "He would have said something to me if he had." She rolled her eyes, and I remembered why I'd liked her so much when I first met her. There was something girlish about her. "He wouldn't have been able to keep it to himself."

"So how did Sunita find out?" I knew I was repeating myself, but I had to know.

Priya frowned. "She said that someone messaged her on Face-book."

"What did they say?"

"I only know this because I overheard her telling my husband this morning. They said that their daughter was involved with someone. A girl. They said this person did not want good things for Magdu." Priya looked at me. "I'm sorry. I know how you feel about my niece."

The anesthetic was wearing off, a painful tingling that made me want to bite down hard on something. "Was it someone Sunita knew?"

Priya shook her head. "No, it wasn't. It was someone who knew Magdu, though."

"Who?"

Priya waved a hand, looking apologetic. "I have no idea."

12

BEFORE

It was a sunny but crisp day, and Magdu and I were going for a hike. It had been a couple of days since Magdu found out about Suze.

We left my car and approached the low wooden sign that indicated the beginning of the track. The letters carved out of dark wood had once been painted white. Now, time and weather had stripped the grooves back to naked wood.

I stopped, turned to see Magdu squinting in the sun.

"So we're looking at a four-hour hike today," I said. "Some ups and downs but nothing too crazy in terms of elevation. I'm carrying three liters of water. What have you got?"

Magdu laughed. "Is your boss around anywhere?" she teased, peering into the bushes.

"Yeah, yeah. How much water you got, Hot Lips?"

She waggled her water bottle at me. "Plenty."

We walked, heaving ourselves up deep steps made from wood

or sandstone slabs. I imagined the men who had hauled the rock into position on this track at the edge of the valley. It would've been backbreaking work. These days, they moved materials in by helicopter.

I tried to set a steady pace, but Magdu lagged behind as the slope began to climb. Then she picked up speed on the downhill parts of the track, getting so far in front of me I couldn't see her as the track twisted and turned.

"Whoa, slow down!" I said.

"I've got to make up time somewhere," she said.

I'd wait for her at the top of the steep bits. At one spot, I turned to set off again as she arrived.

"Don't you fucking *dare*," Magdu said. "You fit people. You think you're so gracious waiting, but when we catch up, after you've had a decent rest, you're all like, *Off we go*." There was a demented cheeriness to her impression that made me laugh out loud.

"Sorry, Mags," I said. I pulled her toward me, kissed her.

She put her arms around my sweaty back. She tasted like her minty gum.

"You're determined not to let me get my breath back, aren't you?" she said.

We moved steadily on. The day was heating up now, even here in the green cool.

"Why do you think you ended up doing the work you do?" Magdu asked, pausing and leaning on a tree that bent over the path. "I mean, after what happened with your sister, a lot of people would have stayed away from all this." She gestured to the dirt and trees and sky.

A feeling of liquid bubbling in my guts.

"Honestly?" I stopped next to her, put my hands on my hips. "Nature feels like the last place left that you don't need words. I don't have to explain myself here. I can just exist, and nature doesn't give a shit, and that's always been kind of a comfort."

Everyone had expected me to avoid the national park after what my sister had done. But I needed what it gave me more than ever after she died.

Leaves crunched underfoot as we padded along.

"So, why psychology?" I asked.

"Well, most psychologists will tell you we're there to figure out our own minds. But it was also the most attractive of the options my parents would approve of."

"Why did they want you to do psychology?"

"It's very important to my mother that it's not my body doing the work," Magdu said.

I raised an eyebrow.

"Not like that, Finn dearest."

I loved it when she called me "Finn dearest." It was one of the few times I could detect what I thought of as an Indian inflection in her voice. A richness and roundness in her otherwise flat American English. When I tried to replicate the sound, I had to let a bubble form in my mouth when I pronounced the "r" in "dearest."

"What I mean is, they're happy that I'm using my brain. They would prefer that I was studying to be a psychiatrist. Then I would be a doctor first. But they think psychology is an acceptable profession while I'm cooling my heels, waiting for them to find me the right husband."

"Is that something that still happens?"

She looked at me like she wasn't sure if I was kidding.

"It's how a lot of Indian families do it." She pulled herself up a high step with the help of a thick vine that twisted over the path. "Besides, you think Mrs. Sunita Fernandes knows that her daughter is a lesbian? Mom likes to think of herself as very modern, because her family wasn't happy when she married Dad and she did it anyway, but some stuff is baked in."

We were far along the path, winding through ferns and tall trees that blocked the sunlight. Everything alive and thick and rich. Like Mum's old joke about how she liked her men the way she liked her milkshakes.

Magdu's phone buzzed with a notification, and she stopped, plucking it from her pocket. She didn't say anything, reading the screen.

"Babe?"

"Huh?"

"Everything all right?" It wasn't like Magdu to get distracted by her phone.

"Sorry, I'm waiting on an email about the details for our end-of-year placement." She flashed a grin. "Maybe then I'll be able to stop obsessing about it."

She put her phone into the front pocket of her backpack.

"What's your dad like?" I asked. I wondered if he was as keen to marry Magdu off as his wife.

"Dad's a marshmallow. Mom's the stick that roasts him over the fire."

"Ouch. Bit harsh?"

"And my little brother is the prince who everyone runs around after."

"What was that like? To grow up with, I mean?" I asked.

"If my brother wanted something, he got it. It didn't matter if I was playing with it. I learned that I couldn't trust them. Your parents are supposed to be fair, but mine weren't."

"You don't realize things could be different, when you're a kid," I said. "And then you grow up a bit." I was remembering what it had been like for me to see how other people lived as I'd got older.

Magdu lifted her backpack by its straps, resettling it on her back. "I wonder what I would hear if I could get inside your head."

I laughed. "No one wants that."

Magdu pulled me close to her. Despite the good weather, we hadn't seen many people on the trail. I relished being like this together, outside. She looped her arm around my neck, her other hand snaking around to squeeze my breast. "You bet those sweet tits I do," she whispered.

————

We walked along in silence for ages after that. A good, companionable quiet that made me feel calm.

I thought of Daphne and the bushwalk we'd been on when I told her about my sister. No. Better to think of a different walk. Daphne and I had been talking about doing the Highsmith Track for over a year, since we'd met, practically. Everything that could have gone wrong had gone wrong on that walk. It'd been getting dark, and I was trying not to let Daphne see how worried I was when she bent down to look at something to the side of the path. "We need to keep moving, Daph," I said.

She looked up at me; she was holding the small stem of a plant between her fingers. To touch the leaves would be to kill it, she explained. "Just like if it was a real little lepidopteran." She smiled. "That's where it gets its common name: moth plant. But it's a good idea not to touch it anyway, as it's quite toxic."

I longed to touch the leaf, to feel the powder between my fingers, something soft and forgiving.

"Look, Finn—there're so many!" Daphne called, straightening and stepping off the path.

"Daphne, stop!" I yelled. "I think we're close to the edge here."

Past the trunk of an ancient gum, the dark valley opened up below, a sheer drop. We almost never spoke about Suze after I'd told Daphne what had happened. But sometimes, in moments like this, I would think about it, even though I wasn't supposed to.

"Fuck, you're not wrong," Daphne said. "It's so close, you feel like you could soar off." Her eyes were shining.

I looked down. Everything in my body was telling me to move away from the edge.

"Okay, let's go back to the trail now."

We were almost back at the path when Daphne bent down again. She was having trouble levering part of the plant away from the rest of it. The stiff stem was thin but obviously stronger than it looked. She wrenched it from side to side, then looked up at me.

I took out my crappy fake Swiss Army knife and, kneeling, cut the stem in one motion.

"Thanks, Finn. I would leave them, but I want to dry this leaf."

We made it back to the campground late and sore and tired but in one piece. I never let on to Daphne how worried I had been.

The day after we got back from the hike, I went to the market and saw a beautiful wooden-handled knife with leaves carved into the sides, varnish gleaming. On impulse, I bought it for Daphne, so she'd be able to cut her own sample next time.

"It's beautiful, Finn," she said, looking into my eyes when I gave it to her in front of her parents at dinner that night.

All I wanted was to give people what they needed. I was small, in a good way; small and compact and useful and shining, like the knife.

———

"Ask me a question," Magdu said. "I need to take my mind off my feet."

"Do you ever ski?" I asked.

Magdu paused, taking a big gulp from her water bottle. "My brother wanted to try, so of course we went once, to Switzerland." She rolled her eyes. "A lot of sunburned white people hurting themselves out on the snowfields. I'm much more into the part where you sit in the lodge, drinking hot chocolate." She was breathing heavily but smiling. "You?"

"I learned at a camp for the siblings of children who'd died."

"After your sister?"

"That's right. I was sixteen. The camp was called—and I shit you not—Crying Eyes Camp. We called it Damp Camp."

Magdu laughed. "Sorry, but that's great."

"It was a pretty bizarre idea. Daphne's mother, Carol-Ann, knew one of the organizers and Daphne wanted me to come. They had sponsors or something, so it was all paid for."

"So, you and Daphne went together?" Magdu's face had gone politely blank.

"Yeah. She already knew how to ski, of course. But I picked it up quickly."

"Of course you did, you're a freak."

She was joking. How to tell Magdu what it was like to pick something up easily for once, when usually you were at the bottom of the class? The only other thing I'd been good at like that was climbing with my dad.

"The Bennetts started taking me skiing after that. They lent me gear that belonged to Daphne's older brothers. They were great holidays."

It had meant a lot to me. They never mentioned the cost of the lift pass, or my food. Daphne's dad said it would be a waste to let Daphne's brothers' ski gear sit around unused.

A sign appeared at a fork in the track. "Wow, that was quick," I said. "We're almost back where we started."

————

Back at her place, we sat on Magdu's couch. I was sitting upright, while Magdu reclined with her legs across my lap, pillow behind her head to prop her up.

"Do you wanna watch a movie? I've got a French comedy Émile loaned me on DVD."

So far, I'd avoided any situation where I had to read in front of Magdu. Now, I wanted to be honest with her.

"I don't read very well," I said. "I'm dyslexic. So I find subtitles difficult." I looked at her. "I probably should have mentioned it before now."

"When did you get your dyslexia diagnosis?" Magdu asked, shifting to sit up a little more on the couch, keeping her feet on my lap. There was something so clean about the way she'd asked it, as if she was asking when I'd got my driver's license. Something even less personal than that, like, *What was the average rainfall in 2012?*

"At the end of year ten," I said. "I probably would have left school if it wasn't for Daphne. She helped me."

Daphne had got in the habit of reading things aloud for me, in an offhand way that would make anyone overhearing think that she was processing the information for herself. When I read aloud (something I avoided as much as possible), Daphne would correct me in a matter-of-fact tone: someone picking up wayward balls from a tennis court and sending them back accurately without a follow-up glance.

"You only found out a couple of years before the end of high school?" Magdu asked, swinging her legs to sit up. "That's rough, Finn. That must have been hard on you."

"I just assumed I was stupid," I said. I resisted the urge to say,

"Still do." That was the problem with Magdu's kindness: sometimes it made me want to say what I thought.

"How do you manage it now?"

"I muddle through. But I tend to mess up administrative stuff. I think I told you that I was supposed to go to Canada to work at a ski resort after high school?"

"I remember you said that it didn't pan out."

"Yeah, well, that was my fault. I messed up the passport application and my passport never arrived. The managers of the resort were angry with me."

Magdu grimaced and placed a hand on my back.

"I'd bought the flights to Canada on a credit card, the plan being that I would pay it off using the wages I would make working, but then my passport didn't arrive, and the resort said I'd annulled my application and dicked them around to boot, and they would never give me work again." The warmth of Magdu's hand through my shirt. "So I didn't go, and because I'd bought the cheapest flights I could find, I couldn't get a refund. And I'd bought all this snow gear. The interest on the credit card was high. When I couldn't pay it off, bigger and bigger amounts started rolling over. It got so bad that I couldn't even open the letters that the credit card company sent. I made a habit of checking the mail first thing every day so Mum wouldn't see them."

"Finn, I think that sort of thing is way more common than you realize," Magdu said. "Any number of things could have delayed the passport application. Bureaucracy is screwy." Magdu made a small, steady warm circle on my back with her hand. "And the credit card debt—that's totally not on you. Those companies are so mercenary. They're the ones who should feel ashamed."

It'd taken me a couple of months after Daphne left for uni to get the jobs I had now, at the visitor center and the café. It felt pathetic not to have made any progress since I was eighteen years old.

Magdu's phone buzzed. She scooped it up, her eyes scanning the screen, then she put it down again.

"Still no word?"

She sighed. "No."

"Did I ever tell you that I went to a psychologist, for a while, when I was a teenager?" I knew I hadn't told Magdu, but I wanted it to feel casual, like normal conversation.

"Oh." Her smile faltered a bit, or was I imagining it? "No, I didn't know that."

"I mean, it was a long time ago," I said. "Daphne went to the same one first, actually, for a year before I did."

"Hmmm, now that's someone whose case notes I would like to see!" Magdu laughed—then, seeing my expression, she put a hand on my shoulder, squeezed.

Magdu loved me and everything would be okay. And I would never need to go back to Jo. The Suze thing was still there, but I wanted Magdu to know as much about me as possible.

"So, did you enjoy the hike?" I asked, when we were settled back into the couch.

"I can see that nature is your element," Magdu said. "And it makes me happy to see you happy."

I smiled. But I was uneasy. I worried that she would leave me if we didn't share the same interests. What if what she liked about me at first was the thing that drove her away?

Magdu added, "I would also say, however, that I'm glad to be living at a time when food and mates and shelter are so readily come by." She winked at me.

The ease of it sent my shoulders back down away from my ears.

Magdu stood, walked over to the fridge, and bent down to get something from the freezer section.

"Häagen-Dazs!" she said triumphantly, holding up a tub of

cookies-and-cream ice cream. "Today was fun. But I think next time it might be just as good to imagine it from my couch with a pint of ice cream in my hand."

I laughed and Magdu waggled her eyebrows, spooning a mouthful of ice cream from the tub and presenting it to me. I took it, and it was cold and sweet on my lips.

13

FRIDAY, SEPTEMBER 8, 2017

I walked out of Priya's shop into a rainy afternoon. I turned toward home, then remembered that I'd driven to the dentist. I scurried to my car, anxious to avoid running into Sunita or Magdu's uncle. The only person who could tell me who had messaged Sunita on Facebook was Sunita herself, and I had no desire to speak with her.

———

I arrived at Indra police station without really thinking about what I was doing. It looked the same as it had the day before. I felt different, though; less afraid. I wasn't leaving without doing what I had to do.

"I'm here to see Senior Constable Gosling," I said to the young woman behind plexiglass.

I put Dale's business card on the counter.

"Won't be a minute," she said, picking up a clunky gray phone. "Grab a seat."

She indicated a row of chairs that were bolted to the floor. I took the business card and slipped it back into my pocket before sitting. I smoothed my wet hair down with my hands.

I wanted to see Magdu's body. I wanted to ask it, *Did I make you feel like dying?* My head was gray and fuzzy, an old television filled with static, the kind we'd had when Suze and I were little.

Dale came out.

"I need to see Magdu," I told him. "I'm begging you."

I knew Magdu would never kill herself. I felt that if I could just see her, things would start making sense. Maybe they had only picked up a bundle of dirt and leaves from the valley floor and put them into a body bag. How could I be sure if I didn't see her?

"Keep your voice down," he said, looking over at the receptionist, who was speaking with a tired-looking woman in a big coat.

He didn't stop or say anything else, only walked toward the front doors. I stood and followed him. I risked a glance back at the woman at the front desk, but she didn't look up.

"You drove here, right?" Dale asked, once I'd caught up to him on the path that ran along the front of the police station. He had a hand raised over his head. Rain was falling steadily.

"Yes."

Dale's eyes moved to the station doors and back to me. A dark shadow on his jaw, like he hadn't had time to shave that morning.

"Okay, follow me, then."

A pocket of air in my stomach, like when you crest a hill on a bike and the hill falls away beneath you. Your body and the bike airborne for a moment.

I waited in my car, which was parked on the street, while he went to fetch his. It was next to the station, in a small lot surrounded by a high fence.

I knew the way to the hospital, but I kept close to the police car, following Dale into the car park and pulling into a space beside his.

He led me past the front desk, into a lift, and down a series of corridors with too many left and right turns to keep straight. Up close, Dale smelled of men's deodorant, something adult and probably expensive. He hadn't actually said that he was taking me to see Magdu.

I swallowed, hard. Pain from my tooth was pushing out the hot, numb feeling. I still couldn't shake the fear that Magdu's uncle had done something he wasn't supposed to, something to make me feel more pain than normal. Adrenaline spiked through my body. I wanted to run into the bush, follow a track, become breath and sweat and salt.

Dale stopped in front of a door. He rested his fingers on the handle and held my gaze. I nodded and he pushed the door open.

In the room, on a high metal table on wheels, lay a body, covered head to toe in a white sheet. I stood in the doorway. I had the absurd thought, *Oh. This is happening now.* Dale ushered me in, glancing up and down the corridor as he did.

For a moment, Magdu could have been pretending. Her breath hot and wet under the sheet, holding in a giggle. At any second, she would leap up and yell, "Surprise!"

I placed my hand on her stomach, on top of the white material. Behind me, Dale shifted on his feet. He must've called in a favor to have her waiting for me like this.

There was no warmth underneath the sheet. Nothing alive. Deeply wrong to put my hand on Magdu's stomach and not feel her respond. I took small, hiccupy breaths between my sobs. It was a room kept too cold, like a cinema, and it smelled of chemicals.

"Wait," Dale said. "Let me do the sheet for you."

He pulled it down to show Magdu's face.

I wiped my tears with my sleeve, fibers rubbing against the raw skin under my nose.

They'd cleaned her face, but I could see traces of blood in her hairline, behind her ears. There was a strange crumpling in her jaw that made me feel sick. She'd been wearing a helmet. We all had. I didn't know what else I was looking for. Some sign of what had happened. What would it have been like, for Magdu? The lurch as the rope had detached, then falling, tumbling through the sky. The sickening feeling of having nothing under or above you. How had it felt, to fall through the trees? And the pain of impact, down somewhere in the valley, all alone. Had she died instantly or had she had time to feel it, to try to call out, try and move her body?

In the years since the night at Brinkley's Leap, I'd imagined so many times what I would do if I could take back my sister's death, if I could have kept her safe that night, if we hadn't had that stupid fight. Looking at Magdu's body, I knew I would unpick the fabric of the universe to bring her back. I would ignore every cautionary tale about raising the dead, block out every warning that she wouldn't *really* come back, not as she had been. I'd make any kind of bargain, no matter how dark.

After a long while, Dale spoke. "We should probably go."

Why was he doing this? Why had he stuck his neck out for me? Cops didn't do things to be nice. He had to want something. I was too tired to think, to work it out. I longed to lie down on the cold hospital floor and close my eyes.

Dale pulled the sheet over Magdu's face. He did it gently, like he didn't want to wake her.

It was so squalid and small. I had to feel grateful for this shitty little favor. This was not how it was supposed to go. I loved Magdu. I'd decided on her. She was everything I wanted for my life. Part of me had always been afraid that she had not decided on me, but that was meant to be the worst thing that could happen. Maybe some weak part of me was happy that she could never change her mind about me now. She'd died loving me, and even in that sad, cold room, some part of me knew I'd won something.

———

We moved soundlessly back through the hospital corridors and through an exit-only door that gave on to the car park. Endless gray concrete, shuttered openings that let in light. There were food wrappers on the ground and it smelled like piss. I'd seen Magdu. Was I supposed to accept she was dead, now?

"Thank you," I said. It wasn't right, or enough, but I was unable to muster anything else.

"Are you okay to drive?" he asked.

"Yup," I said.

"It would be better if people didn't know about this," he said, holding my gaze, making sure I'd understood his meaning.

"I need you to believe that Magdu would never kill herself," I said.

Dale pressed his lips together before speaking. "We're continuing to investigate all avenues," he said, tugging at the epaulet on his shoulder, evening himself out. He spoke like a cop.

A roaring in my ears. As if seeing how much it hurt, he threw me a bone.

"Listen, I did look into Brendan McNamara again. Turns out my colleague didn't do a full national check the first time. Brendan has an assault prior in Victoria."

I grasped one hand with the other and squeezed. I pictured the tall dark-haired man with white teeth.

"He attacked an Indian worker at a service station." Dale raised a hand before I could interject. "But it was years ago. He was only eighteen at the time. He didn't know Magdu; he would have no reason to hurt her."

Something rippled through me. There was something wrong about the way he had come so close to us on the climb. I knew it.

Dale leaned forward. "Daphne and Magdu didn't know each other well. Is that right?"

"They'd only hung out twice," I said.

"Tell me about Daphne," he said, like the thought had just occurred to him.

My heart sank down into my belly. "What do you want to know?"

What could I tell him? That once I'd let Daphne in, I couldn't imagine my life without her?

I thought of the line from Daphne's poem: *no speaking is left in me.*

"You seem like very different people," he said.

"What do you mean?"

I knew what he meant. Of course I did.

I sighed. "I guess when you go through what we went through with our sisters, it binds you."

The opposite could have happened. We might not have been able to bear to look at each other. But that wasn't how it had gone.

"Their deaths were quite close together, weren't they?"

I scuffed the asphalt of the car park with my foot. I couldn't look him in the face. "Yeah."

"How did Daphne's sister Brianna die?"

That made me glance up.

"She took poison," I said.

Dale's eyebrows rose a fraction.

"They kept it out of the papers," I said. "They do that with suicides. Of course, saying a girl died was enough. It's dangerous whenever a young person's suicide is in the paper. My sister died a month after Daphne's." I couldn't complete the thought, turned my mind away from it, out of habit. Steered Daphne's ship into calmer waters.

I needed to get away from this man before he smelled something on me.

"Do you have any siblings?" I asked abruptly.

"A little sister," he said. "You remind me of her, actually. Her name's Bec."

"Is she a cop too?" I asked.

He smiled, and we were somewhere else. Somewhere that wasn't a hospital car park. "Nah. Lawyer. At least, she will be. She's at uni in Melbourne."

"Then she must be a lot smarter than me," I said.

"Book smart isn't the only smart. That's what Bec says."

A car rolled past us, looking for a parking spot.

Dale cleared his throat. "I'd better get back."

I reminded myself that Dale was probably risking his job to bring me here. "I'm sorry," I said. "I mean, thank you. Thank you so much for doing this."

"It's okay. But I'd appreciate it if you didn't mention it to anyone."

I resisted the sudden urge to lean into him for a hug. I didn't want to have to hold my own body up anymore. Maybe his kindness was all a ploy to get me to talk, but I wanted to believe he was good.

"Before you go," Dale said, "a final question. How did Magdu seem to you, on the day?"

"She was nervous," I said. I'd already told him this in the interview. I wanted to tell him about the energy we had for each other, how we were changing each other's lives. In the end, all I could manage was: "But things were good. We were about to move in together."

"She never seemed depressed?"

My answer shot out into the space between us. "No. Absolutely not. She was worried about uni stuff, but that was all."

"Okay then." He looked over his shoulder toward his car. "I'll get going. Are you sure you're okay?"

"I'll be fine," I said.

He nodded and turned away. I felt stupid. He'd asked and I'd answered and he'd believed me and that was it. What else did I think was going to happen?

I found I still wanted him to pull me into that imagined hug, to tell me that it would be all right.

I walked back to my car, opened the door, and slid into the driver's seat.

The only person I wanted to talk to about how much I missed Magdu was Magdu. I was supposed to grow old with her. She had a way of driving her own life. I loved her both for who she was and for who I would be if we stayed together. Ten years, twenty. My life with her could never be damp or cold because she knew how to live, and she had to have the heater turned up all the way. I loved her because she was truly, truly kind. Not in a polite way. Not in a way where she would take shit from people. Kind in a way that did not need to hear back, kind in the same way that you might release a balloon into the sky, with no need or expectation that it would return to you.

The thought of that balloon made the tears well again. My stomach hurt from contracting. I closed my eyes and rocked back and forth. I tried to keep the sobs in, but the sound pushed through my lips. My shoulders rose and my head sank and it was so much less than she deserved. I'd never been what she deserved.

I wiped my eyes, pulled myself together enough to raise a hand to Dale Gosling as he drove past in the squad car.

The rain had eased. Through the openings in the car park walls, I could make out the sun. Thin streaks of fiery orange burst from behind the concrete outline of the hospital. I sat there, thinking of

Magdu's body on that metal table inside that bare room. Maybe Dale did want to help me, but I didn't know why. I deserved this awful thing that was happening. Magdu had been a good person and I was not. I never would be.

————

At home I crawled into bed. I should've called Daphne, but I couldn't bear the thought of it. I heard Mum's car pull into the driveway, then her footsteps in the hall. I turned toward the wall and squeezed my eyes tight, like a little kid. She stood motionless outside my room for a short while, then moved away again toward the kitchen.

When Suze had died, the police had treated Mum like shit. They had no sympathy, had acted like it was her fault. And she'd held her head up high and stopped drinking in the middle of all of it.

I relaxed my face, though I kept my eyes closed. I tried to picture my ship. The rigging, the details on the prow of the boat. I heard pipes bang. Mum must've been filling the kettle. Heavy sadness pinned me to my bed. I pulled the pillow down in front of me, so I was cradling it.

Daphne said it was bad for me, but I slept belly down, my neck turned and face mashed into the pillow. "You look like a superhero when you sleep," Magdu had said once. "One arm up, like you're flying through the air. On your way to rescue me."

I heard Mum in the hallway. The floorboards creaked and something was pushed under my door.

I waited for Mum to walk away before I got up and padded across the room. I bent over to pick up the slip of paper. The words swam and I had to struggle to decipher Mum's handwriting. *I've made an appointment with Jo for you tomorrow. I think it could help. 11 a.m. I'll pay.* She had drawn a small love heart at the bottom of the note.

Jo. It had been years.

———

That night, I had the dream I started having around the time Suze died. I was standing on the edge of a cliff when something I couldn't identify came wafting up out of the valley. I could almost reach it, and I knew that if I could grab it and bring it back to my side, everything would be fine. If I concentrated, I could attach my feet to the ground, which seemed perfectly right and normal in the dream, and I leaned forward until I was almost horizontal. As I was about to touch the shape—a white shag carpet dipped in slick, dark oil, the fibers moved by an unseen current—the force holding my shoes to the earth gave way and I toppled over the edge. I was falling and falling, expecting to hit the ground, but it was taking so long. When I did reach the bottom of the valley, the carpet slid beneath me at the last moment and cushioned my fall, and in the dream everything went black, like falling into ink.

14

BEFORE

I met with Jo for the first time just over a year after Suze died. I was sixteen, as tall as I was ever going to be but feeling more of a child every day. I still slept more than I should. Racked with guilt and shame, pink with it, working furiously on my ship. I'd wake up to find that I'd scratched my own skin while I slept, the way babies do.

"Your father has organized for you to talk to someone tomorrow," Mum had said a few weeks after the anniversary of Suze's death. "A professional."

The following day, Suze would have been dead for exactly a year and four weeks. Four weeks and one year since she had slipped out of my hands. The thought like a single cloud that changes the whole feel of the sky.

"*Dad* organized it?"

Even at her worst, even at the height of her drinking, Mum was the booker of appointments. Dad was inert, passive. He absorbed energy and gave nothing back. The last thing he'd made happen was leaving Mum, and that was only because Gwen had forced him.

When Mum didn't reply, I asked, "Why?"

"He thinks you need to talk to someone about Suze, that's all. And I agree with him."

Part of me wanted to ask Mum if *she* was going to go and see a psychologist. I hadn't seen her drink since the night of Suze's death. I tried to push down the hope that bubbled in my belly.

"What if I don't want to go?"

It stung that Dad was getting involved *now*, and he hadn't bothered to tell me himself. Another, deeper part of me wanted desperately to do what he asked. Even as I was figuring out ways to make myself bigger, trying to make myself into something solid that the wind couldn't blow over, I wanted to be small enough to fit in his field of vision, in his life. To be something he could see and understand. Maybe even pick me up and carry me around with him for a while. Sick guilt that I was thinking about myself.

"He's paying for it, Finn."

That was it, then. If Dad was paying, Mum was in.

I'd phoned Daphne. I didn't need to tell her I was worried. I said that they wanted me to see a psychologist about my sister. "You'll be fine, Finn. Just remember what we've talked about."

———

As I was leaving the house the next day, I slipped on my dad's jacket. The deep pockets were lined with synthetic fleece, and the navy material fell to my knees. I wanted as little of me to show as possible.

I was nervous, the way you are before you have to give a presentation at school. You'd rather be anyone else, anywhere else, instead of yourself in the moment you are in. Was I also a little excited that things might be about to change?

The psychologist's office was in a shopping arcade off the main street. I had trouble finding it at first until I caught sight of a little nameplate: *Jo Richards, Psychologist*. I pressed the small buzzer. The metal on the button had turned hazy from being pushed so many times. I looked up and down the arcade. If anyone saw me they wouldn't guess where I was going unless they'd been there themselves. I steadied myself with a deep breath. I felt on the verge of throwing up. Guilt pulsed through me.

A speaker crackled.

"Hello," said a voice. I wondered if Jo Richards had a receptionist or if it was her voice. "Who is it?"

"Finnlay Young," I said, and a tinny buzz sounded. The glass and metal door, a relic of the eighties, swung open.

Entering the office was like walking into a place that sold botanical oils to people with too much money who didn't realize you could buy them for two dollars each at the little hippie shop across from the camping place. Someone had recently burned one of those pungent, sweet oils, without totally covering up the smell of damp.

The office was all sleek wooden furniture made in some variation of a rectangular box. There was abstract art on the wall: olive green, mustard yellow, and plum stood out and called to each other in the different works that all appeared to have been painted by the same person. Someone who had googled "art for therapists' offices." They seemed more than happy for your eyes to slide right off them. Daphne said the point of real art was to get you a little bit stuck. The moment you were looking at it should feel longer than a moment spent looking at something else.

A door opened and a woman appeared. Her curly hair was cut short so that it puffed around her skull. I was reminded of the head of a dandelion. I'd pictured her with dead straight hair and rectangular glasses—probably because that's how most of the psychologists I'd seen on TV looked. So I'd thought: pencil skirt, brown lipstick. Jo looked like she wouldn't be seen dead in something like that.

"Hello, Finnlay," she said. She had a deep, resonant voice that made it hard to believe she had ever been a child. "Please come in." She indicated the open door with her outstretched hand.

I walked past her and into the room. It was a smaller and cozier version of the waiting area.

"It's Finn," I said.

"Okay." Her gaze stayed calm, her voice even. "Nice to meet you, Finn."

She gestured to an armchair. There was an office chair that I assumed was hers. I sat down opposite it, noticing a clock on the wall that she would be able to see from where she sat but which would be invisible to me. The leather armchair sighed as I lowered myself into it. I should have taken off the jacket, but didn't want to. I resisted the urge to touch my face or tug at my ponytail. There was a small air vent in the wall above her head. I worried that someone in one of the other offices in this old arcade might hear us, like in movies when the mystery was solved because sound had traveled down a vent, allowing the hero to hear what the villains were up to.

"I'm going to jump right in, okay?"

She smiled at me, crossing one smooth leg over the other, somehow bringing her ankles in line with each other. She looked very composed, which I supposed was part of the job.

"The first thing you should know is that there are some ground rules I must follow. You're a minor, so there are certain things I have to report on. And as with all my clients, if you tell me you're thinking about hurting yourself or someone else, then it's my duty to tell someone. Otherwise, anything you say remains between you and me."

We sat in silence. I didn't hear the clock ticking and wondered if Jo had bought a silent clock especially.

"Can you tell me a little about yourself?" she asked.

"I'm sixteen. I live with my mum in a house in Indra. I go to high school." I sounded so young, saying these things.

"Why do you think your dad thought it would be a good idea for you to come and see me?"

When Dad was rock-climbing, he had this way of making his whole body calm and slow in moments of pressure. He was perfectly in his environment, not fighting against it. No wasted effort. It was like he was a different person. When I was a kid, he would see me starting to lose it when we were climbing—getting the yips about some move or another, working myself up into a state—and he would make me take five deep breaths. *The only part you control is you. The rock isn't going to change, so you have to change yourself.*

I shifted in my seat. "What do people usually say, at the start?"

I was calling out into a valley; the strangeness of the statement bounced back to me in layers, the way an echo does. If she'd been even a little bit mocking in that moment it all would have been over. But she didn't say anything, and her facial expression didn't change. In the silence between us, something seemed possible.

"We can start wherever you like." Jo held her pen loosely in her fingers. "I'm glad you're here, Finn. I think you've been through something very difficult."

Hot tears on my face. I couldn't think of how to explain it to her, what filled my body. "Everything is wrong. It's not supposed to be like this."

"You've had a very traumatic experience, one that any adult would struggle to deal with."

I pictured Mum. I put both hands to my forehead, the tug of skin tightening.

"Talk to me, Finn," Jo said. "Tell me what you're thinking about."

I was doubled over in the chair now. I took a deep breath, looked up at her through my fingers.

Mum's sobriety was still a relatively recent development then: one I couldn't quite believe in.

I'd wanted Mum to get better for Suze, but Suze was dead. It was like Suze's favorite Goosebumps book: *Be Careful What You Wish For*. A girl is granted three wishes, and they come true but in a twisted way. She wishes to be the best player on her basketball team. When she gets on the court, the other players stare at her, eyes wide, as their legs refuse to carry them, unable to throw or catch. Suze had read the book aloud to me, and I could still remember the cover: the out-stretched hands of a woman with long red fingernails, raised like she was protecting herself from the image rising up from inside a purple crystal ball. A young girl sat opposite her, her horrified face bathed in a pink light.

I couldn't say what I most wanted to say, so I offered up, "It's been so hard for Mum."

Jo nodded, then in her deep voice asked, "Could you tell me more about that?"

She listened as my words came out in a rush, slipping and sliding over each other. I hadn't been able to protect Mum from the cops, who swarmed around us. And there was the unspoken threat that I would be taken from her, that there had to be something wrong with our family. The police had looked at Mum like she was a woman who didn't love her daughters.

I tried to tell Jo this, sure I was babbling, sure that what I was saying wasn't coming out right. Shame shriveled my insides.

Jo took a breath before speaking. "It must be hard to be worrying about your mother."

"It was all my fault." The words had come out without touching the sides. An unlatched carabiner pulled up, slipping frictionlessly off the bolt. I locked my fingers together, looked down at the lump made by my two hands. More silence between us. Jo, waiting.

"I've been the one who looked after Suze since we were kids. I know I'm only a couple of years older, but she needed me. And I let her down."

"It's completely normal that you would feel responsible for your sister's death."

Something fired through my guts, like that episode of *Myth-Busters* when they'd fired a bullet through ballistics jelly. I'd watched it rip through the piss-yellow goop in slow motion.

Maybe everything would have been different if I'd been able to tell Jo the truth then.

———

I told Jo lots of things, even if I could never manage to tell her the main thing. I told her that sometimes I lay in bed and thought of all the things I could do that would make my mum stop loving me. Some small and bad part of me also knew that I was a scarcer commodity now, and my stomach fluttered.

When I went quiet, she would ask, "What does that bring up for you, Finn?" I wanted her to stop using my name; it made me feel less myself somehow. One patient of many.

I was shaky, like when I drank two cups of coffee. It'd been Daphne who got me on to coffee. She liked to stop at Jimmy's before school, and she would buy me a latte even when I told her not to. I had to add sugar, but I felt like an adult, drinking it. Thinking that meant the opposite—that you *weren't* an adult—but it didn't matter. I enjoyed the feel of the paper cup in my hand, the weight of it. I liked the idea of myself as someone who drank coffee.

I squeezed my hands between my thighs. "I feel like I'm a black hole. I suck people in and then they disappear forever."

Jo wrote something in her notebook. She took her time before speaking again. "If a friend was in the position you are in now, what would you say to them?"

I knew what I would say because Daphne had already said these things to me. I let my voice go flat, to show that I didn't believe the words I was reciting. "Nothing you can do will bring your sister back. She would want you to be happy."

We talked about my parents, about how they had been living separate lives long before Dad left. I told her about Daphne, how we'd met, how strange it was that both of our younger sisters had died. Jo was very polite anytime she made a guess about my life, very tentative. She didn't say that she was also Daphne's psychologist. I suppose she wasn't allowed to.

Eventually she glanced at the clock on the wall behind me. "I'm afraid that's all we have time for today."

She walked me back out into the small reception, with its serene paintings. They looked different, like they'd swapped themselves around while I was in Jo's office.

"You'll come back, won't you, Finn?"

I mumbled something that meant yes.

Then I was back in the arcade, hands deep in my pockets, trying to shrink down into my father's jacket.

15

SATURDAY, SEPTEMBER 9, 2017

When I sat up in bed, the room was dark. My digital alarm clock showed 1:12 a.m. There was someone banging on my window.

Fear. The sound of hissing. Acid moving up from my gut into the back of my throat.

I opened the blind. Moonlight shone into my room. Daphne's face in the window. She pointed toward the front door, a few steps to her left.

I pulled on pants, thought about putting on a bra, skipped it, and tossed on a jumper instead.

I used all my weight to push the door into its hinges as I opened it so it wouldn't creak. Daphne slipped in.

"Finn," she whispered, and buried her face in my shoulder.

She pulled back from the hug, keeping her hands on my arms. I nodded toward my room.

Daphne walked in ahead of me. She threw her damp raincoat over my chair and sat down on the unmade bed.

"Okay, I'm here. Because you don't answer your phone."

"I'm sorry. I know I've been slack . . ."

She held herself like a queen disciplining her subject. "This horrible *thing* happens and you don't even think to call me or come over?"

I sat down next to her on the bed. "I'm sorry, Daph. I'm still all over the place. You can understand that, right?"

"Finn." Daphne raised a hand, cutting across what I was saying. "I'm pregnant."

A sensation moved through my body; the volume of the world around us was turned down. I was aware of the blood moving through me.

"I think I'm almost three months along," she said, smiling like she'd got us tickets to a concert we wanted to see. "I've missed periods, but that happens sometimes, so I didn't really think about it. I did, like, ten tests tonight."

For a moment, I was sitting above it all, someone managing to stay at the crest of a rockfall as it cascaded down the mountain. I could see so much in her face. Her body was made of certainty.

"Whose is it?" I asked.

She waved a hand dismissively. "That doesn't matter."

My mind cycled through the possibilities. Her ex from uni? I didn't think she'd seen him in a long time. There'd been no other steady boyfriend, just guys at the pub. Some of whom she made fun of after.

Daphne picked up my hands and held them in her own. "There's no father. He doesn't matter."

"You're a biologist," I said, blinking. And then, "What are you going to do?"

"I'm twenty-seven. I'm not getting any younger. I don't want to be like my parents. I'd rather raise my child on my own while I have the energy for it. I don't want to be as old as my mother was when she had Brianna."

"What about your PhD?"

Daphne looked down before speaking. "I'm failing my PhD."

"What do you mean?"

"I don't want to talk about that. It isn't important."

"But—"

"It doesn't matter, Finn."

"What will you do?"

"It'll be fine." She squeezed my hand. "I want someone to love me with everything they've got. It will be a fresh start. And I'm going to need your help. Lots of it."

I was a part of her plan. I'd be expected to step up, to be the involved friend.

"So, you'd want to stay here? Not go back to Sydney?"

"I kind of burned my bridges there."

"How?"

The skin under her eyes was blue, and for the first time I noticed how tired she looked. She took a deep breath. "Some stuff went missing from the house, and my housemates blamed me. They also happen to be my only friends in Sydney." She shrugged. "Fuck 'em."

"What? When did that happen?" Daphne had been in Indra for over three months, and she'd never said anything about fighting with her Sydney friends.

"It's the real reason I came back."

A beat of silence passed between us; I was unsure what to say next.

Daphne shrugged again. "I may have borrowed a few things and forgotten to return them."

I hadn't been paying enough attention. I'd been busy falling in love with Magdu. I'd assumed Daphne was crushing her PhD the way she had all her other studies. And she had so many friends from her undergraduate days, I'd imagined a busload of them, sophisticated and worldly types, crowding into her share house, cheering her on. But then, other people didn't always see Daphne like I did. She could fall out with people pretty spectacularly, I knew. For some, she was a bit intense, interested in things they didn't understand, that made them feel stupid. And people could be funny about their stuff.

We lay on the bed I'd had since I was little; a pattering rain started up outside. Daphne snuggled into the crook of my arm. I took a deep breath. She looked fragile, like she might blow away.

I wanted to float away from this room and my problems and be wherever Magdu was. I didn't believe in heaven, but maybe somewhere Magdu was lying on her couch, in the last bit of golden sunlight, reading a book she enjoyed, Celtic symbols on the cover.

"What are you thinking?" Daphne asked, voice low.

"I'm sorry I've had my phone off," I said.

"You've always been terrible with your phone."

Daphne was going to have a baby. She was going to make a new person.

"I'm really sorry that I haven't been there for you," I said.

A moment of hesitation. A car drove by outside, the room lit up by its headlights. "Oh, Finn." She put her hand in mine and squeezed. "I'll forgive you for anything. You know that."

It was true. It had been true our whole friendship.

Daphne tucked her hands up into her jumper sleeves. "So what have you been doing, other than avoiding me?"

"I went to the dentist." I didn't want to tell her that Mum had made an appointment with Jo for me, that I would be seeing her in less than ten hours.

Daphne laughed. "You are so fucking weird."

I couldn't bring myself to tell her about seeing Magdu's body. The thought of it made me start crying. Daphne held me to her chest, let me cry it out.

We fell quiet. I heard something that might've been Mum moving around or might've been the rain.

"Can I stay here?" Daphne asked softly.

My tongue felt fat inside my mouth. I knew I didn't want her to stay but I didn't know how to say it in a way that wouldn't hurt her feelings.

Daphne stood up from the bed, and I knew my silence had been an answer in itself.

"Forget it." Daphne tossed her hair behind her shoulder. "You'll be snoring and I'll be wide awake. I'm going to go for a drive instead."

I reached for her hand from where I sat on the bed. "Congratulations, Daphne. I mean it. You're going to be an amazing mother."

The room seemed to pitch and tilt. And then she was gone. The front door creaked as she saw herself out.

———

I pulled on socks and shoes and a rain jacket and crept out into the hall. Spencer was sleeping in his bed in the kitchen. I was who I was because of Daphne. I owed her, and I always would. She would never leave me.

"Hey, buddy, good boy," I said, reaching for the lead we kept on a hook by the fridge.

Spencer staggered to his feet, so eager to be standing that my heart lurched a little. I thought of Magdu. Of her body lying on a cold steel table at the hospital.

"I'll bet Mum hasn't walked you all day, huh?" I whispered.

He ducked his head. It had been a strange few days, he seemed to say, and my mother was doing her best.

How'd you end up here, buddy? I would ask him sometimes, when we were alone. Golden retrievers were a rich person's dog. I was almost sorry for him that he'd got stuck with us.

I slipped the key I'd left on the hallstand into my pocket, clipped on Spencer's lead, and we stepped out the door.

Outside, it was cold and drizzly.

The cold was good. Clean. You couldn't smell anything when you breathed in. The town oozed out below us as we lurched up the hill, some lights twinkling, smoke rising from the chimneys. Everything dripped with moisture. I could feel the dampness inside the jacket, near my neck. For a moment, I pulsed with shame to think of Daphne, of how she must be feeling.

I'd been self-absorbed, had missed so much that was going on with her. I had only remembered at the last minute to congratulate her on the baby.

Spencer sniffed at a boundary fence.

Mum had brought him home after Suze died. It was Suze who'd wanted a dog, who'd actively campaigned for one. Mum had relented, had organized to pick up a puppy from a friend who had just found out they had to move overseas for her husband's new job—but she hadn't told Suze yet. Maybe Suze's diary entries would have been different if she'd known. Mum brought the puppy home and it was as if my sister had been replaced.

Damp seeped through my jacket. I couldn't stop thinking about what Daphne knew, what she could tell the police if she wanted to. The thought poured mortar into my bones.

"Maybe we should go home, boy?"

Spencer looked at me, panting, agreeable.

We didn't see a single soul on the way back. I let Spencer off the lead in the hall and went to my bedroom. I took off my rain jacket and pants and crawled into bed in my jumper and underwear.

I thought about my upcoming appointment with Jo. I remembered long conversations, punctuated by her nodding silences. The thought of it should have kept me awake, but the familiar, sticky

heaviness came over me and I fell asleep. I dreamed of Magdu falling over and over, a feeling in my body like the rumble setting in
the PlayStation handset Suze had got for her tenth birthday. And I
dreamed of the moth plant, of a blunt blade slicing through a stem,
severing it from the ground.

––––––––

"Hello, Finn," Jo said when she buzzed me in.

There was a café in the arcade that hadn't been there when I was
a teenager. Laughing conversations rang down the tiled space, people
enjoying their late Saturday morning coffee.

Jo looked the same as I remembered, just a few more lines around
her eyes. "Come on in."

I was hit by the familiar smell of essential oil and rising damp.
Like no time had passed.

I followed Jo into her room.

"Have a seat," she said, gesturing to an armchair that could have
been the same one I sat in when I was a teenager, though it looked
too new and clean.

"So, it's been a little while," she said. "How are you?"

This was it. We were starting. "My girlfriend died—Magdu." A
choked sob. "On Wednesday."

"Can you tell me about it?"

"We were rock-climbing. There was an accident."

I assumed she'd heard at least some of the details from Mum.
We'd kept the TV and radio off and we never got the paper, but it had
probably been on the news as well.

What had happened on the cliff, how I'd been trapped on a ledge
when Magdu fell, all of it tumbled out in a sick rush. Jo asked occasional questions, probing into what I'd thought, how I'd felt.

"Sounds like you're still in shock, Finn," she said softly.

Being here made me think of Suze, and I struggled to hold on to the story Daphne had given me.

When I told Jo that the police suspected suicide but I knew Magdu would never do that, she kept her face still. I told her about Magdu's mother coming to the house. Her cool, impassive face. A shaking hand held to her throat.

Jo leaned in. "That would have been extremely confronting."

I was sobbing again. "The stupid thing is I wanted her to like me." I took in a ragged breath. "I wanted her to love me."

"That makes sense." When I didn't reply she kept talking. "Can I ask how long you and Magdu had been dating?"

"I was in love with her. I wanted to marry her," I blurted out. But that wasn't the question she'd asked. "About six months," I said.

"Why do you think you were so certain about wanting to marry her?"

It had been one of the few things in my life I'd been sure of, but I didn't know how to explain it to Jo.

"Magdu didn't *need* me." I looked at Jo. "She *wanted* me." I looked down at the carpet. "She made it possible for me to be a better person."

"And now the police say they think it could be suicide?" Jo said, her voice steady. "That must be very difficult for you."

"At first they were saying we were negligent." I squeezed my right hand with my left, tight. "But this is worse." I looked at her. "Magdu wouldn't hurt herself; I know it."

Jo waited for more.

I crossed my arms. Let her wait.

Rain beat on the roof, and there was a trickling sound. Water rushing down a pipe.

"I read that Daphne was there with you," Jo said eventually, her deep voice catching a little as she said the words.

"Yes. She came over last night—well, this morning, really. Very early. She told me she's pregnant." A thought solidified as I said the words. "Which means she was pregnant when we went out on the climb."

Some girls we went to high school with had kids, but I'd assumed *we* were too young. Even if it wasn't planned, Daphne would never have an abortion, I knew. She believed in fate. Sometimes I thought that she had so much choice, she enjoyed letting the universe make choices for her. Letting the universe make choices for both of us.

Daphne would expect me to be something to her child. Parenthood was hard work and Daphne wouldn't like that. She would grow frustrated. I could picture her saying, *Here*, before shoving the baby into my arms and walking out the door. There'd been a point in the first site survey she'd done for her honors year where I'd had to come and finish for her, bending over thousands of tiny shoots, placing tags and measuring until my back ached. When things come easily to you, I suppose you never get used to doing the hard and boring work. Maybe that had been the problem with her PhD, too.

"So, you still see a lot of her?" Jo asked.

"She's my best friend. Not that I deserve her."

"I've often had the sense that you feel you owe Daphne a debt. Is that fair to say?"

I took a breath. How did she know that?

She looked at me. "You may remember that we talked about Daphne quite a lot in the sessions after your sister died."

I laughed, despite myself. We *had* talked about Daphne a lot.

Jo plucked a notebook from between the chair cushion and the armrest. She found a page that she'd bookmarked and read aloud: "*I feel like I'm a black hole. I suck people in and then they disappear.*" She looked up at me. "What do you think now, hearing that?"

After a long pause, I said, "I guess I'm supposed to feel sorry for that kid." In that moment, I wanted to tell her that Suze's death was my fault. But how could I? It was flickering in my mind in a way it hadn't done for years. The stress of what had happened with Magdu was applying pressure to the ship I had made, that small and perfectly formed object, and its timbers were straining.

When I didn't say anything more, Jo kept talking. "You didn't deserve to have this happen to you. Nobody would. It hurts, and it will continue hurting, and I don't want you to think too far into the future. I want you to focus on right now, if possible. Focus on each breath. When it gets to be too much, which it will, I want you to think about what you can smell and hear and taste and touch. Let that be enough for the moment."

I set my shoulders.

Jo checked her watch. "I'm afraid that's time, Finn. I'm sorry to have to end our session today. I want to acknowledge that this must be difficult. I know you probably don't want to hear that you'll get through it, but you will."

My body flushed with anger. And then fear rippled through me. I was afraid of my own response. And what I couldn't tell Jo was that maybe I would be arrested. Maybe Daphne had called the police after she left my place, after I hadn't let her stay, hadn't been able to give her what she wanted.

I shook my head, rejecting the thought. Daphne wouldn't do that.

"You're right," I said.

"Shall we make another appointment?"

I nodded.

"I'll need to take payment now."

"Oh. Mum said she would pay." I'd never had to pay when I was a teenager; it had all been taken care of before I got there.

"Unfortunately, I need a card today," Jo said. "Could your mum pay you back?"

A wave of shame. I was an adult. I should be paying for myself anyway.

Jo's expression was neutral. I suppose this was part of the job. Getting people to open up and then taking money from them. There should be more distance between the person who might be able to help you and the person who took your card details.

Jo ran my card through her card machine and told me that if I went to my GP, I could get a mental health plan, and then the government would subsidize part of the cost of my visits to her. *Great*, I thought. *Because what people in distress need is to try to get an appointment at the fucking medical center.* I held my breath until the payment cleared.

———

I returned to my car and drove home, rain hurling itself at the windshield.

I pictured Magdu's body under its white sheet. The thought slid neatly between my ribs, blossoming in my gut, expanding to take up all the available space until I couldn't breathe.

16

BEFORE

I was surprised when Magdu invited me home for Christmas. We were at her place, in her kitchen. It was the last day of August. It was warm for that time of year, and I'd just said as much to Magdu.

"Finn, I'm going back to Dubai in December, and I want you to come with me," she said, not ignoring what I'd said, but like she couldn't wait to ask.

My heart leaped. Given Magdu's reaction to seeing her uncle on the street that day—and the way I couldn't move about her flat if her mother happened to ring, but had to sit silent and still, playing *Tetris* on my phone until the call was over—I'd thought maybe I would never meet the rest of her family.

"I know it's a few months away, but Mom likes to plan early. You might not think that a Muslim country would be a good place to celebrate Christmas, but my mom goes all out. The flat will look like a department store window. And the food is amazing. She makes curries and trifles and bebinca—a huge feast."

My mother had never really been that interested in Christmas, especially not after Suze died.

"I mean, we can't tell them about us," Magdu added quickly. "Obviously. But you can stay in my room. My mom won't think twice."

I managed a smile. I would have to let her down gently. How many thousands of dollars would it end up costing? There was no way I could afford it. But it wasn't only that. I would have to take time off work, and who knew if my job would still be there when I got back? Magdu was a student; a few months' holiday a year was part of the deal for her, but it wasn't for me.

Like she could read my mind, Magdu said, "I'll pay for it, Finn— flights, your passport, everything. It's not going to be the trip of a lifetime, trust me. The trade-off will be that I won't feel so guilty for forcing you to sit through all my family stuff."

This wasn't paying for takeaway. This was something else.

"I can't let you do that, Magdu," I said. "It's too much."

She took me by the arm. "Please? I want you to let me do this. It will make me happy." She squeezed my elbow. "You don't have to answer now, but think about it. Mom doesn't know yet that you're moving in with me, but it'll be the perfect opportunity to tell her, when we're there."

How was she going to explain that? Was I supposed to be sleeping on the foldout couch in Magdu's little flat? But Magdu's mother had never come to Australia, had never seen the little flat, so maybe it wouldn't come up.

And I wanted to see the place that had made the woman I loved. I wanted to meet her family. They were there, in the imagined wedding photo in my mind. Magdu needed her family by her side for the picture to be complete.

I'd told Magdu by now that I wanted to marry her one day. I'd done it in one of those moments when you're seized with a calm that sinks into your muscles, your bones, and you can say exactly what you mean in exactly the right words, and the person you're saying it to smiles and you wonder why you were so afraid. Like driving, and you can see a section of road with fresh bitumen up ahead, black and untouched. When you *ker-clunk* onto the smooth section and something inside the car changes.

Magdu had smiled. I didn't know if she believed I was being serious.

"I should be worried, of course, about marrying a bisexual," she'd said, in a tone that was warm and which I knew I was supposed to take as a joke. "The grass will always be greener, no? And when lesbian bed death occurs, you'll run off and leave me for the first virile man you see."

"We're not going to experience bed death," I said. I would never get sick of her naked thighs, her breasts, her lips, her smell.

She wrinkled her nose. "That's what they all say."

"Who's said that to you before?"

"You're not jealous, are you?"

"I want to know everything there is to know about you." After the words had left my lips I worried that what I'd said was creepy.

But Magdu just laughed. It's a powerful feeling, to be in the company of someone who believes there is nothing wrong with you.

"Hannah and I were just friends by the end. I hated it."

"That won't ever happen to us," I repeated.

"She wasn't bisexual, so I don't know why I'm casting aspersions on you," Magdu said. "It's what I've absorbed from the culture." She shrugged.

"Yeah, well, that's not me."

She laughed and kissed me. "I know that!" she said.

I thought about my grandmother's wedding ring. Mum had given it to me not long after Suze died. Mum had cried, said that she'd always felt bad because she had two daughters but only the one ring. The opals on the ring would suit Magdu, I knew.

We couldn't legally marry in Dubai. It wasn't legal in Australia either. But maybe it would be, after the bullshit same-sex marriage plebiscite. *A glorified survey*, Mum called it. Still, it would be safer to have a ceremony in Australia. Or maybe I would *feel* safer because it was a place I knew. But this trip would be my opportunity to win her family over.

That was when I started carrying the ring around with me in my car.

———

After Magdu had worn me down and I said yes and agreed to talk to my bosses about taking leave, I asked, "So, what's your parents' place like?"

"I've got some photos here somewhere," Magdu said. She stood and went to the crowded bookshelf, found a plastic-covered photo album. She seemed to hesitate for a moment before opening it. She turned and looked at me. "So, my mom is a bit . . . baroque in terms of her interior design."

"Okay," I said.

"What I'm saying is that she makes Liberace look minimalist."

I didn't know who that was, but I raised my eyebrows in a way I hoped conveyed that whatever she had to show me would be fine.

Magdu opened the album to photos of what looked to be the foyer of an apartment. Marble the color of old teeth was set off by vases with gold rims and overstuffed chairs in the same bone color. There were mirrors behind the potted plants that caught the reflection of the mirrors opposite, making the plants stretch back into another dimension.

"Whoa," I said.

"I know, it's a bit insane. But more is more in Dubai, you know?"

So, Magdu is rich, I realized.

I'd always known Magdu's attitude to money differed from mine. She didn't worry about it, for one thing—but unlike Daphne, she wasn't blind to it either. I'd never had to ask her for anything, she'd always just seemed to guess what I needed. I'd known that when she finished her psychologist training Magdu would make a lot more money than me, but what did it mean to have grown up in an apartment like that in Dubai? I supposed it meant you had choices. A soft place to land. On some level I must have always known that Magdu came from money, but I hadn't wanted to think about it too hard.

The thought flared in my brain: What must she have thought of me, of my credit card debt?

Magdu couldn't be herself in that fancy flat, I reminded myself. That was something I could give her that no amount of money could buy.

———

I told Daphne about the Dubai trip, and about Magdu's family's golden apartment, over drinks at the Wild Colonial that evening. I was so excited. I didn't tell her Magdu was paying for it, but she guessed.

"Well, look at you and your sugar mama," Daphne teased, leaning back into the green leather of the booth seating. "I hope Magdu realizes how good she's got it."

When I didn't reply to that, she said, "We should all hang out again."

I eyed her skeptically.

She laughed. "Look, I know it didn't go so well last time. But I'll be on my best behavior this time, I promise." She banged the table between us. "I have an idea! Why don't the three of us go climbing? We can do Kamikaze Koala. She'll love it."

"I don't know, Daphne. I don't think that's a good idea."

"We can't go on like this, Finn." Daphne batted her mascaraed lashes at me: a flirtatious gesture, or a parody of one. Her lower lip pushed out. "You know we can't."

I thought of the hot day on the bush track in high school, of everything Daphne had done for me. Of all the things we didn't need to say.

———

Later that night, Magdu and I lay in her bed. The lights were off, but I could see her silhouette beside me.

"Maybe you, Daphne, and I could go climbing together?" Even as I said it, I wondered if it was a stupid idea. "The two of us could do some more belay practice outdoors first. The climb itself is easy."

I had faith in Magdu, and a part of me wanted Daphne to see her like I did. Capable. Levelheaded.

"Are you sure that's a wise idea?" Magdu said. "The three of us, I mean?"

"Look, Daphne wants to make it right between you," I said.

Magdu frowned. "So, her solution is to meet on her turf, doing something she loves?"

I thought of all the times I'd been afraid no one else would ever see what Daphne could. Daphne had never given up on me, and I knew she never would.

"It may not seem like much, but I think it's a big deal, coming from her."

"You say that Daphne has done so much for you, but I don't see it. Maybe when you were in high school, but not lately." There was no anger in Magdu's voice, only conviction.

I sighed. "I hear what you're saying, Mags. I do." Did I? I felt guilty even saying it, as if Daphne might hear me. "But she and I have been through a lot together. I think you'd like her if you got to know her better. You're both super smart." I raised my eyebrows, tried to waggle them suggestively the way Magdu did. "And good-looking."

"Jesus," she huffed. "That's all I need, to be in a beauty competition with Daphne Bennett."

"Daphne suggested this," I said, taking both of Magdu's hands in mine, "because she knows you're important to me." I leaned closer to her. "I know it's been a bumpy start, but she can tell you're not going anywhere." My heart leaped, pushing my lungs aside, because I believed it was true. "We'll have a good time. I'll keep you safe."

We kissed.

"I know, Finn. I do. I'm getting used to the idea." She smiled. "I trust you."

And then I pulled her close, reached for her under her clothes.

———

Magdu called me the following afternoon.

"Finn." From the way she said my name, I knew something was up. Usually, it sounded like something good in her mouth. A big, juicy Werther's Original that she'd popped in. Now, my name was one of those chalky mints in the shape of a hockey puck.

"Finn, I spoke to my mom."

Something in my belly was already sinking.

"She . . . she said I can't bring a friend."

"To Dubai for Christmas?" I said stupidly. "But I thought it was all arranged?" I could hear the whine in my voice.

"So did I. She said she was excited I was bringing a friend home. But something has changed. She's being weird about it. Says it's not appropriate to have someone stay in my room. Says I'm not a little girl anymore. It came out of nowhere."

I could feel my pulse pounding in my neck.

"I bet my brother's been in her ear. He can be such an asshole."

"Don't worry about it, babe."

Magdu must have heard something in my voice. "Oh, Finn. I'm so sorry. I'm an idiot for getting your hopes up. I want you to be there, more than anything, but I couldn't inflict my pissed-off mother on you."

The truth was that it hurt physically, like a blow to the stomach. My chance to meet Magdu's family pulled away like a layer of skin.

I forced myself to take a deep breath. "Don't worry. I was excited, but I'll get over it." I smiled, glad she couldn't see me. It would be a watery smile at best. I wanted to change the subject. "Still keen to go climbing? With Daphne?"

Suddenly, I felt like I shouldn't have brought it up. That maybe I would lose that too. There was a rustle of material, like Magdu was moving the phone from one shoulder to the other. "We've picked a day," she said. "I haven't changed my mind."

I felt relief wash through me.

"I love you," I said.

"I love you too, Finn."

17

SUNDAY, SEPTEMBER 10, 2017

Magdu had been dead since Wednesday. When I woke that morning, it slammed into me with the full force of that afternoon, like no time had passed.

She'd already had a key to her place cut for me. In bright red metal, "So it goes faster," she'd joked. My dad used to say the same thing: that red cars went faster. I pictured the flat. There would be almond milk in the fridge. I thought of Magdu buying it, not knowing it would outlast her. I wanted to drink that almond milk from the carton, feel it run over the corners of my mouth and down my neck. I wanted to wrap myself in Magdu's quilt and sob.

Mum was still in bed and I tried not to wake her as I left for work. Today would be my first day back at the café. Jimmy must have heard about what happened, because he'd called to say they could find someone to cover my shift. But I didn't know what else I would do with myself. I couldn't face going back to the guiding work at the visitor center—you had to be "on" to do that—but I figured if I was going to be miserable, I could do it just as well in an apron.

Daphne had asked me on more than one occasion why I worked at the café. *We're not in high school anymore, Finn,* she'd say. I'd fobbed her off enough times to realize she really didn't understand. Daphne had her PhD scholarship, but I assumed her parents were helping her out, as she never talked about getting a job. She didn't think about money. She would help people out, the same way someone holding a running hose would move the stream from one place to another if asked. But you had to ask. Once, I must have let something slip in the look I gave her, because she said, "I mean, you could pick up more guiding work, couldn't you? You could take people out on longer trips. Maybe even head out to the snowfields and do a season there." My aborted attempt to work in Canada hung between us when she said that. My spectacular failure. "You'd be really good at it, Finn."

Daphne sometimes joked about how much her parents had spent on taking me to the snow over the years. My body was hot metal when she said that.

I'd got the café job when Daphne went off to uni. I took all the early shifts I could get there, and then I'd do the afternoon shift at the visitor center. I was the one who unlocked the doors and turned on the lights at Jimmy's. It was my job to get the food prep underway for the day, so the sandwich bar was stocked, but I rarely managed it, because as soon as they saw the light on, people came in wanting coffee. In the very early hours of the morning it was sometimes mums with prams, more often climbers heading out for the day. I envied them, rugged up in their beanies and their gloves, laughing about the fact they'd need to stop off and shit before the climb now they'd had a coffee. I wanted to follow them out the door.

As usual, I was working the early shift this morning, and there weren't many people on the street. The strangeness of walking to work, like it was a normal day, like Magdu was still alive, sent a spike of nausea rising from my gut up into my throat.

A group of men were clustered under the weather shelter near the train station. They were talking and laughing loudly, possibly still out from the night before. I heard what sounded like, "Where's your bike?" and in case that wasn't clear enough, the single word "Dyke!" yelled and then covered with a fake coughing fit as I walked past. I made sure to keep my face still. This was the ugly flip side of my haircut. I kept my head down and crossed the road, like it was something I'd been planning to do. I would wait until the antique store, where the road bent out of sight, before crossing back over. My gum throbbed. I tongued the plastic cap on my tooth. It still didn't feel right.

There'd been leaflets dropped in our letterbox about the marriage equality survey, and posters urging people to "Protect the Family," whatever the fuck that meant. The plebiscite had seemed to make people nastier, bolder.

"I don't know why you're worried," Daphne had said. "It's going to get up. And besides, we should be able to have civil discourse about this."

"Oh yeah?" I'd replied, fists clenched into tight rolls. "And when are they holding a nationwide vote to decide if *you* can get married, huh?" I surprised myself with my own anger, and I think I surprised Daphne too. I didn't usually talk to her that way.

I thought of kids hearing what the men had shouted. That was who all of this was fucking up, I thought. Kids.

I risked a glance up and back. One of the men, the tallest one, leaned in close to the others, flashing a white smile. It was the guy I'd seen on the morning of the climb. The tall, handsome one, the one with the big, showy knife. What had Dale said his name was again?

Brendan. He wasn't the one who had called out, but he was laughing with the men who had. They were all familiar, I realized. They'd all been there, on the cliff. Something cold and heavy spread through my body. Even with my guts churning, there was something about the tall man in particular that struck me as familiar, and not just from the morning of the climb. Where did I know him from? The question fizzed but couldn't connect with anything else in my brain.

His gaze fell on me, and I looked down at my feet. I wondered if he recognized me. The men had left by the time the cops had winched me up to the top of the cliff. It was hard to imagine that the same guys who'd called the police, had waited for them in the car park, would be the kind to yell at women on the street. *People contain multitudes*, Daphne would say.

The men were all looking at me now. I hurried down the road.

I walked past the closed hardware store, then the bakery. Warm, sweet smells hit me as someone opened the door to leave. I was trying to turn my face away from the men by the train station, or I wouldn't have seen him. Dale Gosling, out of uniform. He was standing next to a taller man, both facing the cabinet that was piled with pastries and pies. The man beside Dale had a beard and wore a big jacket. As I watched, the bigger man raised a hand to Dale's neck, running a thumb into Dale's hairline and back down. In that moment I knew why he'd allowed me to see Magdu's body. Why it would matter to him that her family wouldn't let me.

I walked fast, wanting to put distance between me and the bakery. The men from the cliff and Dale and the glistening pastries swirling in my mind. I kept up a fast pace the rest of the way to the café.

I was on with Amy, who was older. We didn't talk much but I liked working with her because you could see she was present in whatever she was doing. She gave me a wordless hug when I arrived that I melted into. I was grateful she didn't ask me any questions.

I worked the coffee machine, pulling shots and frothing milk. An endless stream of flat whites, lattes, and cappuccinos. If I angled my body right, I didn't even have to see the customers. All I had to do was pack, tamp, pull, steam, pour, shove the completed coffee across the bench in front of me, call out a name, watch as a hand bore it away. The smell of coffee was something I could focus on. So was the smell of burned milk when I over-steamed it, which I did more than once. Hot milk frothed over the side of the jug and I had to run my hand under cold water. Then I didn't put the lid on a cup properly and a person picked it up in a hurry only to have coffee spill all over them.

The morning passed. My black apron was flecked with froth and dusted with coffee grounds. My feet and legs ached, a duller version of the punched-from-the-inside pain in my belly, but it was good to work through it. Like all that pain might be productive. I thought about Dale, and what he'd done for me at the hospital.

A line of people were waiting. The door to the café opened and the queue rippled as a woman pushed her way toward the coffee machine. It was Sunita. Her hair was swept back severely from her face, pulled into a braid. I fought the urge to go out the back and check the milk stocks.

"Finnlay?" Sunita called my name loudly and it was as if our roles had reversed, and she was the one calling the coffee orders.

The person closest to the counter picked up the coffee I'd placed there and turned away. Seeing an opening, Sunita moved forward.

I turned and asked Amy if I could step outside for a few minutes. I didn't want Sunita to make a scene in the café. Amy looked between me and Sunita and then, although there were at least half a dozen people waiting for coffee, said, "Of course."

I followed Sunita out under the awning of the café, drizzle curtaining the edges. We kept close to the building, away from the flow of people moving down the footpath.

As Sunita opened her mouth to speak, I suddenly wished my mum was there. I wanted to run down the main street of Indra, push past the group of dickhead men and jump on a train, head to the city, shrink myself down, get even more lost.

"I have been speaking with my family since leaving your house yesterday morning," Sunita said. For some reason, I was sure she meant Priya, Magdu's aunt. "We discussed my visit . . ." Sunita looked out on to the street.

Priya had stuck up for me, had tried to talk Sunita down from her anger.

Sunita looked around, as if checking that no one was listening. "I am sorry. I should not have come to your home."

Sunita looked diminished, drained of the rage that had filled her the day before. I wanted to say something, to let her know that I understood, that I wanted to talk to her about Magdu, look at photos of her as a child, hear all about her favorite foods growing up. But the words wouldn't come out.

Sunita pushed her shoulders back, as if deciding on something. "When my daughter was small," she said, "we were at a festival, and she had her first asthma attack. She looked at me, kept her eyes on me the whole time she was trying to get the breath in. She knew that I would save her." Sunita ducked her head. I had the sense that she was a very private person who'd been pushed so far that the old boundaries didn't apply. "We took her to the hospital, where they gave her drugs and oxygen, and she soon recovered. When she slept I stroked her and told her I would always save her." Her fingers tugged at her necklace and she looked back up at me. "But then she came here . . ." Sunita wiped at the tears that had been flowing silently down her face.

"I'm so sorry," I said. The words were puny, not enough.

Sunita moved toward the edge of the awning. Then, as if remembering something else she wanted to say, she turned back.

"I hope you can understand how upset I was."

It took me a moment to realize I was being dismissed.

She stepped out into the rain, unfurling a long, black umbrella as she did.

I stood there, not ready for the conversation to be over. I was relieved not to be yelled at, but nothing had changed. I didn't get to be involved with the family's mourning. I was still apart and separate from them. Someone whom Magdu's uncle and mother had warned to stay away. I'd moved the wedding ring from the car after Daphne had given it back to me, placing the box in the drawer by my bed. I wished I had it on me. I wanted Sunita to see it, to know what I had wanted for myself and her daughter.

———

Amy didn't say anything when I returned to the café. She just caught my eye and nodded when I took up my post by the coffee machine, and we got on with catching up on orders.

At nine, Amy urged me to take my break. A rowdy group of teenagers was passing the café as I stepped outside. I didn't like their jeering, resented the sound of them intruding on the quiet. They made me think of the men by the station earlier that morning.

I got my phone out of my pocket and turned it on. Dale Gosling's number was saved under "Cop" in my contacts.

It rang for a long time before it went to voicemail. I was sliding the phone into my back pocket when it buzzed with an incoming call.

"Finn?" Dale's voice sounded cautious. "Is everything all right?"

"Do you remember that you showed me a picture of a guy who was at the top of the cliff on Wednesday? The one who had assaulted someone when he was younger?"

"Yes," Dale replied, voice low.

"I saw him today—in Indra—with the other guys from the morning of the climb. But I know him from somewhere else, from before that day; I'm sure of it. I just can't remember."

"Okay," he said.

The reasonableness of his tone sent a flood of shame through me. He felt much farther away than he had in the hospital car park. I could feel the distance filling my body. I had the urge to run.

"Right," said Dale, when it was clear I had nothing to add. There was noise in the background. "I've got to go."

The wet concrete beneath my feet seemed to grow warm, move. Like the earth's core was overheating and the place where I was standing might dissolve. I shoved my phone deep down into my pocket.

I wanted to call Dale back. I wanted to throw myself on the ground. I couldn't stand it. Everything in me was ready for action but I had no idea what to do.

———

Back in the café, Amy and I moved smoothly around each other. Amy took over the coffee machine while I served. We usually swapped around at the halfway point of a shift, to break up the day. We worked in a gentle rhythm, two dancers anticipating each other's moves.

A woman came in with her young son hanging off her hand. While she ordered, the little boy pressed his face and hands to the glass of the display case where we kept the pastries. He pulled himself up, trying to reach the jars of cookies sitting on top of the unit. He wobbled, began to overbalance. "Watch him," I said, more sharply than I'd intended. The mother grabbed him under the armpits and heaved him down, not looking at me, muttering under her breath.

The door opened and Daphne walked into the café. My heart began to beat faster in my chest. I was glad that I had a few moments to gather myself while I collected the woman's money and handed her a cookie with Smarties in it for the little boy.

Daphne approached the counter, her wet umbrella leaving a trail behind her. I could smell neroli oil and something else, too. Something softer. A different shampoo?

"When do you get off?" she asked, placing her hands on the counter. "I need to talk to you."

I looked down at the order slip in my hand, then slid it into the rack above the coffee machine so that Amy could get started on the mother's drink.

"You need to talk to me," I repeated slowly.

"Shit. Don't just say it back to me."

"I finish at three thirty," I said.

"Well, can you take a break before then?" Daphne had an impatient look on her face.

"I've already had my breaks, and it's only me and Amy on today."

"C'mon, Finn." Daphne's eyes were red. She looked exhausted. "I *need* to talk to you."

Amy had overheard us. "It's fine," she said. "It's not busy. Take five if you need it."

Daphne put a hand on my arm across the bench.

"Thanks, Amy," I said, turning my head to speak to Amy directly, using that as an excuse to pull my hand back toward my body.

Daphne headed for the door. I followed her outside.

I stood with her below the same awning Sunita and I had sheltered under earlier that day. I was so tired, it was like I'd been drugged. My tooth ached. Magdu's uncle had done something bad, something wrong. Fuck. It didn't help that I was now on the heaviest part of my period, which made me sluggish. I longed to go home and crawl into bed. I didn't want to talk to Daphne, to anybody.

From where I was standing, I could see a poster in support of marriage equality stuck on a power pole. A thick strip had been torn down its center. The Blu-Tacked edges fluttered a little. I forced myself to look back at Daphne, who had a frown on her face.

"Daphne." I didn't have the rest of the sentence planned. I wanted to find a way to communicate that I couldn't do this now. It was too much.

"The police came to the house this morning and took everything that I had with me on the cliff that day."

"What?" I could taste metal. "Did they have a warrant?"

"Yes, of course they fucking did."

The rain was coming down hard now. I'd never been surfing but I'd seen videos of huge, crashing surf. It had a score to settle, the way it kept coming and coming. The rain was like that.

"What exactly did they take?" I said.

Daphne looked at her feet. She was wearing her black boots with the heel. "The bag I had with me on the day of the climb, the clothes I was wearing." Daphne ran a hand through her hair. "And then they took me back to that stinking station to interview me again. For hours."

Dale hadn't said anything when we spoke. He'd let me rattle on about seeing the men from the day of the climb and he hadn't said anything about having Daphne in an interview room.

But, then, why should he tell me? His job was to figure out what had happened.

"What did they want?" I said, after a few seconds had passed. I felt fifteen years old again.

"They asked me to tell them everything I could remember from that morning. They went through the contents of the bag with me and said they were taking it all into evidence. They took everything. Even the beautiful knife you gave me." Daphne pouted. It would have looked ridiculous on anyone else.

"Then what? How did it end?"

"They said I was free to go but not to leave town. The same shit they said the first time."

I felt cold, as if I'd plunged into a deep pool. "Okay."

"That's all you have to fucking say?" Daphne said. My sore tooth throbbed sharply where Magdu's uncle had done his work. "You've been distracted for months, ever since you met Magdu. I tell you I'm pregnant, that I'm failing my fucking PhD, and none of it registers. I need you now, and it's like you're a million miles away." Daphne lowered her voice. "Finn, they came to my *house*. I know you're upset about what happened to Magdu, but I need you to take this seriously."

I took a step back from Daphne, nearly falling into the gutter. Everything had always looked so easy for Daphne, this person who memorized ancient poems, who could draw, who knew the name of every plant she saw. "I don't know what to say. I'm sorry."

Daphne looked down the street and then, like she was speaking more to herself than to me, she said, "The weirdest thing is that the cops wanted to know about our sisters, about how they died." Something about the way she said it. A children's TV presenter saying, *I wonder what activity we're going to do today?*

Something in my gut kicked. It happened this way whenever I pushed her on something she didn't want to be pushed on, whenever she needed to tug on a rope to pull me back in. What she knew, what she could tell the police about me, shimmered between us.

I thought of the hospital car park, of what Dale had said. "Senior Constable Gosling asked me how Brianna died," I said.

Daphne waved a hand. "Why are we talking about this, anyway?"

You were the one who brought it up. I thought the words but couldn't say them.

"Look, I've been thinking." Daphne played with the hem of her white blouse. A band of embroidery sat at the elbow and under her breasts, material puffed out over her forearms and waist. A girl from a folktale. Gretel from "Hansel and Gretel," all grown up. "We can move out and get our own place. I know you're funny about money, but I'll pay. Now we can be together. None of this awful stuff that's happening will matter when the baby gets here."

Now we could be *together*?

Daphne could decide to do something and then make it happen. It didn't sound like much, but if you weren't afraid, if you thought that things would work out for you, then it was amazing what was possible. Sometimes that could be exhilarating, to be close to someone who could make things happen. But at this moment, I felt sick. I knew she could do it, but could I?

Daphne pulled my hand toward her stomach, holding my palm to her belly. Was that a slight curve under the fabric? I couldn't tell. I thought of the muscular wall of her tummy, the smooth flatness I remembered from lying beside her in her bed, her shirt rucked up casually. It didn't matter to her that I would be looking; I was no more threatening than a dog or a houseplant.

"You can't feel it yet, but it's in there."

There was no one on the street, only us.

"We just need to get through this," Daphne said. I supposed *this* meant the police asking questions. "That's all I want."

"And you always get what you want," I said flatly.

She laughed and let my hand fall. I had a vivid flash of me with Daphne's baby, sitting on the floor of her parents' house. The house was empty, save for me and the baby. I had no idea where Daphne was, but in my vision I could smell neroli oil.

Magdu had tried to tell me that Daphne was bad for me, that she made me feel bad about myself; Magdu could see it. But wasn't it more accurate to say that *I* was bad for me? Liquid concrete moved through my body when I tried to explain to Daphne what I felt. That was my fault, not hers. I couldn't think. I couldn't swallow. I did it to myself, didn't I? All I had to say was *no*, but I couldn't.

She smoothed the folds of her blouse. "I'll let you get back to work." She pulled me into a hug, and I relaxed into it despite myself. "I thought you should know."

She turned and walked away from me, the tips of her gold hair dark with the water that dripped from her umbrella.

I rushed back into the warm coffee fug of the café. The rich smell made me think of shit, but somehow not in a bad way. I couldn't return Amy's smile as I ducked behind the coffee machine. Luckily, no more customers had come into the shop while I stood outside with Daphne. I made myself a coffee, pumping two shots of vanilla syrup into it. Needed something strong and sweet if I was going to stay upright.

Amy was watching me. "Banana bread?" she asked.

"Yes, please."

She put a piece for each of us into the sandwich press. That was the good thing about Amy: she'd worked there long enough to feel comfortable making executive decisions about what food we could help ourselves to. I knew we'd run out of banana bread soon, because we always did on a Sunday, so it felt good to take it before a customer could have it. I slathered it in butter and cut it into pieces I could eat with one hand while I worked.

We had a couple of waves of people, busloads traveling together. Despite the rain and the cool weather, I made a surprising number of iced coffees. Some days it was like everyone had woken up having dreamed of the same thing. We'd get runs of a weirdly specific sandwich order, or a handful of people would ask if we had peppermint syrup, then no one would ask about it for months.

At closing time, I checked for any remaining customers before locking the front door behind me and flipping the sign.

"You all right?" Amy asked.

The kindness in her voice had cleared a path for them, and tears came. Amy put her arms around me, and I put my head on her shoulder and cried them out.

After we'd said goodbye, I took out my phone and dialed Jo's office. To my surprise, she answered. I knew she worked on Sundays, but I had no idea what time she finished.

"Jo Richards speaking."

"Hi, Jo. It's Finn. Finnlay Young." There was a wobble in my voice and part of me was glad, because I needed her to say yes. "Is there any chance I could see you again today?" I squatted on my haunches. I was under the awning but rain still fell on my pants. "I haven't been to the doctor for a mental health plan yet, but I . . . I need . . ."

I burst into tears. I couldn't afford a session, but I couldn't imagine going home either. Not yet. If Mum saw me like this, it would drive her out of her mind with worry.

"That's not a problem, Finn." Jo's voice was tired, calm. "I could see you at five o'clock?"

18

BEFORE

I should never have told Magdu about the stupid wallet thing that happened with me and Daphne. I hadn't anticipated how upset she would get. Hadn't thought about the end of the story before starting. Words were treacherous like that.

We were lying in Magdu's bed, talking about practical jokes. Her brother had loved them when they were growing up, and she wanted me to know that she'd had enough to last her a lifetime. I took her hand, threaded my fingers through hers. Dim light came through her suncatchers, which caught the red and orange of the couch, blankets, and bed. As I spoke, it was like we were inside a red-and-orange lantern.

———

It had been a cold, rainy day in August, in the stuffiest classroom in the whole high school. The gas heaters were blasting, and I had to keep wetting my clay birds so they didn't dry out.

I was working in clay for my final-year project. I liked the solidness of it in my hands, dense and wet and slippery. They were simple birds. Little swallows, with their wings outstretched.

I was in no danger of being included in the year twelve art showcase. I was trying to be the kind of person who was into art, but woodwork was my favorite class. That was the one subject I took that Daphne didn't. My major piece for woodwork was a delicate, to-scale model of a Greek ship. I was too embarrassed to tell Daphne that. As it had come together, I'd realized it was such a dumb thing to pick. I could never show her, because she would know exactly what it meant. Daphne had never asked about what I did in woodwork, and I was grateful.

Mrs. Strauss, our art teacher, was in love with Daphne. Daphne's year twelve visual art project imagined that the Daphne from mythology had been allowed to turn back into a human at will. Her drawings showed the moments of transformation. *We put a wreath of laurel on people's heads to celebrate an achievement, but the laurel tree is a symbol wound up in the downfall of a woman who did nothing wrong*, Daphne wrote in her artist's statement. They were beautiful pictures, haunting. In one drawing, you could clearly see Daphne's breasts. The delicate pink nipples, which I tried not to look at when Daphne got changed, rendered in graphite.

Mrs. Strauss was talking about what Daphne was going to do after the HSC, about art school. That's why I'll never understand why she did what she did. Maybe it was because Mrs. Strauss had complimented me that day. Mrs. Strauss was not a fan of mine. My clay creations often blew up in the kiln, destroying the work of students whom she liked better. But that day there was something quick and light about my bird. It might have been made of something other than clay, that's how delicate it was. Mrs. Strauss walked past me and commented, "This is a delightful surprise, Finn."

The smell of wet school jumpers and the drumming of the rain on the roof. Time stretched longer on rainy days, something to do with the smell of the gas heater in the poorly ventilated room. That smell was high school for me. Huddling next to a heater, our hands stretched out, our jumpers singeing before our fingers were properly warmed. Blue metal, black vents.

I was starting a second bird, hoping that I could keep alive whatever had made the first one work. I smiled to myself as I wet my hands and thought about how Mrs. Strauss had praised me.

Daphne hissed at me to stash my backpack under the table. "Quick, Finn. She's coming."

"What?" I whispered back.

I could never be as quick as Daphne. Always two steps behind. I was the one looking down at my feet, while Daphne saw things that I would never have noticed.

My hands were wet and covered in clay. Later, I would think there was no way I could have hidden my bag in time. It was impossible.

Maybe if Daphne had given me more warning. I'd covered up countless little things before. That was what being a friend in high school was all about. Finding the limits, skirting them, dragging a match along them to light Daphne's cigarettes. I hated smoking, but had taken the fall for Daphne when she nearly got caught by the principal. Daphne ducked behind a tree and left me standing next to the still-smoking butt on the ground. I got a week's worth of detentions for that one.

"What's in your schoolbag?" Mrs. Strauss said the words slowly, her tone curiously flat.

It took me a moment to reply. "Miss?"

I looked at Daphne, who was staring off into the distance behind me, a look on her face that I couldn't decode.

Mrs. Strauss put her hands on her hips. "I can see orange leather through the opening. Do you mind telling me what that is?"

"Orange leather?"

"Is that my purse?" The muscles in Mrs. Strauss's face contorted. I could smell her breath. Instant coffee gone sour.

I had a vivid flash of being a little kid, picking at bark on a tree with a stick. Then the bark came away and a swarm of ants shimmered into life. There were hundreds of tiny white dots that I knew were their babies. Panic. Fear. I was a bad person and I would be found out. Terrible, terrible, terrible. Something that should have been kept hidden had been exposed to the light.

Then, when my mind caught up with my body, I was angry. It was one thing that Mrs. Strauss hid my work, that she didn't want me in the class. It was another thing to accuse me of stealing. I reached for the old towel thrown at the far end of the desk and wiped my hands.

I stood up to my full height. "Are you calling me a thief?"

My anger surprised me. It filled every muscle in my body.

As if sensing the weight advantage I had over her, Mrs. Strauss took a step back. That made me angrier. She thought I was going to *hurt* her?

She plunged her hand into my bag and pulled out a chunky orange wallet. It had a brass zipper and an intricate pattern worked into the leather. She held it up between us.

"I didn't take that," I blurted.

Mrs. Strauss's voice was pleasant, like the automated announcer on the train line. "I want you to leave the room now and go to the principal's office."

"But I haven't done anything wrong." Despite my anger, I couldn't summon anything stronger. It was so obvious to me that I wouldn't have done what I was accused of that I felt fixed in place, behind thick glass. I looked at the wallet and then at Daphne. "I . . ."

"I'll go with her, Mrs. Strauss," Daphne said.

"That would be a good idea, Daphne. It's going to be a lot worse

for Finn if I find out she hasn't gone straight to the principal's office."
Mrs. Strauss looked at me, and I longed to punch her in the face. She
turned to Daphne. "You'll see she gets there."

––––––––

Magdu had taken her hand out of mine, crossing her arms over her
body and sitting up in bed. "So, Daphne walked you to the principal's
office and let you take the fall?"

I shrugged.

"You seem so calm about all this, Finn."

"It was a dumb joke that went wrong. She had a better relationship with that teacher. Art meant a lot more to her than to me."

Magdu shook her head. "She used you. And in the end, she gets
you to think that it's your idea."

I shrugged again. "She's my best friend."

What else could I say? I couldn't tell her the truth: that all
Daphne had to do was threaten to tell about my sister and I would
do whatever she wanted.

I wished I hadn't told Magdu. I could see the story swishing
around in her brain, taking on a meaning I hadn't intended. We were
going climbing with Daphne that week, and I wanted everyone to
get along.

I didn't tell Magdu the rest of the story. How Daphne had kept her
face neutral while Mrs. Strauss was talking. How something kicked inside of me. I wanted to get into the hall and talk to Daphne, so I gath-
ered up my bag, shoving in my stuff. The orange leather wallet was on
the table between me and Mrs. Strauss, where she'd left it. She leaned
forward and picked it up gingerly, like she wanted to avoid messing
up any fingerprints. I zipped my bag closed and slung it onto my back.
Daphne left her bag on the table, as if signaling she would not be gone

long. Mrs. Strauss's mouth was a cranky little line. I stormed out and Daphne followed.

"*You* took that wallet," I said, once we were in the hallway.

For some reason I was keeping my voice down. Daphne walked on a few steps, as if wanting to put some distance between us and the art room before replying.

"I panicked." Daphne went to take my hand, but I shook it off. "Thank you for not saying anything."

"Daphne, I could be expelled."

"Say it was a joke. That you meant to show me and freak me out and then put it back."

I looked at her. "It's a good excuse, Daphne. So why didn't *you* say that?"

"What?"

For once, I was made of steel. I wasn't afraid, even though I could hear my heartbeat in my ears, feel the heat in my face. I was speaking louder now. "You could have said *you* were only fooling around, that you'd planned to put it back. That it was stupid, but you never meant to steal it. They would believe it, coming from you."

Daphne looked at me coldly. "It's not like I've never done anything for you," she said, so quietly I almost didn't hear it. The truth about my sister's death moved between us. Daphne smiled.

We'd arrived at the door of the principal's office. Why had I come here? I could have walked out into the afternoon. Left it all behind.

Daphne put a hand on my shoulder. "What are you going to do?"

All the anger had left my body. I was empty. I couldn't imagine going in there and saying it had been Daphne. No one would believe me, and now Daphne would owe me something, wouldn't she? Maybe this was what true friendship meant.

The principal must have heard voices, because he stepped out of his office into the corridor.

"Finnlay," he said, eyebrows drawn together.

Daphne came close to me, whispered urgently in my ear. "Be apologetic, Finn. Say you don't know what came over you. They won't expel you."

And they didn't. To Daphne's credit, I think she spoke to Mrs. Strauss and asked for leniency. I'm sure my dead sister was mentioned. It was too late in year twelve for me to transfer out of art, but I moved from Mrs. Strauss's class to Mrs. Nakamura's. Mrs. Nakamura liked my clay birds. It was nice to sit and work and not have to talk to anyone. The ninety-minute class passed quickly. Sometimes, I'd get so absorbed that I wouldn't hear the bell ring. I'd look up to find that everyone had already left the room. It was just me, hands slick with clay, the sounds of laughter floating in from the quad outside.

19

SUNDAY, SEPTEMBER 10, 2017

How stupid it was for me to come here, I thought, in Jo's waiting room. Jo couldn't help me with this. An urge for a whiskey or beer. Or—and this came out of nowhere, a bat startled from a fruit tree— some of the cheap and nasty white wine that had been Mum's tipple of choice. I could taste it, the vapor on Mum's breath, hanging sharp and tangy in the air after she'd had a big night, pickling us all alive.

When she came out to greet me, Jo looked different. Her hair was pulled up into a small, tight bun instead of puffing out around her head. She seemed rumpled in a way I'd never seen before.

"So," she said, once we'd sat down inside her office, "you seemed distressed on the phone."

Now I was here I didn't know why I had called Jo. What could she say? What did I want her to do?

I had come to talk about Daphne, about her being questioned again, but instead I told her about visiting Magdu's body on Friday, that a cop had helped me to see her even though her family didn't want me to. I said I hadn't been ready to talk about it in our session the day before, but now I needed to.

I caught the rise of one of Jo's eyebrows before she looked down at her notebook and arranged her features in a blank expression. *Maybe I shouldn't be telling her this. I could get Dale in trouble.* I didn't tell her that I thought I knew why. Why it would matter to him that I be allowed to see my girlfriend.

I talked about Magdu, about our plans for the future. I talked and talked. Relieved that I could speak in a muddle without Jo pulling away. I didn't know what I needed to say, so I kept going, hoping something would leap out at Jo, that she would stop me and direct the conversation. She didn't.

After a long time, I fell silent. I wanted to tell her about Suze, but I didn't know how to begin. It was too late. Had been too long.

"Finn," Jo said, breaking the silence between us, "I expect it won't help much, but I want you to know that everything you're going through right now strikes me as quite normal."

I leaned forward, propping my elbows on my knees. "I don't know what to do."

Jo put her pen and notepad down.

A thought occurred to me, quick and skittering, a cockroach across a kitchen floor. "Today, Daphne . . ." I couldn't finish the thought.

Jo resettled herself in her chair. "Daphne strikes me as someone whose opinion is very important to you," she said.

A ripple of anger moved through me. Jo didn't have the first fucking idea what we'd been through together. I stayed quiet.

Jo looked down at her hands. "It's just an observation."

"She's my best friend," I shot back. "It's normal to care what she thinks."

"You told me once about something that happened between you

and Daphne in high school," Jo said, steepling her fingers. "It seemed like there were a lot of situations in which she hurt you. And yet you remained friends. Why do you think that is?"

Jo was wearing glasses, I realized. That was part of what had made her look different. The rectangular frames made her eyes look smaller.

"Are there things you feel you can't share with Daphne? Certain emotions?"

I gave a strangled laugh. "Isn't that why I come here? To tell you all my deep, dark thoughts so you can tell me I'm not crazy?"

It was meant to be a joke.

What would happen if Jo turned to me and said simply, *You are crazy?* What then? I still hadn't told her what had happened with Daphne that afternoon, what had sent me into a spin in the first place.

"Daphne came to see me at work today. She told me the police had turned up at her house with a search warrant. Then they took her in for questioning again. She seemed so mad at me; it's like I can't give her what she needs. Things happen and I feel . . . numb."

I folded my arms around myself, slumping forward. Jo was writing furiously in her notebook.

"She's pregnant, and I know that she needs me." My heart battered against my chest. "But I just can't seem to—"

Jo raised a hand to stop me, gazing at me steadily over the top of her notebook. She looked tired. "It's been a long day, Finn. And I'm going to level with you. I think you need to focus on yourself right now. Take all the time and space you need. You are not responsible for Daphne."

It was a relief to have someone tell me that out loud.

Jo appeared to be wrestling with what to say next. She looked at her notebook. Underlined something. She was quiet for so long that I was startled by her deep voice. "Maybe it wouldn't be a bad thing to keep your distance from her for a while?" She said it like someone who cared about me, who didn't want to see me get hurt. "But I'm afraid that's it for today." Jo straightened in her chair. "I'm glad you came to see me, Finn. I've been worried about you."

I turned to look behind me at the clock. We'd gone well over. I felt a little flutter of satisfaction, like I mattered.

———

I drove straight home after my appointment with Jo. I couldn't think of anywhere else to go. I pulled into the driveway, the house squatting on the low side of the street, water streaming from its full gutters.

I entered through the back door, went into my bedroom, and put on my hiking jacket. I needed to go for a walk, and I couldn't take Spencer with me. I needed to move, slip into some bush and bash through it.

"Is that you, Finn?" Mum called from somewhere in the house.

I'd been hoping to get in and out without talking to her.

I heard her bustle down the hall toward my room. She stopped in my doorway.

"Where are you going, love? It's pissing down outside."

"I have to get out of here," I said, walking toward the front door without looking at her.

"Are you going to Daphne's?"

I laughed. It sounded like one of Spencer's barks. "No, Mum. I don't want to see anyone. I want to walk, and then I want to go to bed."

Mum gave her crooked smile, one tooth missing on the left side. I pictured her as the chubby kid she would have been. Her genetics had been passed wholesale to me, skipping my sister altogether. The only thing I'd got from Dad was his height.

"Maybe it's a good thing for you to stay away from the Bennetts for a bit," Mum said. "I thought it was strange how much time you spent there after your sister." She had her chatty voice on, the one she used to talk to her friend Sandra. "They acted like you were an orphan or something, like there was no one to take care of you." She leaned against the doorframe. "I tried not to take it personally, because I could see how much it meant to you, but I thought it was odd. Daphne was always off, if you ask me. And you were a completely different person when you spent time with her. I don't think it was good for you."

Something inside me roared, shook its fist, rattled its cage.

"Good for me?" I snarled. "Who the fuck are you to talk about what's *good for me*?"

Rage suffused my body. I knew the guilt would come, but I couldn't feel it yet, didn't want to. In that moment, I didn't give a shit that Mum had been younger than I was now when her parents died; that she'd been an only child with no one in the world to support her. These were old thoughts, too well-worn to be of use in this situation. I wanted to blaze at her. I wanted her to experience my anger as something physical. Deep down, I knew it wasn't her fault that my father had been weak, had turned away from us, but in that moment I wanted to punish her, and keep punishing her.

A silence hung between us.

I was filled with poison that had nowhere to go but out of my mouth. "And you're going to tell me you don't know why they took me in? You're going to act all fucking wide-eyed and innocent about why I may have preferred their house to ours?" There was spit on my chin and I wiped it away with the back of my hand.

Mum wasn't looking at me, her eyes trained on the stained carpet. I was reminded forcefully that whatever had happened between us, she was my mum and I cared deeply what she thought of me.

"Why did her death make you better?" It was only as I spoke the words that I realized the truth of them, that I needed to know the answer.

The pale skin of Mum's chest was mottled with pink now. "It didn't make me better, Finn. How could you think that?" Mum tapped her chest and sobbed. "She's here, Finn. All the time."

She was still hunched in the doorway. She wiped at the tears under her eyes.

For a moment, I'd wanted to be as ugly and as awful as I could, for Mum to overpower me, to hold me like a little kid having a tantrum, to love me so hard that I came back to myself, that I came back to the kid I was before Suze died, maybe even before Suze was born.

Instead, I was the one who pulled her into a hug, held her head to my shoulder.

"Oh, Mum. I'm sorry. I'm so sorry."

"I'm glad you're here, Finn," she said into the synthetic material of my hiking jacket. "I get so scared when you leave me. Even if it's just to go to Daphne's."

I thought of how hard it had been to get away for a hike after Suze had died. The one place I could be myself was on a bush track. That was as close to peace as I got. But it cost Mum something, to let me go. To have me out of phone range, worrying that I'd slip and fall. That's why I never went alone. I could have gone anyway, could have lied to her about it. I was capable of it. But whenever I was tempted, I would remember that I was the last one left. The only one she had.

"I'm sorry, Mum," I said into her hair. "I really am." I breathed in her smell: lemon balm and Winnie Blues.

I realized that as we'd spoken, some part of me had already been getting ready to call Magdu, to drive over to her place. A sick, stupid thought.

"How about some tea?" Mum asked. A watery smile.

"I'm going to go for a drive, Mum. But thanks."

———

I drove in the direction of Magdu's flat. Her red key was on my Tasmanian Devil key chain, and I intended to use it.

I parked down the road from her row of flats; I didn't want her neighbors to see me. The same metal knocker on her door as the night I'd come to apologize. Useless now. I unlocked the door with my key, slipping inside and shutting the door behind me. The flat was dark, blinds pulled down over all the windows. I wondered if Magdu's family had a key too. Her tote bag was still in the passenger footwell of my car. They might think I'd stolen the bag. Maybe I should have handed it over to the police? It honestly hadn't occurred to me that anybody would want it. I'd tried not to think about the fact that there was an investigation, and hadn't given a thought to her family at all, not really. Only myself.

I took a few steps into the room, then stopped. I was still wearing my black runners. Magdu didn't like shoes in the house. I returned to the front door and kicked them off next to a pair of ballet flats.

I looked at the couch, where we'd sat so often, Magdu's feet resting on my lap. I ran my hand along a line of books on the shelf. A series Magdu loved, the spines cracked from the harsh treatment she dished out to all her books. She'd bend them all the way around, so that she could read one-handed. I turned to look at the bed, which was neatly made. Magdu always made the bed. I lay down on it, curling into a ball at the smell of her in the sheets. I moaned but couldn't seem to cry. I was all dried out inside. The room had sucked all the moisture from my body.

I don't know how long I lay there, but after a while I heard footsteps outside. I sat up. What if it was Magdu's family? Sunita would be furious to find me here, scrabbling through her daughter's belongings.

My heart pounded, my tooth pulsing with pain to the rhythm.

The footsteps moved away, but I swung my feet off the bed and headed for the fridge. Took the half-empty carton of almond milk from the door and poured it down the sink, then rinsed the carton and put it in the cardboard box Magdu used for recycling. I padded on socked feet back to the door. There was a floor-length mirror on the wall next to the front door, so you could see your entire outfit on the way out of the house. I kneeled down in front of it and, instead of picking up my black runners, I grabbed the ballet flats. Magdu and I wore the same shoe size. *Not that it helps me much*, Magdu had said. *I wouldn't be seen dead in most of your shoes.* Seeing the hurt in my face she'd laughed. *Don't get me wrong. They look great on you. Very lesbian-in-the-woods.*

I smiled to think of that. I stripped my socks off, arranging the ballet flats so that I could step into them. A curve that her foot had impressed into the sole over time. Magdu wouldn't even have noticed the ridge because it would have been in the shape of her foot. But I felt the curve of Magdu, the lack of her. I kept my eyes down and away from the mirror.

A braided bracelet that Magdu always wore was lying on the small table next to the door. I would've assumed she was wearing it the day of the climb, but she must have taken it off, worried it would catch on something. I picked it up and smelled the leather. I tied the bracelet tight around my own wrist, enjoying the feeling of it on my skin. With a sense of urgency now, I picked up my black runners, stuffing them in the crook of my arm, and stepped outside, locking the door behind me. Magdu's ballet flats were on my feet, and I could finally cry.

20

BEFORE

About a week after the incident with the wallet, Daphne caught up with me outside my English class as the bell was ringing for the start of lunch. I'd been avoiding her, and we hadn't spoken since the afternoon she'd walked me to the principal's office. I was amazed that I'd managed to hold out so long. Of course I was still scared that she would tell everyone my secret, but something in me had solidified. If Daphne was going to tell, she would tell. I couldn't keep doing this, being frightened of what she would say. If she decided to go to my mother or the police, at least it would be over.

Daphne must've left her own class early to make it to my classroom in time. She seemed out of breath.

"Come to mine after school today," she said, her tone pleading.

"I don't want to."

I'd spent a lot of time alone in the art room, on the oval, in the library, in the computer room. I knew I wouldn't be going to uni, but while searching online for jobs I could do outdoors, I'd found a ski resort in Canada that took applicants fresh from high school. The thought lit me up from inside, but I had no one to talk to about it. And if Daphne revealed my secret, I wouldn't be going anywhere but prison.

Daphne ran a hand through her hair. "We need to talk. You know we do."

A group of younger kids were setting up handball squares in the quad not far from us, with plenty of good-natured jostling and laughter.

"I'm begging you," Daphne said.

It was like being out on the rock in the sun, being tired at the top of a climb, knowing you had to make a big move if you were going to drag yourself up and over the edge. Daphne had been sitting with the girls who hung out in the year twelve common room. She didn't need me. And yet here she was. I was hanging, suspended, trying to summon the strength to do what I needed to do. Something had to give. I was going over or I was going down.

"All right," I said, and she smiled. "But I can't stay long."

———

We had sport that afternoon. I did athletics, and had changed into the school polo and shorts. I took my time walking to my car after the bell rang. The Suzuki had been a hand-me-down seventeenth-birthday present from Mum's friend Sandra. The first time I'd done the registration on it had been like missing a stair at nighttime, pitching forward, indignant and scared. It cost so much money to keep a car on the road. I'd used all my savings and had to ask Dad for money, which I hated doing.

I drove out of the student car park and turned in the direction of Daphne's house. She did yoga for her sport elective, which finished before athletics, so I knew she'd be home already. I wondered for a moment what it would mean to lose this familiarity. To not know what Daphne was up to. Year twelve would be over in November. Maybe we could go our separate ways, leave this thing behind us. Be adults who didn't know each other. I would go off to Canada and shape myself into somebody new, somebody better. I could picture that, and yet also see myself in a green prison tracksuit, holding both ideas in my mind at the same time.

———

The front door of Daphne's house was ajar. I let myself in, the way I'd done countless times before, closing the door behind me. A long Persian carpet runner stretched down the hallway. I wished we had one at our house. Anger swelled inside me. There were so many things I wanted, but I'd never stolen anything.

"Hi, Finn."

I turned to see Carol-Ann in the kitchen doorway. "Daphne mentioned you'd be coming over."

Carol-Ann worked part-time as a social worker, a job she'd started shortly after her youngest daughter had died. It must have been one of her days off.

I smiled, not sure what to say. Had Daphne told her what had happened? While she didn't mind telling stories that showed her in a bad light—almost seemed to enjoy it, with me and her family—I didn't think she'd want Carol-Ann to know what she'd done, that she'd let me take the blame.

I nodded my head toward Daphne's bedroom, not trusting myself to speak.

"You go on. She's waiting for you." Carol-Ann waved a hand dusted in flour. "It's been Sturm und Drang all week." She turned back to her baking.

I walked down the hallway and knocked on Daphne's door. I didn't know what the words Carol-Ann had used meant, but I could guess.

"Come in."

Daphne was sitting on her queen-size bed. The cool blues of the quilt were soothing. She alternated between this cover and a green one, I knew. Daphne patted the bed, inviting me to sit beside her. I sat a little farther away than she'd indicated.

"Thank you for coming."

Why was I here? Why had I agreed to come? She was the one who'd fucked up, not me. Sure, I'd let Daphne down in lots of little ways, by not being fast enough, interesting enough. I'd been living on borrowed time with her for as long as I could remember. But now she was in the wrong—about this, at least. For all I knew this conversation would end with her telling her mother what I'd done, and Carol-Ann calling the police. Still, I wasn't going to back down.

"You knew what you were doing," I said. The sentence I'd practiced. "Why did you put the wallet in my bag and not your own?"

The unfairness of what had happened rushed through me again, and I clenched my fists.

What Daphne did next surprised me utterly. She raised her hand to my neck, tucking her fingers behind it with the neat, quick movement of someone slipping a Christmas card in an envelope, and looked me in the eye. "I'm sorry," she said.

I'd never had a direct apology from Daphne. Usually when she'd done something wrong she'd refuse to admit it, and I would decide that what I was mad about was not more important than keeping the peace between us.

She stood and turned away from me. For a moment I was confused, but then I heard the sound of the bolt hitting home.

She returned to the bed and kissed me, hard, then brought her hands to my waist. I tried to mirror the action, but she caught my hands before they reached her body. A politician intercepting a high five, turning it into a more dignified handshake.

She sought the skin under my uniform. Her hands found their way underneath the fabric of my school shirt and inside my bra. My lips parted in surprise. She licked the corner of my mouth. She was leaning into me, and I made to lie back. With the hand holding my breast she gestured for me to move, and I laughed, wriggling up the bed so my head was closer to the pillows. Daphne followed, swinging a leg over so that she was on top of me, pinning me down. She removed her hand from underneath my shirt and began to unbutton it, then reached around to undo my bra. I arched my back to make the job easier for her. She got it in one smooth motion and freed me. I was sexy, laid out on the bed. Daphne's hands found my breasts and she leaned in to kiss me, her hair falling over us in a shiny curtain.

Daphne lowered her head and I felt like I was breathing in through the space between my legs. I tried to pull her further into me and everything pulsed and was pink and warm. I took big, shuddering breaths. Aware that there was sound but not entirely sure if it was coming from me.

Daphne didn't look at me; she kept her eyes down. A Greek maiden, anointed in oil. I felt a sharpening. Everything in me coming to a point. I rocked against her, moaning as quietly as I could. The final exhalation, the pleading sound coming from somebody else. I was salty and slick and trembling.

She pulled her hand away and looked at me again. Her hair was messy and she smiled.

I kissed her. Ran my hands along her body. She didn't respond, seemed tired. I let my hand rest on her waist, her body snuggled into mine.

She murmured, "We'll always keep each other's secrets, won't we?"

"Yes," I whispered into her hair.

Everything I wanted, everything I'd been too scared to say I wanted, was suddenly mine and the feeling was so overwhelming my body did what it always did when there was too much emotion. I fell asleep.

When I woke, the sun had set and Daphne was gone. I found her drinking tea with her mother in the kitchen. Carol-Ann was strange. She sounded like her usual self, cheery and chatty, but I caught her looking at me. Her eyes moved between me and her daughter, and it was like the barometric pressure had dropped, like when you're on the ridge and a storm is coming. I retrieved my bag from Daphne's room, saying I should get home. Daphne waved from the table, like she was stuck to her chair.

Carol-Ann walked me out, which was unusual. I'd been coming and going from the Bennetts' place for a long time. She looked like she wanted to say something, but in the end she waved me off and closed the front door behind me.

Outside, I couldn't keep the smile off my face. I believed it was the beginning of something different. It wasn't, it would end up being just a pause before more of the same. But I didn't know that then.

We never talked about the wallet again.

———

A few months after that, Daphne and I went to a party at Emily Maddox's house to mark the end of year twelve. Emily's parents were away. Why parents would even consider leaving their teenage children at home alone was beyond me. Hadn't they ever seen a movie?

Nothing had happened since the afternoon at Daphne's. We didn't speak about it, and I'd been forced to acknowledge that it probably wasn't going to happen again. Still, it burned as a good secret inside of me.

Everyone had been talking about how smashed they were going to get at this party. I'd never trusted myself around alcohol. Sometimes, I wanted to rub up against it, see if it would break the skin. See what all the fuss was about. Maybe I wanted to prove to myself that I was better than my mother. But I only ever took a couple of beers with me to parties. They were expensive, for one thing, and hard to get, because I was still only seventeen. And I was afraid of what might come out, I guess. And that I might be like Mum. The ship I'd built with Daphne's help was only a couple of years old then.

Daphne, on the other hand, loved to drink. I think she was someone who needed an excuse to let go. To do what she wanted. Eat the food she turned down normally, flirt with the people she wouldn't usually bother with or want to be seen bothering with. And sometimes, when she was drinking, she would look at me, and something in her eyes would say, *I know. I know, and in this moment I am choosing not to say.*

Daphne was not a sad drunk. Not like some of the girls in our class, who could be found curled into corners at parties, mascara flowing down their faces and into their tube tops. Once, Daphne told me that she tried thinking about her sister when she drank, to see if she would cry, but she never did.

I stood in Emily's kitchen. Photos on the fridge, labeled Tupperware drying on the draining board, varnished wood everywhere. They had wooden chairs, gingham curtains, and a wall hanging with a painting of a hen sitting on a nest. It was both musty and comforting. I'd managed to fill my beer bottle with water without anyone seeing, which meant I could stop drinking without anyone giving me shit for it.

Daphne came in, trailed by a few girls from school.

"There she is!" she exclaimed. "Settle a bet, Finn?"

"About what?" I took a big swig from the beer bottle, aware that if I was found out it would be embarrassing. What if someone made a grab for the beer? Daphne could do impulsive things like that: take my drink and help herself, winking at me, feeding the flames of the gossip that we were a couple.

"Which one of us is most attractive?" Daphne looked across at the other two girls, spoke loudly. "Come into the light, Emily, Beatrice. No fair to rely on a low-light situation."

The three young women, a little unsteady on their feet, lined themselves up in front of the kitchen cabinets, each with a hand on her hip, like this was some kind of demented Miss World competition. Daphne was in the middle.

Why had I been chosen to make the decision?

"You're all beautiful." I meant it. I would have happily rubbed my face in the soft bellies of any one of these girls.

"No, no, no," Daphne said. "That simply won't do."

I knew why I had been asked to judge. We all did. I wasn't sure how it had got out, but I figured it was better that the girls in my class knew. I'd lived in fear of being accused in the changing room. At least now they knew to turn their backs.

"See? I told you she wouldn't do it." Daphne smirked at the other girls. "Finn is too pure for this world. She's not the same as us. She does things. She's an outdoors woman. She has a big, rich inner life and she spends time in nature."

Why was Daphne saying this? We lived in the mountains: everyone spent time in nature. But part of me flushed with pride to hear her. Daphne knew me better than anyone, and she could still praise me to others. I could see the other two girls looking at me quizzically, as if they struggled to see the shining woman Daphne was describing in the lumpy, chubby-faced idiot in front of them. It felt wonderful for someone to see me that way—as only and purely good. But then it felt like I was tricking her—a similar feeling to the one in the changing room before the girls knew what I was—and there was something oily about it, something that stained me. Or maybe that was how being a teenager was supposed to feel?

––––––

I'd never found a way to explain any of this to Jo. Never found a way to put into words what it was to be angry at someone for not doing something, something that you couldn't reasonably expect that they would do, which was love you back. I stuffed the hurt down.

It was also true that Daphne had been there for me when my sister died. When everyone else had turned away, unable to look at me, we'd had each other. And even though I realized Daphne and I would never be together, not in the way I wanted, it felt good to be seen with her. When she would absentmindedly take my hand in hers, or drape her arm over my shoulder, I would imagine how we would look to people walking past us; if they would think we were lovers. The thought made me glow, strong and steady like a torch beam in the gloom of an unexplored cave.

21

MONDAY, SEPTEMBER 11, 2017

It took me a moment to register the phone ringing on the wall in the hallway on Monday morning.

The home phone never rang for me. Mum was at work, or I would have presumed it was Mum's ancient boss at the grocery store; Mr. Crean was single-handedly preventing the fade-out of the landline. Or it would be Sandra, forgetting Mum had an early shift.

The ringing stopped, but as I continued on my way to the kitchen it started to ring again.

I picked it up. "Hello?"

"Finn, is that you?" I recognized Dale Gosling's voice.

I reached for my phone in my pocket. It was switched off. I held the power button, and the screen illuminated. A wave of missed calls came crashing in. That missed-step feeling.

"We've arrested Daphne Bennett and we'd like to speak to you again."

The ground seemed to move under my feet. "What? You've arrested *Daphne*?"

"I don't want to talk about it over the phone. Can you come to the station?"

Looking over the edge of a cliff, mind screaming, *Jump*. "I'm on my way."

I hung up and a second later my mobile started ringing. I held it to my ear without checking the number, assuming it was Dale calling me back, maybe to tell me it had all been a mistake.

"Finn? It's Carol-Ann."

I stabbed with my thumb to end the call and threw my mobile down the hall away from me. I'd done it instinctively, like flicking off a spider crawling on your hand.

As my mobile rang again I walked into the kitchen, shutting the door behind me. I couldn't speak to Carol-Ann now. I needed to think. A scratching in my chest. I'd swallowed something with sharp edges, something alive.

In the kitchen, I found my car keys on the table, where I'd left them.

I went back into the hallway, picked up my phone, put it on silent, and put it in my pocket.

I took the back steps two at a time. My phone was vibrating, Carol-Ann calling back, but I ignored it. The broken clicker hung useless on my key chain as I unlocked the driver's-side door. I wrenched the black piece of plastic from the metal loop and flung it over the back fence. The radio came on when I turned the key in the ignition and I slammed it off with my left hand, shocked by the sound.

As I pulled out into the street, the thought came to mind like something slipping from your hand and smashing to the floor. I realized where I had seen the man with the white teeth before. It was when I saw Daphne leaving the Silver Fish the night of the gig, after

Magdu had already left. Daphne, walking out of the venue with a tall dark-haired man whose arm was around her waist. The two of them laughing, him taking one last look back before they walked out the door, as if to make sure people were watching them leave together. Bright, smug smile. I buzzed with the realization that Daphne already knew Brendan; the knowledge surged through me like a series of static shocks.

What was I even going to the police station to do? And what would Daphne say about me to the police, with her back to the wall?

———

At the station, Dale was standing near the front desk, talking to a female colleague. He looked up when I walked through the doors.

"All right, Finn?" he asked.

I followed him to the pale blue interview room with the battered toys in the corner. There was a picture book with its cover ripped off splayed open on the floor. I imagined the kid who'd done it, who'd been upset enough to tear pages from a book while their mother or father talked to a strange person in a blue uniform.

Dale waited for me to sit. Everything was slowed down. My brain knew I couldn't handle what was happening and was lowering the frame rate for me.

There was too much saliva in my mouth.

Dale fiddled with the device set into the table and warned me that it would be recording our conversation.

"Thanks for coming in," he said.

"Sure." It was hot in the small room.

"I know you've done this before, but can you take me through everything that happened on the day Magdu died?"

And so I repeated it all for the third time.

"And where was Daphne at that point?" he kept interjecting.

I wanted to ask him why he had arrested Daphne, but it was all I could do to answer his questions.

Eventually, he poured me a glass of water. I gulped it gratefully.

After a pause, he said, "I think you know that we brought Daphne in again on Sunday, and that we conducted a search of her house."

"Yes. She told me, afterward."

Dale rubbed his jawline. "What did she say?"

I couldn't swallow. I didn't want to be here, sitting on this government-issue chair, my hands pressed between my thighs. That Daphne had been arrested seemed bizarre. A schoolyard rumor you couldn't trust. She was somewhere in the building. I felt so old in this police station. I wanted to be young. I wanted to be sitting in a bar somewhere, laughing at someone's dumb joke. Maybe it was all a trick. Maybe Daphne had finally told them about Suze and they'd just said that Daphne had been arrested to get me to come to the station.

"Nothing, really. Just that it had happened." I wondered if Dale knew she was pregnant. Something itched at the back of my brain, but I couldn't take a deep enough breath, stop long enough to address it.

"The blue rope we recovered was damaged. Scruffy on the ends, like a rope would be if it snapped. You would have seen that yourself on the day. At first glance it looked like an accident."

I remembered Daphne pulling up the blue rope. I'd seen the damaged end. After I'd been winched up, we had stood waiting for them to bring Magdu. I'd seen Daphne looping her rope neatly, like she would at the end of any normal climb. We were both in shock, I figured, going through the motions automatically.

"As you know, we took both ropes and all your gear for forensic examination. We also examined the section of the rope still attached to Magdu's harness, of course. We were preparing a case for the coroner. We need to be thorough."

My heart filled with Magdu, just for a second. It was a relief to hear her name. She existed.

"You light up when I mention her," he said, voice soft.

"What are we actually talking about?" I asked, wanting it all to be over. To lie down on the cool linoleum floor of the room.

"When I asked you if Magdu had a knife, you said no."

"That's right," I said.

"Daphne told us that she had loaned a knife to Magdu."

"I didn't see her do that." I sat up in the chair. "Maybe it was after I'd already belayed down."

"Based on the information provided by her family, and on examining the rope, we were operating on the hypothesis that Magdu might have cut the rope herself with the knife Daphne said she had given her."

"But that makes no—"

He raised a hand, cutting me off.

"Where she fell there is a series of ledges, which are difficult to access and search adequately. It's also possible that the knife bounced off a rock and landed outside our search area. Whatever the case, we never recovered a knife."

Dale put his palms flat on the table. "Without going into too much detail, we had sufficient cause and were able to obtain a warrant to search Miss Bennett's residence. We took her bag and the clothes she was wearing that day. And this time, we *did* find a knife."

I thought of the knife I'd given Daphne, with the delicate carving on the handle.

"While the blade itself had been wiped, the striations on the rope were a match for the cut pattern." Dale looked at me. "Do you understand what I'm telling you?"

Something settled in me, a stone being rolled into place. This was why he'd brought me here.

Almost gently, Dale said, "Daphne put Magdu on the rope knowing she was going to die."

I pulled at Magdu's bracelet beneath the cuff of my flannelette shirt. The pressure against my skin was suddenly unbearable.

Dale kept his voice low. "Daphne must have cut the rope once you'd gone down to belay. When Magdu's weight was fully committed, the rope snapped and she fell."

My pulse seemed to slow, blood evaporating through my fingers. I thought of Magdu falling, of the sound of screaming. The pain from the tooth with the plastic cap on it spiked. A radio frequency, asserting itself in the hiss of static.

I fought an impulse to grab Dale by the lapels of his uniform and shake him. I wanted to seize the picture book from the floor and hit him in the face with it.

"Daphne is my best friend." My mouth gaped open and closed again. I bowed my head, my mind scrambling to make meaning from what he'd said. "What about the men who were there? What about that guy I saw?" I put my hand on the table. "I saw him, that guy I told you about on the street. With the same group of men. They called me a dyke."

It sounded so unconvincing to my own ears. How could I make Dale see? The thought of Daphne in a cell, of Daphne going to court, of Daphne being a *murderer*, was ridiculous, absurd.

"He knew Daphne before that day at the cliff, but he acted like he didn't."

I thought of Daphne, her eyes bright in my bedroom, telling me she was almost three months along.

"He went home with Daphne," I said. "Brendan. After a gig at the Silver Fish. Three months ago. And now Daphne is pregnant."

Dale pushed the heel of his palm into his eye socket.

The words came out in a rush. "He's the father of Daphne's baby.

I know it." It was like scrabbling on rocky ground, looking for something stable to stand on. "And you said yourself that he'd hurt someone before, right? He attacked an Indian worker."

Dale bit his lower lip. "Finn. You're not listening to me. We have solid evidence to prove Daphne did it."

"But why would Brendan climb so close to us?" There was a wheedling tone in my voice that I didn't like. I sounded like a little kid. "And why did he pretend not to know Daphne?"

"You might ask why Daphne acted like she didn't know him."

I put my head in my hands. My jaw pulsed with pain.

Daphne could not have done this. It wasn't possible.

"Finn, in her very first interview, Daphne told us you were behaving strangely on the cliff that day. She tried to make it sound offhand, but in her latest interview she started to panic." He stopped, like he was unsure what to say next. "She threw you under the bus pretty hard."

My heart turned to gravel, shifting and sharp-edged in my chest. Had Daphne said something about Suze?

"She said you set the anchor, were responsible for the ropes, that if something had gone wrong it was your fault."

The gravel slid and came to rest. I took a deep breath. He had not said Suze's name.

"But we have the knife in her bag, with only her prints on it." He let his hand come to rest on the table between us. "I know this is hard to accept. I also know you loved Magdu."

Something in my chest stung and sweated, a flaming lighter held to my insides. I knew my best friend didn't do this, wasn't capable of it. Daphne couldn't be the answer. She couldn't. She would do what she had always done. Step behind a tree, leaving me with the still-smoking cigarette butt. Daphne would tell them about me, about what I had done to my sister.

I started to cry.

Dale took a deep breath. "I am terminating this recording at nine thirty-three a.m."

I looked down at my hands. We sat without speaking for a long while.

Eventually, Dale said, "I was one of the first people on the scene at a homicide once. A man had killed his wife. As we got him into cuffs, he kept saying, 'She wouldn't pass me the tomato sauce.' That's why he killed her. She refused to pass him the sauce." Dale's mouth and nose puckered, like he'd smelled something bad.

"That can't be the real reason," I said.

"His lawyer advised him to shut up and he never offered another motive. He pleaded guilty and got some bullshit sentence. What happens to the next person who doesn't want to pass him the sauce?"

"Daphne barely knew Magdu."

Dale stood, put a tea bag in a Styrofoam cup with two sugars before filling it from a boiler mounted on the wall. He put the cup down in front of me.

"Drink it," he said. "It'll help."

He raised his gaze to the clock on the wall. "I need to go."

"Okay."

We both stood.

Dale looked at me, holding eye contact before turning and moving toward the door.

I followed, still holding the cup, afraid that I might be left in the small blue room, that he might lock the door behind him.

Dale walked me back to the front doors of the station. "If you remember anything else, anything at all, I want you to let us know."

"I want to help you," I said. I remembered seeing him in the bakery with a man I presumed was his boyfriend. "You were the reason

I . . . I got to see her." I breathed deeply. "But I don't know what to say. Daphne's my best friend. She didn't do this. I can't abandon her."

He must have seen something then, some hardness in my face, because he leaned in close and asked, "Whose idea was it to go climbing, Finn?"

A beat. "Daphne's," I said.

"Well, this morning she told me it was *your* idea. Think about that, okay?"

He turned and left, and I had to sit down in one of the hard plastic chairs in the waiting area.

Daphne had said it was my idea? Suddenly, I didn't give a shit if I ran into Carol-Ann. She must have heard us all those years ago, in Daphne's bedroom. She didn't want to see me as Daphne's girlfriend. Not that I had ever been that, anyway. I was an object of pity, a pathetic friend—those were the only acceptable roles for me in that family.

I downed the tea, which was still too hot to drink. I felt it burn on the way down.

My mobile rang, buzzing between my thigh and the hard plastic seat. I resisted the urge to throw it across the room. The caller ID read: *Jo Psych.*

I hesitated before swiping to answer.

"Jo?" I said, thinking that perhaps she'd pressed the wrong contact on her phone.

"Finn! I'm sorry to call you, but I haven't been able to stop thinking about you since yesterday." There was a clacking sound that I thought might be Jo's earing hitting the phone. "It's not strictly professional to ring you like this, but sometimes you can tell when it's the right thing to do."

I looked around the crowded waiting room, wanting privacy. I ducked into the grubby disabled toilet through a door off the waiting room, locking the door behind me. "Ah, well. Thanks for calling." My voice reverberated off the seventies tiles.

Jo's deep voice in my ear. "Where are you? It sounds as though you're underwater."

"I'm at the police station," I said.

"Oh, goodness. Is everything okay?"

"Um. Not really." A telltale hitch in my voice. Would I ever stop crying?

"What's happened?"

"Daphne's been arrested." I could hear the squeezed sound I made. I was still having difficulty swallowing.

"What?"

I shook my head. I couldn't make sense of it.

Realizing she couldn't see me, I said, "I don't know what to say. The police brought me in and asked me more questions, and"—I took a deep breath—"they told me they think that Daphne cut the rope that Magdu was climbing on."

As I was speaking, I kept expecting Daphne to burst in, to say she'd been listening at the door, that I'd failed the test she'd set for me.

"What happens now?"

"I don't know. But Daphne wouldn't do this." She was a lot of things, but she wasn't a killer. Not like me.

Jo fell silent, like she was weighing something up.

"How much do you know about Daphne's life before she came to your school?" Jo asked.

I couldn't bring myself to answer, not because I didn't care but because I was zapped of energy. It was like someone had laid a heavy blanket over me. The truth was that we'd never really talked about Daphne's life before she came to Indra.

When I didn't say anything, Jo continued, "You can't repeat what I'm about to tell you. Do you promise?"

I looked toward the door of the bathroom. "Yes," I said.

"I could lose my job," she said. "In fact, there is no *could* about it. I wouldn't be allowed to practice psychology anymore."

"I understand."

Jo took a breath. Something clacked against the phone again. "There was a nasty business with a fellow classmate at Daphne's previous school. It went on for almost a year. Apparently, Daphne had information about the classmate that she was threatening to reveal."

"What was it?"

"Even if I knew, I couldn't tell you that. All I know is that the girl in question was very shaken up by the whole thing. Apparently . . ." Jo hesitated for a moment. "It seems Daphne treated her like a slave before the girl's parents got an inkling of what was happening."

I crossed my arms, tried not to think about the secret of mine that Daphne had kept through all those sessions with Jo. "The girl could have said no," I pointed out. "She didn't have to do whatever Daphne said."

"I'm not saying it's conclusive, but it suggests Daphne has a history of manipulating people, hurting them, to get what she wants."

I leaned against the tiled wall, phone held hard against my ear. Hadn't we joked that Daphne always got what she wanted?

"Listen, Finn. I have reason to believe that Daphne's attitude to the actions of others is different from that of a normal person. Particularly when it comes to things she perceives as deserving of punishment. I'm worried for you. Even when you were a teenager, I wanted to warn you off her. When you told me on Saturday that she was pregnant, I grew concerned. And then you told me the police had brought her in for questioning on Sunday without seeming to give any thought to why that might be."

"They brought me in twice as well," I said.

"Well, yes." Jo sounded almost exasperated. "But they never served you with a warrant to search your house. They never accused you or arrested you."

"No," I said. Would Jo regret telling me all this once what had happened with Suze came out? That was the only possible outcome I could see to Daphne being held for any length of time.

The knowledge settled in my gut like a lump of rock.

Jo spoke again. "Daphne's sister's death was ruled a suicide at the time, but what's odd is that the poison Brianna Bennett took wasn't a household poison. I looked it up. It was something she would have had to extract from a plant using quite an involved process, by all accounts."

"Brianna looked up to Daphne," I said. "They both loved nature. Daphne said Brianna was a curious kid."

"Curious enough to plan her own suicide? To track down such a rare plant?"

Was Jo accusing Daphne of faking her sister's suicide?

"Maybe Daphne loved botany, so Brianna loved it too," I said. "Little sisters can be like that."

Not mine. I pushed down the thought. Suze, feet swinging in a camp chair. I stared at the dirty bathroom floor, refusing to let tears come.

"Did you know Daphne was the one who found her sister?" Jo asked.

"No." The small, grubby room contracted around me. "I didn't know that."

"Daphne was the one who found Brianna, in a cave on land that ran behind their parents' property. It was an easily overlooked spot. The poison Brianna took was slow-acting and she would have been incapacitated. It was far enough from the house that no one would have heard someone cry out. It was assumed she'd hidden herself for privacy—that's what Daphne said—but I'm not convinced." Jo paused, as if waiting for me to catch up.

I moved the phone to my other ear. We'd moved into a fantasy realm now. Daphne, hurt her sister? How could Jo believe that? I hadn't known that Brianna had been found anywhere but her own bed. But where had I got that idea? Had anyone ever said that? Had Daphne? What Jo was doing was wildly unprofessional. I never would have thought her capable of it. What had she written about *me* in her notes?

Something in my chest was turning hot.

"If Daphne has been arrested, this is serious. You can't just explain it away. I want you to promise me that you will keep yourself safe, that you'll work with the police."

I stood in that old, tiled bathroom with my legs shaking. I said goodbye to Jo, promised her I wouldn't tell anyone what she had told me. I just needed time to think.

I knew that Daphne was willing to ignore me, use me, to get what she wanted. She'd done it before, no matter how hard I'd tried to push down the memory. The thought burned through my body and I wrenched the door open, stepping out into the curious stares of the people in the waiting room.

22

BEFORE

In those long weeks after year twelve ended, Daphne wanted to spend a lot of time with me. We mostly hung out at her house, talking in her room or watching things she liked—more than once she put on a DVD of a production of *Oedipus Rex* where all the actors wore large full-head masks and long robes. There was a lot of yelling and fist-raising. Sometimes, the villagers chanted in unison. It put me to sleep. She acted bored when I wanted to talk about what I would be doing the next year. I'd never spent so much time imagining a place I'd never seen as I did thinking about what it would be like in Canada. They had some photos of the resort on the website, including the accommodation for staff. It was weird to think that one day these places would be familiar to me. I would live in a country with different power sockets, among people whose faces I didn't yet know. I was tingly with it. I spaced out sometimes when I was hanging out with Daphne, imagining the new person I would become.

It was mid-December when the stuff-up with my passport led to the job offer being withdrawn. Daphne came over to cheer me up after I'd called and told her what happened.

"We've been through some shit, you and me," she said. "But you're going to be okay. I wish it hadn't taken something awful to bring us together, but I'm glad we found each other."

I didn't say what I was thinking, which was that she would be gone soon. She would be moving to Sydney to start uni at the end of February.

———

Even after Daphne had gone off to uni, she still came home to visit occasionally. We immediately fell into our old patterns when she did. I was as in love with her as ever. I realized now that was what it had been. Love. And that she was never going to love me in return. That wasn't her fault, though. It was my problem.

She called me one night in April of her second year. "God, it's not worth sleeping with people at college," she said. "As soon as you do, everyone knows about it."

I wasn't sure why she needed to tell me, if she didn't want "everyone" knowing about it.

"Yeah, well, the mist is my only friend," I said.

Daphne laughed. "I wish you were here on campus with me," she said.

By then I was seeing Beth, who I'd met climbing, but I never mentioned her in my conversations with Daphne.

We agreed that I would visit her in Sydney.

I drove down, and slept on the floor of her room in the college. We ate in cafés and drove to the ocean. Maybe I could have been an ocean person, if I'd encountered it when I was young. But when I stood in the shallows, I didn't like the way waves sucked at my calves and ankles, as if trying to pull me off balance.

I liked the university, though. The wide avenue that ran through the heart of the campus, lined with old sandstone buildings. I was struck by the thought that this was where politicians went to university, and famous heart surgeons and people who would go on to do things that changed the world. Daphne refused to take any of it seriously. She was living in an expensive college on a partial scholarship. She'd wanted the scholarship, to prove something, but she made fun of the dinners, of college life, of this idea that any of it was preparing students for the real world. When it came to her course, she loved the field trips but would skip her lectures as often as not. "They're lucky to have me," she said, and you could tell she meant it. "I have an aptitude for science." It should have sounded arrogant, but it didn't. I wondered what it would be like to be as smart as Daphne, to feel as blasé about it as she did. But, then, why would she need to tell me how smart she was if she really didn't care?

She wasn't supposed to have overnight guests in her room, so I made myself scarce when she had classes. When she came back from her last lecture on the final night of my stay, she was brandishing a bottle of vodka and a carton of pineapple juice like they were trophies. I forced a smile; Daphne knew I didn't drink. I could either play along, against my own wishes, or ruin the moment. It was the same old dynamic, and it pissed me off.

Sometimes, being around Daphne was enough to make me feel that something exciting was about to happen, like holding a burning match, or getting ready to make a prank call.

Sometimes, I could almost grasp the fact that Daphne needed me more than I needed her. If nothing else, I was someone who could bear witness to how superior she was to other people. But I could never hold on to the thought. It was like trying to hold your own body weight while hanging from a metal bar. Something gives, and you let go.

We never talked about the secret she was keeping for me, but it was always there between us.

It was a Thursday, and there was a celebration in the college common room for the beginning of the study period. That struck me as odd, because they had exams coming. We could hear the thumping music through the wall of Daphne's room. The building itself was a strange mix of old and new. Brass fittings, wood paneling, and dark green carpet with a floral pattern that was faded in the high-traffic areas. A newish, cheaply built kitchen on each floor. There were signs indicating where fire extinguishers were stored and laminated notices with warnings and instructions. It was like a rich old woman's house that had been turned into a youth hostel.

We were sitting on Daphne's bed, our backs pressed against the wall. She looked at me over her glass of vodka and pineapple juice. "So, have you missed me?"

She hadn't introduced me to any of her college friends. Her latest boyfriend had broken up with her before I came. As far as I knew, it was the first time Daphne had been dumped. She tried to act like it didn't bother her, but there was something off, some part of her that had been deeply shaken.

"Of course I have, Daph."

But the truth was that when she came back to Indra, now, it was sometimes hard to slot Daphne into my life. I had my climbing friends. I had Beth. A lot of things had got easier for me since Daphne left.

"Do you think about Suze much?" Daphne asked.

My heart plummeted into my guts before rising again to thud in my throat.

When I didn't reply, she said, "I've been thinking about my sister a lot. Maybe it's because Alex dumped me. Like, I just want an excuse to feel sad." She gave a short, sharp bark of laughter. "That's pretty awful, isn't it?" A pause, and she turned her body to face me. "I'm a bad person, aren't I?"

"No, you're not, Daph. Of course you aren't."

Daphne leaned in, bringing her mouth to mine, hard, as her hand found the waistband of my jeans. I pulled away. Tried to pull her hand out of my underpants.

"Relax," she said. "This is what I want." A wave of neroli oil hit me as she pushed me down onto the bed.

The words *It's not what I want* were inside me, but I couldn't make them come out. I was small in the face of her need.

I lay there while Daphne did what she wanted to do. She would sense my reluctance eventually and stop. Wouldn't she? I'd never been so far outside of my own body. I was watching myself from space.

The overhead light was on in the room, a glaring fluorescent, and somehow that made it worse. I could hear the song "Barbie Girl" pushing through the thin walls, blasting from the speakers in the common room. They'd played that song at my little sister's funeral.

Daphne tasted of pineapple when she pushed her mouth against mine. This was not seduction. I didn't feel sexy. I was a tool, something less than human. Like in one of those old cartoons where a character is hungry and other characters appear to them as food. A floating chicken drumstick, a hot dog on legs. The hungry character can only see what they need, not who the other characters really are.

At that moment, I could see the incredible need coming off Daphne, thick waves of it. Things were not going the way she thought they should, and I was going to help her to make it right. I couldn't be the one to tell her, *No, you can't have it. I don't want you anymore. Not like this.*

"Only you understand me," she said, grabbing my arms and pulling them around her. "I know what you want."

She had already wrenched my jeans and underwear down. She

lowered her head between my legs. My body was limp. I didn't want this. I couldn't move.

Some drunk boys banged on the door to her room, screaming the words to "Barbie Girl" at the top of their lungs. Their big hands slammed the door so hard for a second I thought they were going to break it down. Daphne pulled away. I refused to return the look I could sense she was giving me.

"We should go out there," I said, looking down at the floor. My shoe was lying where it had been thrown off, turned on its side. I was relieved when she said yes.

We went out to the common room and drank more, and danced. Daphne held her bottle of vodka aloft while she moved to the music, taking big, showy swigs. When she passed out, I half dragged, half carried her back to her room and laid her on the bed. I crawled in alongside her, keeping as far away as I could, my body pressed to the cool white wall.

When I got home, I broke up with Beth, couldn't tell her why. Daphne didn't call for a long time. When she did, it was like nothing had changed. I didn't know how to name what happened between us that night in Sydney, and because I'd stayed her friend I supposed I couldn't claim that it was something. I just knew that now I hated the smell of pineapple.

———

The following year, Daphne sent me a photo of her with some friends at Mardi Gras. She'd gone back to campus a couple of days early for it. She was dressed as a forest nymph in a short white lacy dress covered in fake vines. Green glitter on her cheekbones. Her hair hung damp and close to her head. All the friends were straight, though sometimes they kissed each other at campus parties, she'd told me once. The whole group was laughing and the light in the photo was beautiful, and an anger flowed through me that I didn't completely understand.

I told myself that I was being unfair to Daphne. I was weak and so I blamed her for my problems, and she bore it with good grace. I was lucky to have her. And sick in my stomach when I was supposed to see her. I was gripped by a fear that no one else would put up with me the way she had. And then I would see her and I would realize how stupid I had been. It wasn't Daphne's fault that I was this way.

There was so much Daphne never *asked* me to do. So much of it I took upon myself, the need for it burning and clear, but I couldn't say, *You made me do this. You ask too much. I can't.*

I was the one who hadn't said no to her that night in her college room, who followed along when she acted like it was no big deal. I'd never been strong enough to resist her.

————

I didn't expect Daphne to come back to the mountains after she moved out of college in her honors year and got her own place in Sydney. But then she enrolled in a PhD that involved fieldwork around Indra, and she would visit sometimes.

When Daphne came back, she would call me, drunk, and say she was getting a taxi, and I would say that I was coming to get her—I was worried that a driver or passerby would take advantage of her. There was one time when I left Magdu alone at the flat to go and fetch Daphne. She must have known I would insist on doing it, I think now, or else why would she call me?

And then she told me that she was coming back to Indra for the winter break, maybe even for good, because she needed to finish her PhD and it would be easier to do that away from the distractions of the city. She said it was time she met my girlfriend. It was time for all sorts of things, according to Daphne. I didn't know if I was ready.

————

Sometimes, being close to Daphne was like being trapped with someone in the boot of a car. I pushed against her, aware that it wasn't her fault we were locked in there but unable to forgive her for the space she took up. I'd read somewhere you should punch out the taillights if someone ever locks you in a boot. What would it be like, to punch out the lights of our life together? She could blow my life apart, if she chose. I wanted to tell her I wasn't okay, and I wanted her to know it without me telling her. The bond I had with her was something inside me, like my spine, something you couldn't take away without leaving me wet and pulpy on the floor. The only thing holding me up. I'd had so many opportunities to pull myself together. Daphne wasn't holding a gun to my head—except for the one I had loaded for her. She didn't know how I felt. It was my problem, and it always had been. And I couldn't see how that would ever change.

23

MONDAY, SEPTEMBER 11, 2017

As I emerged onto the police station steps, still reeling from my phone conversation with Jo, I looked around, worried that I would run into Carol-Ann.

Instead I saw Sunita. People walking along the footpath outside the station had to step around her as she cut in front of them to get to me. One man rolled his eyes, as if to say, *How rude can you get?*

"Sunita. Hello," I said. I sounded calm. My head ached.

It was dry under the awning that stretched over the police station steps but there were drops of water on her shoulders and in her hair from the rain that fell beyond.

I wanted to ask her, *What are you doing here?* I also wanted to hug her, to find a suggestion of Magdu in the curves of her body and wallow in it, even for a second. I wanted to be physically close to my girlfriend.

"The police have informed me this is now a murder investigation," she said, something cold and high in her voice. It was strange to hear it phrased that way. *Murder.* "We were supposed to be flying to Goa with Magdu on Wednesday." A sob escaped her, like someone slipping through the briefest gap in traffic. "Now I don't know if it will be allowed."

"I'd like to come to the funeral in India," I said. I knew it wasn't the right thing to say even as I was saying it. But I couldn't talk about the murder charge, didn't want to talk about Daphne. Didn't want to know how much Dale had told them.

"It will be a small, private ceremony," she said, looking in my direction but not at me. "We wouldn't expect you to travel that far."

"I want to," I said. If it was commemorating Magdu's life, then I wanted to be there. I'd figure out a way to pay for it. Even if I had to put it on a credit card.

She spoke louder. "You misunderstood me. I am telling you that you're not invited."

My hands were shaking. I was struck again by the image of Magdu and me getting married. A big Goan Catholic wedding, Magdu in a beautiful white dress.

I was so sad and so tired. My body was heavy. My jaw ached, I was hot. Sunita was standing in front of me expectantly, waiting for me to speak. For me to say, *No, of course I won't come to Magdu's funeral. I wouldn't dream of it.* With the tips of my fingers, I felt for the edge of Magdu's bracelet. It was hidden underneath my sleeve. I wondered if Magdu had owned the bracelet before she came to Australia. If Sunita saw it, would she want it back?

This woman was not seeing me, not seeing how much I loved her daughter. She was seeing only her own fear, her own loss. She hadn't been able to stop Magdu from loving me, and now she never would.

Sunita took a step closer to me. "This friend of yours that they have arrested," she said. "She contacted me on Facebook. I recognize the name."

I pictured Daphne's Facebook photo. I'd taken it in the kitchen at her house. She had looked clean and pure, the sun falling on her face through the windows, wearing a light dress that covered her cleavage but not her collarbones, which were somehow sexier than full-on cleavage would have been.

Sunita's eyes narrowed. "She told me about you. That you didn't care about my daughter or her family."

What I'd suspected locked into place. A certainty. Daphne was the reason Magdu's mother had said I couldn't come to Dubai for Christmas.

"I *love* your daughter." The present tense brought tears to my eyes. I'd used it without thinking. "I would do anything for her."

Sunita pointed her finger at me. "You don't know what love is," she snapped. "Magdu is dead because you thought you loved her. You brought this Daphne person into my daughter's life. I hope you're happy."

I let my hands fall open, unable to stop the next sentence coming out as a rasped whisper. "Don't you *understand?* You never loved the real Magdu. You loved the person you wanted her to be."

"How do I even know that you weren't involved?" Sunita demanded. "That this wasn't something you cooked up together?"

I turned away. I couldn't look at the woman any longer. I was going to be sick.

I pushed past her, walked blindly across the street to my car. I fumbled with the key and threw myself into the driver's seat, locking the door behind me.

Her grieving family members were the ones with the real claim to Magdu. They would have her body and I would have nothing.

I thought of everything Jo had said about Brianna's death, which had happened so soon after she and Daphne came to Indra. Her dead sister had been the first thing I knew about Daphne.

Then my sister had died too and everyone had called it a copycat suicide. And Daphne had told me what I needed to do. If it weren't for Daphne, I would have found a way to tell my mother. The worst part was that Daphne had been right when she told me it would be possible to forget what I'd done. There were long stretches of time in which I did.

Why would she tell Dale it was *my* idea to go climbing?

I thought of how Daphne had taken over my life, slowly at first, until there was no one else left. Like a vine that snakes around a tree until the tree and the vine can no longer be separated, because they are holding each other up. What had Jo said about that girl at Daphne's old school whose life Daphne had controlled? I thought of the TimeKeeper gig when Daphne had managed to push Magdu's buttons so successfully. How Daphne always got what she wanted.

And it had been Daphne who contacted Sunita; my best friend had been trying to tear me and Magdu apart.

I sat in the car. I could see Sunita speaking on her mobile phone out the front of the police station. She was crying.

Gray skies, wind moving through the trees. I focused on the waving leaves. There was an antiseptic taste in my mouth as I started the engine.

I thought about what Dale had said and my desperate need for him to know about Brendan. I'd said that because I'd known that Daphne and I were tied together, that if she went down she would drag me down with her. It was strange that Brendan was there on the cliff that day, that he'd been standing so close, but that didn't change the most important fact: that none of it would have happened without Daphne. I tried thinking the thought very fast, the way you might tap a finger against a hot plate to see if it's working.

————

When I pulled into the driveway at home, Mum's car wasn't there. I walked toward the kitchen, calling for Spencer. He looked up from his bed but put his head back down and closed his eyes. So much for a warm welcome.

My phone rang, buzzing in my back pocket. It was Daphne's mother.

I took a deep breath, held it in my lungs before breathing out. "Carol-Ann?"

I sat down heavily on one of the kitchen chairs.

"I'm so glad I caught you." There was something almost breezy about Carol-Ann's tone. I wondered if she even knew what had happened to Daphne.

"Listen, Daphne has been arrested but Frank and I are in Melbourne. A lawyer will be there any minute, but can you go to her? I can't bear to think of her alone."

It was so like Carol-Ann to think that someone would be able to sit with her daughter, that allowances could and would be made.

"Are you there?" Carol-Ann's voice jolted me from my thoughts. "How soon can you get there?"

"What did they tell you they had charged her with?" I asked, gripping the phone. Had Carol-Ann forgotten whose death we were talking about here?

Carol-Ann's voice rose, a note of panic at the edges. "It's utterly ridiculous. How could they think that Daphne would hurt anyone?"

I heard the sound of the back door opening.

A voice called, "Are you there?"

It was Mum. I wanted to tell her what had happened. I wanted to ask her to make me a cuppa.

"Hold on a sec, Carol-Ann."

What Dale had told me moved through my body. In a moment of perfect clarity, I could see how it would go. The knife. The damaged blue rope that Daphne had put Magdu on at the last minute. Motive. Daphne would do anything to get what she wanted. That would make sense to the jury. And the pregnancy. A good prosecutor would tell the story so that it made sense. Maybe Jo would even be called to testify about what she knew of Daphne as a young woman. The knowledge moved into my body, filled it, changed it.

I brought the phone back up to my ear.

"Finn?" Carol-Ann was still on the phone, waiting for my reply.

Daphne had never been good for me. I knew that now, deep in the core of me. That was what Magdu had been trying to tell me the day of the climb.

"I'm sorry, Carol-Ann. I can't." I hung up.

24

BEFORE

"We're picking up Daphne," I said on the morning of the climb, as Magdu and I headed out her front door.

"Why?" Magdu whispered as we headed for the back of the row of flats, where my Suzuki was parked. It was so early the sun hadn't risen yet and we were trying not to wake the neighbors. "She has her own car, doesn't she?"

Magdu seemed to have lifted herself out of the somber mood from the kitchen, which was a relief, but there was something different about her. A set in her jaw that I didn't recognize. She was just tired, I told myself.

It was only when we were seated in the car with the doors shut that I answered her question. "There's not much parking at the top of the Goat Track. It makes sense for us all to go together," I said.

"Finn." She looked at me. "You were really upset when you came home from Daphne's last night. You tried to pretend you weren't, but

I know you were." I went to say something, but she raised a hand. "I think you need to seriously consider the possibility that Daphne is a narcissist."

I thought about Daphne's bedroom the night before. I could almost smell it, see myself lying on her white carpet.

I forced a laugh. "She's not a narcissist because she wants a lift, Mags," I said, putting the key into the ignition. "I pick *you* up all the time."

Magdu crossed her arms. "The trouble with narcissists is that they don't see you as a person with needs and wishes of your own. They see you only in terms of how to manipulate you to get what they want. They need to be in control."

I started the car's engine, my hands gripping the steering wheel tight.

"I'm not being a bitch, Finn," she added gently. "It's a clinical diagnosis. And the diagnosis tends to be more helpful for the people around them than for the narcissist themselves. Because part of how narcissists operate is by making you feel crazy."

"Daphne is the reason I'm still standing." I thought about lying in the grass outside school with Daphne after Suze died. Asking her if this was what grief felt like. About the ship that she'd helped me build. I shifted through the gears. "Besides, I thought psychologists weren't meant to use the word 'crazy'?"

"Who told you that?" She snorted. "That's like telling someone who works for the fire department they can't say the word 'smoke.'"

"It sounds weird when you say 'fire department,'" I said. "Some words make you sound so American."

I didn't want Magdu to return to the tears of that morning, which had frightened me. We were on more familiar ground now, and I wanted to stay there.

Magdu looked at me. She wouldn't be put off so easily. "I'm

not asking you to do anything drastic. I just want you to think about it."

"Look," I said. "I know Daphne can be difficult. Of all people, don't you think I know that?" Magdu leaned forward as I spoke, already anticipating my *but*. "But she's one of the smartest people I know. Aside from you, of course. And she cares about me."

"Okay. But I want you to ask yourself: Does Daphne ever get you into situations you don't like? Does she end up convincing you that she's doing *you* a favor when you know the opposite is true? Does she refuse to let things rest until she's the good guy?"

I thought about what Magdu had said. It'd always felt like Daphne was the only person who could ever know all of me, and that was worth what it took. I thought about it as a price that had to be paid. But what if I couldn't pay anymore? What I'd learned in her room the night before rose up before me once more. I'd seen something I wasn't supposed to see, and it had shaken me.

I moved back down through the gears as we headed up the hill that would take us to Daphne's place.

"I thought narcissists didn't care if they were good people?" I said, letting my eyes flick to the heat gauge. The car could be temperamental on steep hills. I was oddly giddy and light, like we were talking about something fun.

"Narcissists need others to confirm what they already know—that they're better than other people." Magdu tugged on her seat belt, turning in the passenger seat to face me. "In those situations when she seemed attentive, was the focus genuinely on you? Has she ever given you a meaningful apology when she may have hurt you? Did she apologize for your reaction or for her actions? It's the difference between, *I'm sorry you feel that way*, and *I'm sorry that I did this thing that caused you pain*."

I let the words roll around in my mind, examining the feeling that flooded through me at having Magdu put it into words.

Was Daphne sorry when she hurt me? Or did she think I deserved it?

"If you want to get married one day, then you need to acknowledge that there are no fix-alls. You can't just apply a label like 'best friend' or 'wife' and assume that solves everything." Magdu looked tired again and fear burned in my belly.

One day? I thought about the wedding ring I'd hidden in the back of the car. I'd reconciled myself to a relationship with Magdu that wasn't fully honest, because it seemed like the only option. Maybe it wouldn't be enough for her.

Magdu's tone softened. "When you refuse to face reality, something fractures. And if you do that too often, you break a healthy mind." She took my hand in hers. "Just promise me you'll think about it, babe."

We pulled into Daphne's drive.

"I will," I said.

A hand waved in the window next to the front door, then disappeared. Magdu leaned forward and turned on the radio.

Daphne ran out, dropping her gear in the boot. Magdu's side of the car was closest to her and she stood near it for a single awkward beat. She was waiting for Magdu to move to the back seat. Magdu rummaged in her bag for a hair tie, took her time pulling her hair back into a low bun that would fit under a helmet. She avoided looking up, her movements slow and deliberate.

Daphne finally opened the back door and lowered herself into the seat behind Magdu. The swing of her shiny French braid and the smell of neroli oil brought back a memory of when we'd been at school.

One lunchtime, after history, Daphne had said, "Do you know what gets me about Narcissus?"

Daphne had a way of charming teachers into letting her set her own topics and was doing her assessment on ancient Greek myths. She'd wanted to draw an intricate Greek design around the border of a huge piece of card but she'd got bored and I'd finished it for her. It was soothing, following a pattern.

Daphne widened her eyes. "He was *cursed*."

"What do you mean?"

"Okay, so everyone knows the story of Narcissus, right?"

I did not know who Narcissus was, and Daphne had to know that.

"Basically, he lies beside a pond and stares at his own reflection. He's so entranced that he's unable to pull himself away. He stays there until he dies, still staring at himself, admiring his own beauty."

"Okay," I said.

Daphne piled her blond braid on top of her head, before letting it swing to her shoulders. "Well, everyone says he died because he was so in love with himself. But if you read Ovid, the story goes that one young man who'd had his advances spurned put a *curse* on Narcissus. So, he's actually the victim of a man who couldn't handle rejection. He had a high self-regard, so people think he deserved what he got. But he wasn't responsible for what happened to him. He died alone and crazy."

———

I looked in the rearview mirror and saw Daphne staring out the window. I put both hands on the wheel. No one else made me feel the way Daphne did. No one else would have kept my secret. Magdu didn't know the truth, and if she did, she would leave. I had no doubt Magdu loved me, but she was not made of the same stuff as Daphne. That was part of what I loved about her.

Daphne's eyes moved from the window to meet mine, and I brought my gaze back to the road in front of me.

If Daphne had moved back to the mountains earlier, Magdu and I would never have got together. I knew it.

Magdu kept her eyes on the road ahead. When my eyes flicked back to her, Daphne was looking down at something in her lap. Probably her phone.

As we neared the Goat Track turnoff, I reminded myself to focus on what I was doing. You had to keep an eye out for the entrance, which was a bit overgrown.

Once I'd found it, I relaxed a little.

"We should talk about the plan for the climb," I said, wanting to break the silence that'd fallen over the car.

Daphne shifted in the back seat but didn't say anything.

"You've still got my rope in your bag from our last climb, right?" I'd meant to check before we left.

"Yes." Daphne slipped whatever she had been looking at into her pocket.

"So, I'm thinking we'll set up two ropes. I'll come down to the ledge first. Then I can fireman you and Magdu as you abseil down."

I was looking at Daphne in the rearview mirror as I spoke, but Magdu was the first to respond. "Is that a good idea?" she asked. "Me and Daphne going down at the same time? Won't it be too heavy?"

"That anchor is a bomb," I said. "There's no need to worry; it could have ten people hanging off it and it wouldn't matter."

I put a hand on her thigh.

"Besides, this way you'll have someone next to you, and I'll be right below you. If you panic or get flustered or let go of the rope, I can pull on it at my end to arrest your fall. Daphne will check your gear before you come down together. Then, at the next ledge, Daphne can go down first and you and I will do the second abseil together." I smiled at Magdu. "We can get a killer selfie." Magdu was much more into photos than I was. She smiled back. "And then we'll climb back up."

It was a good plan. Daphne and I would get to do a multi-pitch, work on our rope management, and Magdu would have a fun climb with someone always beside her.

I turned to look at Daphne. "What do you reckon?"

Daphne snorted. "Sounds good, Finnbo."

"Daphne . . ." I tried to keep my frustration out of my voice.

She looked at me, took a breath. "Yes, Finn. I acknowledge the plan."

Despite the hint of sarcasm, I was satisfied.

————

We pulled into the tiny car park for the Goat Track to find two cars were there already. They'd both done crappy parks, and Magdu had to hop out so that I could squeeze the car in next to a tree.

When I opened the boot, Magdu picked up Daphne's rope bag, which was sitting on top of our gear.

"Leave that," Daphne barked. Then, softening, she put a hand on Magdu's shoulder. "I've got it. It's heavy."

Magdu stepped back, gesturing toward the bag with an open hand, a look of perfect blankness on her face. Daphne smiled, without it bringing any warmth into her eyes.

I turned away from them both, not wanting to see the tension that so obviously filled the air between them. Instead, I looked toward the cliff, breathed in the smell of the wilderness around us, and thought about what it would be like, out on the rock.

25

WEDNESDAY, SEPTEMBER 13, 2017

Two days after they arrested Daphne, I drove back to the car park at the top of the Goat Track. It was late afternoon and getting dark, so I had the place to myself. I left my phone in the car and bush-bashed my way down to the spot Magdu had fallen from, rushing to get there before the sun set. I wanted to see it in the light. They'd released Magdu's body to her family after all, I'd heard from Priya, who'd taken my phone number and texted me occasional updates and sometimes photos—a kindness that never failed to make me cry. I'd thought the police might keep the body, because of the charges against Daphne, but it seemed not.

Magdu's body would be in the air right now, on the way to Goa with her mother.

It felt like I'd done nothing but cry in my bedroom, my body tucked around Spencer's, since Daphne had been arrested. The reassuring hay smell of his fur, slightly rank but also sweet. My tears leaking from my face into his coat. Then, that evening, a restless energy crackled in my fingers and toes. Daphne's parents had come to the house twice since my last phone call with Carol-Ann. Mum had sent them away both times. Dale said it was possible that Daphne might get out on bail, that he would give me a heads-up if that happened, and that I should tell him if she tried to see or call me. Still, I didn't want to be at home, just in case. I'd told Mum I was going out, seen her wanting to ask where and stopping herself. Her face had arranged itself into a permanent frown of worry. I wanted to hug her but I didn't feel worthy of touching her. I'd thought maybe it would be better here on the cliffside, where no one could see me and I didn't have to say anything.

I was standing in the place where I'd stood a week earlier, fitting Magdu's harness. I bunched my hands in the pockets of my dad's jacket. Fog bothered the tree line, sinking down into gaps between the trunks, hovering.

It'd stopped raining. My period had stopped too. The sun was sinking, clouds smeared across the sky, which was somehow green. A wind came up. The light cast a strange glow on everything, and it was so beautiful it made me want to push a fingernail into my own skin, to let that be added to the feeling of looking at the sky.

Magdu would have liked it. I wondered if they had green sunsets in Goa. I wanted to be able to picture where she was buried. That was the kind of thing I had left to want, now. The thought cut through me clean and cold, an icicle sharpened into a blade. Her mother wouldn't tell me, but maybe her aunt would.

Soon the sun would disappear altogether and the landscape would turn gray. I stepped close enough that I could see over the edge and felt my guts drop, my body tensing. From where we'd started the climb that day, I could see the part of the valley that Suze had fallen from. I had refused to see it on the morning of the climb. The place where I had done something I could never take back. It wasn't the only thing I hadn't wanted to think about or examine closely that morning.

———————

The day before Daphne, Magdu, and I were due to climb together, I'd gone over to Daphne's place. Magdu had an assignment to finish, so I was making myself scarce.

Daphne and I were in her bedroom. She sat on her bed, and I lay on the white carpet, near her desk. I was stretching my back, sore from being on my feet all day.

When I said how sad I was not to be going to Dubai, Daphne snapped, "Why would you want to force yourself on her family if they don't want you?" She flicked her blond bangs out of her eyes. "Honestly. Have some self-respect, Finnbo."

That stung, but I held my tongue.

She got up to go to the bathroom, leaving me alone.

I'd spent so much time at Daphne's in high school that her bedroom had been an extension of my own. Lying on the floor, on the thick, plush white carpet, I had the bizarre impression that nothing had changed. That Daphne would emerge from the bathroom in her school uniform.

There was a stack of papers piled on the floor next to her desk. As I stretched out my leg, which was cramping, the movement caused the top sheet to flutter to the floor. I scooted onto all fours to pick it up. It was the first page of some kind of scientific-looking article. The bottom drawer of Daphne's desk was ajar, just a sliver. I could see the corner of a passport.

I pulled the drawer open quietly and reached for it.

I wanted to check out the photo so I could make fun of her if it was bad, but when I turned to the page I saw a younger version of myself looking back, alongside the name *Finnlay Louise Young*. A roaring sound filled my ears. It was the passport that had never arrived, the reason I'd had to cancel my trip to Canada.

Breathing quickly, I put my passport back where I'd found it. Pushed the drawer closed. Then pulled it back out a fraction. My heart was pounding.

I replaced the dislodged page that had brought me to that side of the room on top of the stack and lay facedown on the bed, trying to look relaxed.

"Oi, wake up!" Daphne said when she returned, slapping me on the bum.

Who would I be now if I'd been born into this house? If they'd carried me home and placed me in a room with white carpet, everything would have been different. Something happened to my anger in that moment. It turned flinty and cold.

There had been nothing wrong with my application all those years ago; Daphne must have got to the letterbox before me, intercepted my passport. The knowledge crawled on my skin like tiny spiders. Daphne had made sure I wouldn't leave Indra before she was ready. She had no idea how much losing all that money on the flights to Canada would mean. That I would still be in Indra all these years later; that I would never have left.

I didn't stay long after that. I was due at Magdu's anyway. Daphne tried to convince me to stay, but I could tell her heart wasn't in it. In my car, I turned the radio on to find that the TimeKeeper song, the one I'd stayed to listen to the night of the gig, was playing. My throat felt too wide for my neck. I needed to be a person who Magdu could love. I tried to get my fingernail under how it would feel to be worthy of her. To hold on to a sliver of its jagged edge. I drove and let the road get sucked under my tires as I drummed my fingers against the steering wheel.

When I got to Magdu's, I tried to pretend as if nothing had happened, but she could tell something was up.

"What did Daphne do?" Magdu asked, voice flat, one hand on her hip.

"Nothing, Mags. It's fine."

That night, in Magdu's bed, I lay awake thinking about it. It seethed inside me, a surge of pressure looking for a spot to rush up and out. Daphne saw things she didn't like in my life, and she made them go away. But what she had done paled in the face of what I had done.

I rolled into Magdu, kissed her hair.

I pictured my passport lying in the drawer in Daphne's room. The weight of it dragged me down into sleep. A dream in which I was running, trying to escape something I couldn't see that was always on the verge of catching up with me.

I woke the next morning determined to be cheerful. Determined to push down what had happened, like I always did. Magdu had slept badly, was in that strange mood. Upset for some reason of her own. But later, in the car on our way to pick up Daphne, she said things that were good to hear. That Daphne's behavior was strange. That I needed to get myself out from under her.

———

Wind hits the tears that are falling on my face. The valley is getting dark now. My tooth is no longer hurting. The plastic cap that Magdu's uncle put in is still there. But the pain has left my body, slipping away now my period has ended. I'm always more sensitive to pain in the lead-up to and during my period itself. I'd forgotten. I feel bad for suspecting Magdu's uncle, who'd just been doing his job, whatever he felt about me and Magdu.

Standing here, wind whipping through the trees, the noise of it is coming from inside of me. I know with absolute certainty that if Suze hadn't died, if I hadn't killed her, then Magdu would still be alive. Maybe we would never have met, but she'd be somewhere right now that wasn't the belly of a plane. Warm and laughing and alive. I love her so much it fills me and has nowhere to go. It makes my body ache.

Maybe Magdu had only been playing along when I talked about marriage. After all, we'd only known each other six months. But I know in my gut that she believed in our future. I'd have made her feel safe and loved, and her family would have come around in time. She could be the one who wouldn't budge for once.

The wind shifts, coming from behind me, making the treetops swish. The smell of neroli oil floods my senses.

A sound in the bushes.

A voice calls, "Finn."

I whirl around to see Daphne.

She takes a step toward me. "I thought you might be here."

Her presence here seems wrong. A cartoon character suddenly appearing in the real world.

"What are you doing here?"

"You mean, how did I get out?" She looks at me. Looks through me. Shrugs. "Amazing what a good lawyer can accomplish."

I think of my phone in the glove compartment of the car. Dale has probably been trying to call me.

I don't say anything.

We're alone. No one will come out here this close to sunset.

Daphne looks more beautiful, more regal than ever. There's something strange, I think, about the fact that beautiful people are always beautiful. It's wasted here. Her beauty is ridiculous. I could have been free any number of ways. I could have left with Magdu. We could have moved to Sydney, left Daphne behind. The thought makes me want to vomit on Daphne's boots.

"How did you know I would be here?"

She shrugs again. She knows me better than anyone, is the unspoken assertion.

"I found the passport, Daphne. In your drawer. The day before the climb."

When Daphne doesn't reply, I ask, "Why did you do it? Why would you want to blow up my life? What did I ever do to you?"

Daphne takes a deep breath. "It's hard for someone to live up to all the things you think I am. The truth is, I'm a fuckup. And you thought I was so good, so in control of everything. But it's not like that, Finn. I've always just . . . done stuff. Said things I shouldn't, taken things that weren't mine. You could never understand that. I never have a master plan." Daphne wraps her arms around herself; she's wearing a deep blue dress over tights, no jacket. She must be cold. "The passport was stupid. I saw it in your letterbox, and I took it. I was going to let you sweat for a couple of days, and then . . ." She trails off.

I raise my voice over a gust of wind. "You took my passport, you messaged Magdu's mother about us. You . . ." I could hardly get the words out. "You killed Magdu."

Cold stone beneath my feet. The valley stretching out behind my back. Things alive and moving in the growing shadows. A long way down.

Daphne's withering stare. "No one is as good to you as I am. No one else would have kept your secret."

I think of the thousands of ways Daphne has reminded me of her generosity. The tally of what I owe her that she keeps in her head.

"Tell me what happened at your old school," I say, feeling bold suddenly. "Tell me about the bad thing you did."

"That's none of your business."

"I think it's all my business."

Daphne looked around, like we were at a party and she was hoping for someone more interesting to speak to.

She sighed. "A girl in my class was sleeping with our teacher. She knew it was wrong, and when I found out she promised she would do anything if I kept her secret."

I thought about what Jo had said about Daphne, about what she did to people she thought were deserving of punishment.

"I got in so much shit. Everyone said I should have told as soon as I knew, but that wasn't what she wanted. And, okay, I couldn't help myself. She said she would do anything and maybe I took her a little too seriously."

She's downplaying it. But I can imagine exactly how it would go. Innocent-seeming requests, thinly veiled questions in front of other people to remind you of the hold she had over you.

"But that's ancient history. How about we talk about why we're really here? Since you met Magdu, you've been avoiding me. Did I really deserve that, after all these years?"

"Why did you tell the police it was my idea to go climbing?" I ask.

"Because it was." Daphne's face is so blank I almost believe her. Maybe that really is how she remembers it.

I take a deep breath. "Magdu is dead because you will always hurt the things I love."

The wind has swept Daphne's blond hair in front of her face; it twists around her neck.

"*I'm* the love of your life, Finn. Admit it."

I think about Daphne, about our hike on that hot day when I was fifteen.

"I wish you'd told someone. I wish you'd told *me* to tell someone. You never saw me, never saw what I needed."

"Oh, I see you, Finn. No one else has ever seen you the way I do. You need me. Besides, *you've* never seen how much *I* hurt. You think it's all so fucking easy for me."

Daphne looks out into the darkening valley.

"Do you know what they said to me? The Aboriginal cop said that I didn't like the fact you were seeing Magdu, the same way I didn't like that my little sister was trying to convince our parents to move back to Sydney. At the time, Brianna's unhappiness here was seen as evidence of her state of mind, he said, but he thought I was used to taking extreme action to get what I want." She smiles a strange, cold little smile. "And that got me thinking. About you."

A swelling in my chest. If I look down, I will see that my feet have left the ground.

"You told the cops about Brendan," she says, her voice loud, clear. It's a statement, not a question. "You were trying to muddy the waters, weren't you? But you know, better than anyone else could, that I didn't do it."

Daphne looks at me. I am the only thing in the whole world, and not in a good way.

"Have you told them yet?" I ask.

For a moment, Daphne stands there. Face unmoving, eyes looking toward the sky. A hand moves to her belly, resting there. She is refusing to answer my question.

Then she looks out into the valley, looking into a memory. "I just don't understand, Finn. Why would you try to kill me?"

———

It's important to say that I didn't plan it. The idea was like a side trail you notice in the middle of a long hike, one with more shade and better elevation. Getting ready to belay down to the ledge, I'd seen that Daphne was already tied into the blue rope; it had been threaded through her belay device, with enough slack in it that she could still move around easily to tie Magdu in on the red rope once I had arrived down at the ledge. The idea unfurled in that moment; I saw how easy it would be.

Magdu must never learn what Daphne knew about me, could never find out what I'd done. She would never marry me if she did. Daphne was the last remaining piece of the old ship; she didn't belong on the new ship she'd helped me to build. This could be the moment when my life truly started anew.

The night of the TimeKeeper gig, a thought had risen in my brain: *You can't have them both.* I'd managed to win Magdu back that night, but who knew what Daphne would come up with next? Standing on the cliff, I thought of how Magdu's mother had changed her mind so abruptly about me coming to Dubai; it was Canada all over again. Something in me had hardened. I didn't know how, but I was sure Daphne had interfered.

In that moment, as I belayed off the clifftop, I saw what I could do. It felt like a premonition, as if it had already happened.

The knife tucked in the long pocket of my pants was an object sent back by a time traveler in one of the books Magdu liked, the significance of it only apparent in the moment it was needed. After the bushwalk where Daphne had shown me the moth plant, when I'd had to cut it for her with my knockoff Swiss Army knife, I'd wanted to give her something that would show how much she meant to me. I'd bought two knives, good and sharp with decorated handles, from a market stall.

Daphne's parents had seen me present her knife to Daphne over dinner that night. They'd shifted a little uneasily in their seats, and only then had I realized it was a weird gift to give. Embarrassed, I didn't mention that I'd got myself a matching knife. And seeing how much Daphne liked hers, I realized that it would seem less special to her if I told her I had one exactly the same. So I'd put my knife in my bottom drawer with my vibrator and condoms and other things I didn't want Mum to see.

When I went over the edge, I'd been attached to my rope, the red one. Once I was out of sight of Daphne and Magdu, tucked into the cliff, I'd pulled that knife out of a zippered pocket and used it to score the blue rope. Not too much; I needed it to stay in one piece so that Daphne wouldn't suspect anything. I severed it just enough so that it would snap once a person's full body weight had been committed. And if for some reason it didn't snap, from my position on the fireman's belay I could yank it until it did.

It felt like something the universe was deciding should happen instead of something I was doing. I couldn't imagine Daphne dying, but I could imagine people saying, *How unlucky could Finnlay Young get?* A vague image of a funeral, Carol-Ann and Frank in black.

But I'd been distracted by the grit in my eye and hadn't noticed that Daphne had changed the plan we'd agreed on and sent Magdu down on the blue rope. Maybe Daphne had sensed that something was off, though I'm sure she would never have imagined that I'd hurt her.

I told you at the beginning, didn't I? About the thought you have when you're close to the edge of some high place? *What would happen if you went a little bit crazy, for even a second?*

It only takes a couple of out-of-your-mind seconds to change everything.

Magdu fell and the world fell with her.

After it all went wrong, I only ever wanted it to look like a terrible accident. The only way I could talk to the police, could stand to be in the same room as them without throwing myself on the floor and yelling, "I did it," was to tell myself over and over again that I would never have hurt Magdu. And then Dale had found Daphne's knife.

The blades on our two knives must have been identical. Close enough, anyway, for Dale to think it had been Daphne's knife that scored the rope. It had never occurred to me at the time that this might happen. My own knife was a backup only. I kept my multi-tool on my harness and the knife in a calf pocket, just in case. I never climbed without it, but I'd also never needed to use it, so Daphne had never seen it. When Dale had asked for my gear, I'd only given him my multi-tool, with its small blade.

You must not let yourself think the bad thought; you have to believe that things happened the way you wish they had. Daphne taught me that. She was going to tell Magdu about Suze if I didn't do something—that much had become clear to me. It's hard to think about what I did; so much easier to take it apart and think of it another way. I'm better at it than some people. I've had practice.

And maybe I could only construct a new version of myself because Suze had so completely obliterated who I thought I was. Not just what she said that night on the cliff, which still hurt, but what I'd done. What I'd seen in myself that absolutely had to be buried, the timbers ripped off and thrown into the sea, the old Finn weighed down with rocks.

Daphne and I were twins in some important ways: our sisters had both died young in horrible circumstances. But looking at Daphne now, standing in front of me, I don't believe she poisoned her sister. I think Brianna Bennett died because she couldn't see anything changing. But if I was capable of murder, then why couldn't Daphne be capable of it too? For Jo to think that Daphne might have killed her sister had been sickeningly exhilarating. And Dale. He was so close to me, so close to what I had done, but he'd been too busy looking over my shoulder at Daphne. I'd been scrambling when I told Dale about Brendan, trying to persuade him to look elsewhere. It had been a stab in the dark. A wild attempt as my body filled with fear and guilt and shame.

———

Darkness is pouring into the valley now; I can smell the undergrowth. Wallaby and wombat shit, leaves breaking down in the water and mud, becoming slick little memories of themselves.

When I speak, it's to ask a question I've asked before. "Why did you send Magdu down on the blue rope?"

Daphne is shivering. "I told you already. I put her on the newer rope because I could see she was nervous. She was an inexperienced climber. And you know what, Finn? Magdu *thanked* me for putting her on that rope, for talking her through what I was doing. You were so convinced that she had it all under control, but she was shit-scared. You should have known better."

"Did you really give Magdu a knife?"

"I gave her my multi-tool. She didn't really need it, but I was trying to make her feel more secure. It must have fallen out of her pocket when she fell."

"Could you see that I'd damaged the rope?"

Daphne screams. It echoes over the valley, only faintly audible over the wind.

"You think I would see that and send her down? *You're* the fucking psychopath here, not me." I remember that girls' bathroom, how meeting Daphne had felt like meeting a creature from another world. I think of a sphinx, now, face twisted in rage.

"I never wanted anyone to suffer," I say. The words stupid and ugly. What have I done but make people suffer?

"One thing I can't figure out is how you got my knife back to me before I noticed it was missing," Daphne says.

I feel nothing but the anger that pumps in my gut, rises in my throat. All the roads on every map end with me, and what I have done. I look at Daphne's neck and I want to squeeze it. Do violence to it.

"I have the same knife," I say. "I bought two of them."

She moves forward and my stomach lurches; without thinking, I take a step back, closer to the edge.

"We could have been all we needed," she says, her eyes wide with hurt.

I step forward again, away from the drop-off. In a moment of blinding certainty, of pure, shimmering anger, I press my lips against Daphne's. We're standing near the edge, my hands in her hair. I can imagine more than feel the firm rise of her stomach between us. There is power in me kissing *her* this time. It's a kiss goodbye.

And then, pressure on my shoulders. The sickening wrongness of it. And I'm falling.

———

Only, I'm not falling. I have imagined the pressure. Imagined that Daphne would push me, that she would be capable of the things that I have done. The kiss was real—I can still feel it on my lips—but it's over now and will not happen again.

"You should go," I say.

Daphne has already turned away. She knows everything now; she can tell the police about the second knife, and about Suze, too, if she hasn't already.

As she walks off into the bush, I realize I could run after her, overpower her. I am stronger than she is. I think of Mum, breathing in lemon balm as she moves around the kitchen, Spencer waddling behind her. I could turn and give myself to the valley. Part of me wants to die in the same place as my sister and the only woman I've ever loved the right way. A few steps backward and I would be with Magdu. If I could give my life for hers, nothing would hold me back. I think of Dale Gosling standing in a too-cold room with my body laid out on a metal slab, and it almost seems better than the alternative: a room full of questions. A courthouse. A cell.

Even so, I wait until I am sure Daphne is gone and then walk back to my car. I will go home. I will tell my mother what I have done. There's no way she will ever understand the broken pieces of ship that I put in front of her, but she deserves to hear it from me anyway. And when they come for me, I will be ready. The world will know what I have done, who I am. I breathe in the smell of the damp earth around me, feel the wind pushing against the car door as I open it. And then I drive.

ACKNOWLEDGMENTS

I'll be honest—I find acknowledgments can be jarring when a book is written in the first person. Give yourself a break, maybe, between Finn's words and mine? A deep breath?

I wrote most of this novel on the unceded lands of the Wodi Wodi people of the Dharawal Nation. I pay my respects to Elders past and present. I also spent as much time as I could on Dharug and Gundungurra country during several visits to Varuna, the National Writers' House of Australia, while writing *Girl Falling*. I am indebted to First Nations people and I honor their connection to land and waters. Even though the towns in my books have been fictional, I am always aware of how lucky I am to write on country.

Books are strange things: it never really feels like you get started writing one, and then one miraculous day—it's done. I am endlessly grateful for the miracle, and always thankful that the writing ends up being smarter than I am. All my books are dedicated to my mum.

I love you, Mum. Thanks for making all things possible, and for any-one who read the acknowledgments of my first book, you'll be pleased to know Danina is doing well and living her best life. It's honestly exhausting just trying to keep track of her movements these days!

My first novel outstripped every expectation I had for publica-tion. My eternal gratitude, forever, to Grace Heifetz, agent extraordi-naire, who has taken me and my writing to places I never imagined. A big thank-you to the Marsh Agency, for all your work getting *Dirt Creek* into translation around the world. David Forrer and InkWell—bringing my books to North America has only been possible because of you, and I am excited every day to know my books are available to American readers.

To everyone at Flatiron Books, I am so grateful that my novels benefit from your passion, professionalism, and dedication. Christine Kopprasch, in particular, it was such a joy to know you wanted to publish my second book. I feel honored to be part of the Flatiron family. A huge thank-you to everyone who helped place this book in people's hands. From amazing sales reps to tireless booksellers, and to everyone who has ever recommended my book to anybody else: thank you.

I feel so lucky to have a connection to the University of Wollon-gong and its fantastic creative writing department. UOW folk—Emma Darragh, Shady Cosgrove, Cath McKinnon, Chrissy Howe, Joshua Lobb, Luke Johnson, Camille Booker—here's to you.

And then there are the friends who I complain to the most—Julie Keys, Jackie Bailey, Helena Fox, Donna Waters, Eleanor Whitworth, Eda Gunaydin, Sara Rich, Emily Gray, Suzanne Do, Wendy Dorrington, Adara Enthaler, Lore White, Mel Hall, Sam Coley—for your friendship and for putting up with me every time I say, *Yeah, the writing is going pretty slowly*. Bitching about the writing process is my love language—thank you for always indulging me.

A huge thank-you, as always, must go to Jemma Payne and Linda Godfrey—still the first readers of my work. You put in the hours when I need them most and when the work is at its most vulnerable stage. Thank you, thank you, thank you.

I want to thank Nadine Davidoff and Ali Lavau for their essential contributions to this book. I shudder to think what this novel would be without you and I'm grateful to be able to benefit from your knowledge and talent. This book is better for it.

To the Team Awesome crew who helped jog my memory about all things climbing! Hala and Kent Horsley, Marie-Claire Demers, and Axton Conrad Aguiar—I absolutely could not have started this book without you pushing me to try things I would never have done alone, and I couldn't have finished it without your specific skills, know-how, and admirable patience with me. Shout-out to Caity Woods, who features in my fondest climbing memories, and thanks to Serena Edward for being an inspiration and true friend—the original Outdoor Type™.

Thanks must go to my wonderful therapist, Alex. I hope you don't feel like I took liberties with your profession! Thank you for your truly tireless work and watching on so patiently as I roll the heavy ball of my anxiety up the hill only to have it roll back down again. Therapy gives the benefit of distance from big thoughts and feelings and I'm grateful to be able to access it.

My grandmother Antoinette Scrivenor passed away while I was in the final stages of writing this book—I'm sorry she'll never get to read it. She was a singular person and I'm glad there's even a little bit of her in me. To my family, who have been so supportive, and my household, who never let me get too far into my own head, I love you. And to you, if you've read this far—thank you for following me into the places my mind goes. Sorry-not-sorry.

ABOUT THE AUTHOR

Hayley Scrivenor is the *USA Today* and #1 internationally bestselling author of *Dirt Creek*. *Dirt Creek* won the ILP John Creasey (New Blood) Dagger, the Lambda Literary Award for LGBTQ+ Mystery, and the ABIA for General Fiction Book of the Year. Scrivenor has a PhD in creative writing from the University of Wollongong and lives on Dharawal country, on the east coast of Australia.